THE

BOY

I AM

For Maud - *K. L.*

The Boy I Am contains content some readers may find triggering, including sexual aggression, trafficking, murder and surgical procedures.

STRIPES PUBLISHING LIMITED
An imprint of the Little Tiger Group
1 Coda Studios, 189 Munster Road,
London SW6 6AW

www.littletiger.co.uk

First published in Great Britain by Stripes Publishing Limited in 2021
Text copyright © K. L. Kettle, 2021
Cover copyright © Stripes Publishing Limited, 2021

ISBN: 978-1-78895-122-7

Printed and bound in the UK.

MIX
Paper from
responsible sources
FSC® C020471

The Forest Stewardship Council® (FSC®) is a global, not-for-profit organization dedicated to the promotion of responsible forest management worldwide. FSC defines standards based on agreed principles for responsible forest stewardship that are supported by environmental, social, and economic stakeholders. To learn more, visit www.fsc.org

10 9 8 7 6 5 4 3 2 1

THE

BOY

I AM

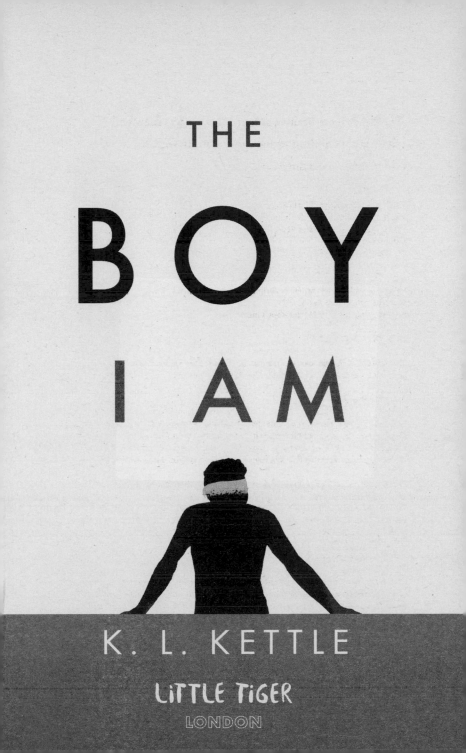

K. L. KETTLE

LiTTLE TiGER
LONDON

THE HOUSE OF BOYS

We blind ourselves to beauty.

Our speech is sacred.

To love is illusion.

1

My name is Jude Grant and I am alive.

Centre stage, I face the deafening crowd.

And I smile.

"Tonight's final lot!" Mr Walker, Head of the House of Boys, introduces me over the theatre's loudspeakers. "Number one hundred and fifty."

Pinned in the spotlight, I squint. I shade my eyes with one hand and wave with the other. Cheers from the audience smack into my chest hard, skewering skin through to stomach, stomach through to spine, spine through to sparkling scenery behind me. Can't tell if it's the floor or my knees that are shaking more.

Smile number one we call *gracious-without-being-smarmy*. That's what I'm aiming for, to hide my locked jaw. Sweat crawls from my hairline. As I adjust my collar, cold dread snakes down my neck.

Pose. Wave.

Offstage, Walker reads out my stats. "Age sixteen," his disembodied voice hums.

Too old, drones the voice in my head. These days it always sounds like *your* voice, Vik. Are you trying to make me laugh?

You've lasted longer than I did.

"Five foot nine," Walker says.

Too short. Your voice. *I was taller.*

"One hundred and forty pounds."

Too fat.

Shut up, I want to say and I laugh like the ghost of you is right there, thinking you're so funny, and proud you got me to react even if it was in my head. My performance slips; for a second, I'm not in the mouth of the Great Theatre, being sold for the dark-hours to the highest bidder, reserved for purchase at the auction. For a second, it was the two of us, back in the kitchens below ground, laughing. For a second, you were alive.

Smile one makes my face hurt but it's easy to hide behind.

Squinting into the darkness, I look for *her* – the Chancellor. Remembering the vast layout of the underground theatre, how it's not so scary with the house lights up. The endless rows of frayed red chairs, ancient, worn carpet, dusty chandeliers and her balcony, now in the dark, in the centre of the dress circle. Dead ahead. Above it all. Is she there yet?

A woman in the audience drops a glass and the theatre goes awkwardly quiet. My silk-slippered toes curl, squeaking against the rubbery stage floor.

Walker coughs. "Yes, so, lot one fifty is a fourth year at the House of Boys. Last year available for auction."

After I turn seventeen, they'll pack me off to the mines. There aren't many boys who survive even a year working down there – the heat, the hate, gangs scraping for minerals, fighting over food, water. That's a few weeks from now.

Walker keeps going. "No previous reserves on the books so I'm pleased to announce the House of Merit can offer a discount on request."

"*Ooooooooooooooo,*" goes the audience.

"A much-improved lot on his previous years, I'm sure you'll agree."

The audience laughs and the spotlight moves forwards, a cue for me to follow. There are bugs that thrive in the dorms below. They fizz and pop in the blue lights they chase.

In the glow of the limelight, low-lit tables in front of the stage swim into focus as I step forwards and bow. The women lean closer. Hungry shadows. Their faces completely hidden behind blank white masks. There must be hundreds of them in the stalls, thousands in the surrounding seats. Rumours are that the richest of them, the ones that live on the top floors of the Tower, get the front tables. They pay the most merits for a spot to judge us best.

Time to deploy smile two. *A-little-bit-defiant.*

Bad choice. The masks retreat, disappointed, into the darkness.

Another drop of sweat slides between my eyebrows, along the inside of my eye socket. It's salty. Stings like needles.

Pull it together, says the part of me that sounds like you, Vik. And it's strong like you were, brave like you were. It's the voice of the boy I want to be. *You owe me*, it says. *You're still alive.*

Wiping my eye, before I turn to find my place among my brothers upstage, I make sure the women see the kind of smile you said would make them all reach for their merit books.

Number twenty-nine. You called it the *I-just-need-you-to-fix-me* smile.

"*Awwwwwwwwwwww*," goes the audience.

See, you can do this.

I know.

All I have to do is <u>kill</u> the Chancellor.

2

Upstage is stacked high with glittering platforms. The band plays me to my mark: the furthest platform, back row. There's that familiar push and pressure behind my head. I'm holding my breath, my teeth locked. I'm doing this for you, Vik, for freedom I remind myself. If I count the beats in the music, focus on that, there's some relief. Tapping my thumb against my index finger, hoping they don't see.

My place is last in the line-up behind 149 other boys displayed, choir-like, on sparkling stage terraces, in matching grey suits. Our outfits were designed by students at the House of Expression again and I swear this year the theme must be discomfort. Whoever made them has never worn a suit. With high-necked collars, jackets with boning in the back, every one of my brothers seems taller they're standing so straight. It makes for a strong jawline, the House Fathers said, complementing the look.

It's hard to be graceful while weaving between my brothers. But that's the second I get to turn my back, to slip a finger between my neck and the stiff collar, stretch my jaw and try to loosen the knots in my stomach. That second is everything.

Walker's deep voice continues. "Ladies, when Chancellor Hyde asked me to host this year's auction, I did what any sane gentleman would do…"

Walker is normally onstage but usually one of the madams actually hosts the auction events – choosing the theme, the showcase event, stuff like that. It was meant to be the Gardener – Madam Dunn – hosting again this year. Did that change last minute?

A man, even Walker, hosting alone – it's not normal. Something's wrong.

Clunk! Up go the stage lights, full beam, swinging, sweeping over the boys surrounding me, all grinning, waving and cheering like their lives depended on it.

"I said to myself: one hundred and fifty handsome young men?"

Slicing my own smile into place, I wave too. I should come up with my own numbers and names for the smiles now you've gone.

"I picked out my outfit and I said yes please!"

All you have to do is…

Swoosh! Spotlights move from us and into the crowd.

You ran, they said. You attacked the Chancellor and then you ran. You gave in to your urges, your base animal instincts. More likely you were scared. There's no air in my lungs. I wonder if they'll say the same about me?

There, ahead, the distant silver fabric drapes of the Chancellor's balcony gleam. All I have to do…

Walker was the Chancellor's only ward last year, when she reserved you. No one ever believed she'd take another ward but she took pity on you they say.

Who says?

Everyone. But you were a bad one, corrupt. You must've just broken, the ladies say. They hear that can happen and it's been happening too much, they say. It's our hormones; we just can't help ourselves.

Bitter bile jumps in my throat. Before I can even try to swallow, snap, the view is gone. Spotlights creak, flooding the stage as the silhouette of Walker sashays between us and the audience. They all coo at the sight of him. That's Walker: perfect smile. Perfect poise. Perfect man. In the light, his sleek silver pinstripe gleams. The Chancellor's man.

Next to me, lot 149 leans close. "Is it true you know him?"

"No," I lie.

Walker leads the applause. "Let's give a big hand for this year's boys." His painted nails shine black but his hands are starting to look old. If I've noticed, so have the women. Two in the front row whisper to each other, giggle. The Chancellor bought him to be her ward when they were both my age. Reserving another ward may have surprised the ladies last year, but not the House Fathers who care for us. Perfect as he may be, they say she's been looking for a younger model to replace Walker for years. She's never settled on one, though.

Until now, you say.

I can't do anything stuck onstage. I have to get the Chancellor on her own. She has to bid on me. I lose my grip on smile three: *patient-not-too-bored*. It's not going to work. I'm the final lot, like you were. But there are cuter, hotter, taller, thinner, more muscled boys with better skin, squarer jaws.

I've a powerful need to scratch my neck but I'm meant to stay still so I clench my fists. She's never going to bid, not after last year. This is a stupid idea. Could I run?

I ran.

Walker's still going, of course. "So, ladies, you know the drill: tonight you get one evening with your personal favourite." The women whoop and whistle at his classic *this-one's-for-the-girl-at-the-back* wink. "Generous bids, please. Your merits tonight set our gentlemen's opening dowries at auction."

Walker jokes. "I have to say, the rumours are true: the Gardener and the House of Life keep breeding our boys cuter. Where is she?" He looks into the audience as the light searches the seats for the head of the scientists who made us all.

"Oh well, I'm sure she's busy planting up a new batch. Let's hear it for the House of Life, our ladies of floor one ten." He stops. The audience cheers and whoops as the spotlights catch something else in the dark aisles.

They're the shadows that the shadows hide.

"Why…" Walker pauses. Is he trying to be dramatic? "They'll be giving yours truly … a run for his … merits soon enough." He has a habit of odd pauses but he never, ever fluffs his lines.

There are Lice in the dark. That's what you called the police. You said they made you itch.

The audience laughs, but not as much as before, as Walker draws the light round the stage, tidying the corners of his slender moustache as he goes. He does that when he's thinking.

"A show of hands – how many debutantes do we have here tonight?" he asks.

The house lights go up. Hands lift above a sea of bright dresses, smart suits, identical masked faces, but I don't count. Surrounding the hundreds of women in the stalls, the circle, the gods, there are swarms of Lice. They're at every exit. Wrapped in black fabric and strapped into scales of armour. The fog mask air filters they never take off hang like stretched snouts.

Walker coughs. "Well, aren't you just gorgeous?" he says as the house lights go down. *Clank.*

"So what are we waiting for?" Walker coughs again, stalling because of the Lice. My fingers pick and scratch at my nails. There's a metallic ache in my throat. If I run, they'll catch me, like they caught you.

No way out, you say.

There are Lice in the wings too, watching, their filtered air sucking in, pushing out.

The women aren't cheering. They know. They see. They're expecting something.

"Oh yes!" Walker clicks his fingers, full of confidence, as if he's just remembered the most important thing. The masked faces of the women snap back to his razzle-dazzle as he cups his hand to his ear. "You want me to announce this year's programme?" He side-smiles, pretending one of our potential guardians has asked him personally. A wink. "Well, after tonight's Reserves, there's your favourite talent show…"

Pause for effect. Drum roll.

"Swimwear!"

No one cheers, someone coughs, but Walker doesn't blink. He continues full tilt.

The stage screens light up with pictures of past events and words I've never been taught to read. Images of a thousand boys of the past fly by, yours too. Your scarred face. The pucker in your cheek below your right eye, through your top lip, that you wore because of me.

I want to crunch my eyes closed, imagine myself fighting the Lice dead, standing on top of piles of them, triumphant. I'd bow, then run. Into the desert like we'd always planned. "Ha ha!" we'd cry and fight monsters, survive on our wits. And the Chancellor would find us in the desert and apologize and offer us anything we wanted. And we'd take all the other boys into the desert and start a new world.

But the light's on me now and I have to smile, an *it's-OK-this-is-OK-I'm-OK* smile. Call it number thirty-one.

"Next week we've the Unmasked Ball for those gentlemen lucky enough to get reserved tonight!" Walker lays it on thick as if any of this is a surprise, as if it's not the same schedule every single fogging year.

Reserves, talent show, ball, auction.

Thanks to last year's disaster, when Madam Bocharov cancelled my reserve, I've never made it to the talent show, let alone the rest of the events. Now I never will. Neither will you.

Truth is I do know Walker. Today's the only day for months I've not had his company, preparing for tonight. I wanted freedom, I said. Not fake freedom being warded off to one of these faceless women. Real freedom, like you and I dreamed of, Vik, remember? Outside in the desert. Walker said he can't give me that. No one can. But when I kill the Chancellor it'll make that ache in my head better, that urge to kick and hit the world until the pressure behind my skull goes away. Revenge, Walker called it. It's the only freedom on offer.

It's still there, pounding, as the audience applauds and Walker turns towards us, tidies his suit, his silver-sided dark hair – Saints preserve him from having anything out of place. Now he catches my eye, checking I can do this.

He nods, slight and deft, cranking up his speciality smile. Number ten, his *this-is-the-best-thing-ever-and-it's-even-better-because-I'm-pure-charm-doesn't-it-make-you-squirm?* smile, before he spins back towards his audience.

If you were still here, I wouldn't have wanted to hurt anyone, let alone the Chancellor. But she had you killed. That's what I've got to hold on to. She's a murderer.

There's a flicker of light in the silver-swagged balcony dominating the dress circle above. Movement, I think.

She's here.

The Chancellor. 'Top Floor', the Single Most Important, Most Merited, Most-Most at Everything EVER. But why should that matter? We all live; we all die. Sure, she didn't grow up in the tunnels. Sure, she's seen the sky. Sure, she's a woman, in charge, and I'm just a boy, but … I bet she bleeds the same as us.

Despite the heat, the bones in my spine shiver.

Not knives, Walker and I decided. A fall. It's the cleanest way. She has to fall, which means I have to push.

3

There's a sign above the stage we can't read but we know when it flashes there's applause. The women clap as lot one twenty is led from the stage, some kid from B-dorm. We all shuffle forwards.

Despite the ache prickling behind my eyes, I maintain smile eleven, my best. Walker calls it my *butter-wouldn't-melt* smile. He gives them names, like you did. Did he pick that up from you, or maybe it was the other way round? The reserve bidding's almost done: boys led one by one from the stage for their 'interviews'. We all know what that really means.

With each bid, my guts tighten. What if the Chancellor wants someone else? What if the Lice arrest me before she decides?

Walker reaches the last row in record time. Less than twenty of us left winding our way into the spotlight.

Nineteen, eighteen, seventeen…

One of your old dorm gang steps up. In all his muscled glory, Toll says, "My name is Hector Dent," as he slicks his hand through his dyed golden hair. Side-smiling and winking like a pro. Roids brush up OK for the auction events. 'Roids', that's what your old friends have taken to calling themselves, on account of the pills they get slipped in their appointments by the women who favour them.

No one has ever given me drugs in my appointments. Every day, from lights-up to dinner, it's the same. Hours of tuition in dance, decorum, deference. Except for when the women pay the House of Entertainment for our private services. Of course we're not allowed to see them, so – with a lot of practice – we learn to serve tea, dance the old dances, ask them about their day and make them feel special, beautiful, interesting, all while blind to the world. Apparently, it's a real privilege to spend time with us, costly too: only the top-floor women can afford it. A luxury. Tell that to the boys who come out of their appointments crying or bruised in places the House Fathers can hide.

Walker leans away from the stink of Toll's cologne.

"This is the best day of my life," Toll oozes. "I've been training hard, very hard, really hard. It'll be an honour, a real honour, to be with any one of you."

Bet you the Chancellor can tell I'm distracted. She'll buy Toll, or Aye-Aye, one of the beefcakes. Whatever he promised, there's no way Walker could make sure she'd reserve me. No way. I told him he should've put me on steroids too. He said he needed my mind perky, not my pecs.

Half the top-floor women in the pit raise their hands before Toll finishes speaking. There are bids from the madams in the balconies too. The reserve settles at 300 merits, to Madam Van Gelder, Chief of Entertainment. Toll winks at Aye-Aye, next in the queue, and strolls into the wings, grabbing his crotch in the dark to make his friends laugh.

The candlelight in the Chancellor's balcony doesn't even flicker.

Only ten left. If it wasn't for Walker, there wouldn't be a sound between bids. With the Lice there – not normal – everyone's waiting for something.

Nine...

Revenge, I remind myself, not murder. There's a difference, right? Taking her out on to her Pent House balcony, right at the top of the skyscraper towering above us, saying I'd like to look over the edge, getting scared to make her feel as if I'm vulnerable, need her help. It's OK, she'll say, let me show you, it's not so scary, and she'll look over the edge and that's when I'll do it. Just one push. All the way down.

Eight...

We move closer. As Walker interviews the boys near to me, I can smell the oil in his hair, feel the heat coming from his skin.

Seven...

Imagine the Chancellor up close: her skin, her bones, her breath and her blood. She'll be real. Like Walker, like my brothers, like me. Could I push Walker?

Three...

No. Walker didn't have my best friend murdered.

Two...

My only friend.

One...

Lot 149, who introduces himself as Paulie, gets reserved by Madam Cramp, Chief of Expression. Lucky kid – every boy

21

says being chosen by Cramp is about as close to freedom as you can get.

My throat tightens as Walker gets to me.

We've practised this. Don't look him in the eye. Focus on the balconies. Keep smiling. Don't panic.

"And now our final gentleman this evening," Walker announces.

I swear the Lice take a step forwards. But I can't hear them breathing any more.

Clearing my throat, I bite my lip and peer into the crowd. My brain's actually died. Right here. Right now.

"I... My..."

Walker gave me a speech! I have to use the exact words! What were they?

Shit.

In the pit, a scratch echoes across the floor as a chair moves. I flinch, expecting a surge of police. And yes, they're moving but not towards me. They're closing in on the middle of the stalls. They're here for someone else. There's whispering, movement, getting closer, closer. Walker peers through the glare of the lights.

"Get off," a voice says.

A top-floor voice, brittle. She sounds familiar. The police push towards her. Other women try to pull the girl into her seat. Plates and glasses clatter. Women snap, "Sit down!" But she keeps moving. Closer. In the limelight, I can see the blood-red colour of her hair. There's only one debutante I've heard of who has hair like that.

"Leaving so soon, Ms Vor?" Walker asks. The audience laughs. A drop of sweat appears on his perfect forehead. I have *never*, not

22

once, not ever seen him sweat.

When she stops, the Lice stop.

Walker presses on. "Were the gentlemen on offer tonight not good enough for you?"

No one embarrasses Ms Romali Vor. We've all heard the stories. If you believe them. There's one that claims one of her mothers, the one who was the Chief of Exploration, had her after meeting some Hysteric in the desert. They made a daughter so unstable that her mother would rather stay in the desert than come back to the monster she produced. And that's not to mention that the mother who raised her is the Chief of Peace, the woman in charge of the Lice. We hear it from the ladies in our appointments. Rumours sink down to our basement dorms like heavy air.

Ms Vor's answer is muffled behind her mask. Strong muscles in her neck tense like string pulled tight, angry. What right does she have to be angry? Shuffling in my spot, heat crawls up to my ears.

"Do you want to bid?" says Walker slowly as if each word could push her back into her seat. It never could. No lady could be told what to do by any man, even Mr Walker.

She's right at the edge of the lime-lit stage. The Lice try to move in but she puts out her hand and again they stop. Even they're afraid of her!

In a flash, I remember my speech, lean into the mic and let the garble begin. "My name is Jude Grant and I—" Distracted by the sight of her – she hardly seems the monster the gossip made her out to be – the last words of my speech are lost. Stop it. Pull it together! "And I?"

23

Swallow. Start again.

"My name is—"

Ms Vor interrupts, breathless, almost panicked. "Wait!"

Recognition hits me like a wall. I do know that voice. You don't forget something like that when it's all you have of someone.

"Ms Vor?" Walker prompts.

The spit in my mouth is sticky, so I swallow. That voice can't belong to Romali Vor, can it?

Behind her bright white mask her eyes are as green as broken bottle glass. She's staring at me.

"You heard me. Wait," she says, firmer now.

Wild and changeable. I know that voice from my appointments. Once a week, every week this year.

Hurriedly, she reaches behind her head, pulling at the knotted ropes of her hair, hair I've combed into buns and plaits and twists.

It can't be her, can it? The girl that came once a week? The girl that never paid for food, or drink, or entertainment, only my time. In my appointments, I'd know it was her because of her perfume. It made my head dance. Fresh rain, she told me, from the storms Outside. We spoke but of course I never saw her, not one inch.

Even if I don't believe the gossip about the Chief of Exploration, Romali Vor is still the Chief of Peace's daughter too. Madam Vor: leader of the Lice. The officers who caught you, that beat boys found out of their dorms in the dark-hours, that blind boys who break their oaths, that deliver all flavours of the Chancellor's mercy.

"Ro—" Walker begins but cuts himself off with a shout as something comes hurtling through the dark towards me.

I swerve out of the way as it slices through the light.

The stage flats behind shake as it hits them. Bouncing back, it smashes on the stage. Shards of porcelain fly in different directions.

After the silence, I stand. Find my light. Try not to let them see me shake.

The shattered thing on the ground is a mask.

Romali Vor stares up at me as the whole audience gasps. Rain Girl talked about how much she hated the auction process, how it was a joke. Said she'd smash her mask, mock the show of it all…

Her large green eyes blink.

Given the rumours about her birth, I can't help but stare, expecting some beast to look back.

I never knew what to imagine when I pictured a woman's face. I thought they'd look different under those masks, but they're not that different to us. So why hide?

Beneath her stare is a blunt nose. Dark freckles mottle her skin. Beneath that her smile. A gap between her front teeth and smile twelve: *the-look-of-a-person-who-won-a-fight*. Relaxed. Satisfied. A hint of pride.

I've broken the first law.

Hers is the only female face I've ever seen. I should be afraid. I should be worried about the Chancellor, about the Lice, about Walker, about being thrown in the cells, a million things. Men can't control themselves, we're told; to look at a woman is to lose our innocence. I don't feel any different. Searching for the fear I've felt all year, the ratcheting ache in the pit of my stomach, it's not there.

Walker steps between us, blocking the audience from my view. I peer round him to keep looking at her.

Are you stupid?

"Now you've *got* to arrest him," Romali tells the Lice.

Unblinking, her wide eyes wild, she points at me, her voice shaking. She looks up to the balconies and shouts towards where Madam Vor must be. "Go on! Arrest him then!"

Anger and fear flood in a wave and I can't move. All this time, Rain Girl was Romali Vor ... and now she wants me arrested?

The swarms of Lice in the wings move closer to me. Confused, the Lice surrounding her turn and begin to climb the stage towards me too.

"No, wait, I—" I begin and bite my tongue. No need to break another law. Speak when spoken to, Jude.

Romali shouts her order over and over as Walker tries to calm the audience, talking fast. But I can't hear because my heart is going to explode, because as the Lice turn from her they move towards me. I'm going to be dead whatever I do. Run, I'm dead. Don't run, dead. Madam Vor's Lice kick and crunch the broken pieces of mask. With every step, all I hear is the sounds my bones will make as they shatter beneath their black boots—

A soft voice from above sighs. The sound slices through the terror, turning my blood cold. The tap of a finger on a whistling microphone.

Even Walker goes quiet. No gasps. No coughs. No creaks in seats or shuffling of feet. The silence makes my jaw clamp tight.

The sigh swims over the speakers again. Long and round and tired.

The audience of faceless women stands as if shot through with electricity. They knock glasses and cutlery. Tables shift on the ground. The whole theatre shakes as if the ancient Tower has pulled its spine up from a slump.

A third sigh, and the women all sit with a thunderous thud. The spotlight moves fast, juddering in the rafters. The light traces the heads of the crowd up, and up, until its glow floods the Chancellor's box.

She's too far away to see clearly. A curving shape that shifts and curls, swimming smoke in the light.

Walker steps aside, catches my eye with his burning blue glare before snapping back into the showman the women know. By then, I've remembered his instructions on what to do when the Chancellor stands.

I want her to want me. I want this, I remind myself, trying not to look at Romali Vor and how she keeps staring at me.

No. Focus on the Chancellor. I bow, full charm turned up, squeezing down the fear in my gut. This is about you, Vik.

The Chancellor's sweet, slow tones offer her reserve. "One merit," she says.

The silence is loud enough: no one's going to outbid her.

I think the woman I'm meant to kill may have just saved my life.

4

The shifting ribbon of smoke drifts away, leaving the beam from the spotlight empty.

Walker was certain the Chancellor would buy me. He knew her tastes, he said: vulnerable, expensive, nice to look at.

Can't hear my heart now, only the applause. Wild, as if every single woman in the audience wants her hands to be heard beyond the walls, beyond the doors, up into the highest rafters of High House.

Clunk, every light goes out. *Swoosh*, the curtains close, separating me from the thunderous audience and the one person in the whole theatre who didn't turn to look at the Chancellor: Romali Vor. As the Lice close in and pull me into the wings, I can still feel her eyes on me, bright cat's globes in the limelight, burning through the curtain fabric and into me.

Walker chases after the Lice, his long legs reaching me in a few strides.

"I can take him up," he insists.

The largest of the Lice laughs with a snort inside her mask. "You're not allowed in the Chancellor's rooms. You know that, old man."

Walker had told me the Chancellor had banned him from her floor. "Paranoia," he'd laughed. "Sometimes it's justified."

The officers pull me down the narrow backstage corridors, past the House Fathers retreating from the swarm of Lice. Walker pushing behind between ancient stage sets and dusty boxes, over snaking cables, round open-mouthed theatre prentice with brooms in hand to clean between the seats.

There's a thud as the Lice push open the exit leading to the front of house. This is where I last saw you alive.

You, kicking and screaming.

You, calling my name.

You, going quiet.

Walker holding me. "He ran. There's nothing to be done. He's gone."

But that was then. Now warmth and light burst into the backstage corridor.

"We'll talk in the morning!" Walker shouts as the troops pull me through, into the atrium.

Looking back, I search Walker's face for an *it'll-be-all-right* smile. It's not there.

5

LESSONS IN RESTRAINT

Did you ever hear the story about the boy who danced? They tell it all the time in the dorms. No one ever saw him so a lot of boys don't believe the tales.

It started down in the Surrogacy, so the stories go. Even as a baby, the boy couldn't stay still, bopping and bouncing to the music on the radio. Boys need discipline, they said, so Madam Hyde took away all the radios. But, as he grew, he was always tapping his foot. A jiggling little thing. He could hum and spin round for hours, laughing, they say. Hard work to get him to stand still, behave, be good, be quiet. Stay there, they'd tell him. But the boy could find music anywhere.

He'd sniff it out, filtering through the pipes from the Great Theatre. He'd stalk the humming of the Nurse Fathers, skip at the squeaking feet of the cleaning prentice, tap along to the chatter and gossip of mice. And then he'd go, running and laughing, skipping and jumping off the walls, drumming on the tables, clicking his fingers, kicking his feet until they caught him.

Dum-da-da, dum-da-da.

Then the top-floor women would come; the ones that lived above clouds that were myths to us: the madams, the highly merited, their daughters. Figures from Above with different voices and strange faces he'd never see. "Dancing?" they'd tut when they heard of the boy. "The horror of it! Think. How would that passion mutate when he reached manhood? No, no, we can't have dangerous outbursts like these." The Surrogacy would have to make sure he wouldn't dance again. He wouldn't be worth anything to any of the houses as a prentice if he couldn't do as he was told.

I can't remember how old I was. Sometime before I turned five. But I remember the Nurse Fathers in the Surrogacy well enough; how I ran, how they'd catch me, how it was a game when they chased me. And then there were the smacks, the bruises. It was for the best, they said. The twisted wrists and ankles as they tried to beat it out of me. You need to be good, they told me. Eventually I kicked back. Harder. Harder still. The Nurse Fathers would get fewer merits for a boy only fit for the mines. I had potential, they said, just took a little disciplining.

I remember the darkness too. My eyes got used to it fast. When they couldn't stop me kicking and biting and screaming, they'd find places to shut me away. Filthy, cramped cupboards, and boxes and chests blurred black with age. They'd let me rot in the dark unless I learned to be a good boy.

Eventually I locked that boy in a dark box myself, buried him deep. The boy they made me into would do what he was told. He'd be their good boy. But there was this pressure in my head that would burst out sometimes. It happened a few times after they sold me to the kitchens. The longer I'd hold it in, the worse it got, that ache, and I'd just start hitting, couldn't stop. Hitting at one of the cooks, the wall, my own head, anything to get all that noise out of my bones. But I learned fast; learned to hold it in tight.

My brothers' story says the boy who danced made it into the House of Boys. There are steps they teach there, old, traditional dances from the Saints' days. Slow, elegant, respectful dancing. Each movement has meaning. We tell stories when we dance for the women at our appointments. The guests applaud.

He'd never dance for the women the way he danced alone, the story says. But maybe, if you're lying awake in the dark-hours, you can hear him dancing in the corridors. You can hear the slide of a slipper on wood or the swoosh of a body spinning in the air.

That's how they tell it and I'm not going to spoil their fun. It's been a long time since that boy danced without being ordered to. But there's always the story and then there's the truth of it, right, Vik? They aren't always the same.

6

We're alone, the Lice and I, crossing the vast atrium of front of house as the closing music from Reserves gets quieter. Past high white walls, falling green plant curtains.

Was it only a year ago that I saw the Lice arrest you?

The shuffle of my slippers on the marble floor seems to echo all the way to the top of the world and down again. High House Tower touches the moon, or so they say. Beyond the fat pillars, there are the balconies. They spiral up into a vast space, reaching into a dark point above, further than I can see.

My gaze stops at a gap in one of the balconies, and a ball of bile catches in my throat.

Below the gap, behind a trickling fountain as high as the chandeliers, there's a roped-off area mottled with unmistakable pooled stains. The bleach the prentice use can mask the coppery tang of blood, but can't get rid of every mark the bodies leave behind. The men that break their oaths. The atrium pours with them.

One little push.

I close my eyes, squeeze them shut. I can almost see you at the balcony edge, your body falling, twisting in the air as they all look up, almost hear the sound as you hit the stone. Silent. Broken.

And I wonder how old the cleaning prentice were that took away your bones, that mopped up your blood.

By law, men who break their oaths are *meant* to be sent to the mines by the House of Peace or pay a 'sacrifice' depending on why they were arrested – an eye for a misplaced look, a hand for a forbidden touch, a tongue for an out-of-place word – but now even that's not enough for the Chancellor. She needs to break us into pieces, like Romali Vor's mask. And she calls it mercy.

If it was mercy, the Chancellor wouldn't invite her ladies to watch.

It won't be long after I've killed the Chancellor before I'm up on that balcony. Looking down on a new audience. Taking a last bow. Maybe there's some sort of freedom, on the other side.

The tallest of the Lice has her hand tight on my shoulder, leading me past the stains. "Cleaning house is a full-time job now," she grunts.

She laughs with a snort, pinches my collarbone until I squirm, then it changes to a sort of massaging that I don't think is trying to make me feel safe. It's like the way the cooks used to tenderize meat, her thumb circling.

Tapping my thumb and fingers together with nerves and curling my toes as we walk, the pressure behind my ears gets worse. The stink of bleach makes my eyes water.

Distracting myself as we walk on, staring at the huge murals on every available wall. The paint is so old and damp it's run in places, bubbled and mildewed in others. We're not allowed to draw on the walls in the dorms, but up here the rules are different. Here there are words and colour and painted figures as tall as twenty women. They seem to laugh and point, their eyes following us as we pass.

The tall officer sniffs inside her mask. "Anyone would think you'd never seen the Foundations before. Don't they teach you anything?"

Of course I know the Foundations, the people who protected High House Tower during the war. The cooks told us to pray to them when we were children. Not that I can tell the officer this: we're not meant to answer back.

"Come on." She leads me closer to the murals, the other officers laughing behind me. "That's the Construction."

The House Fathers talk about history in our weekly classes, but what I know best comes from you. You'd worked in the vents as a prentice, so you'd overheard the madams at the House of Knowledge. The Foundations weren't gods, you said, they were just people. Scientists and artists and politicians. Women, sure, but men too.

The tall officer slows her voice like I'm stupid as she points out the murals. "That's the Arrival."

The Saints: the people that built the Tower, that started their wars for the gods they worshipped. Oil, Gas, Money and Speed.

Don't look back. Give her that *show-her-you're-interested* number nine smile. Don't wonder how many men the hand on my back has pushed…

"The Lockdown," she says. "The Last War. Tunnel life…"

Stories in paint. Proof of the history you told me when we were kids, before the House of Boys.

"That's the arrival of the refugees." The painted faces are of grey men and women, small, sick, being welcomed to safety beneath the Tower.

"The 'Many Womb' plan," the officer continues. To repopulate they needed more women than men, so we're told. "The Exploration. That's when the Foundations' ancestors went into the world to find what was left."

I always loved the expedition stories. Rain Girl would tell them best, talking and talking. Romali Vor's triumphant smile slides into my mind and I try to shut it out, just as the tall officer's hand slips from my shoulder, down my back.

Everything inside goes cold; my toes cross in my slippers as her hand keeps moving down. "They went to the edge of the earth and there was nothing," she says. "We're alone."

Alone.

Don't react. My chaperone's cold hand edges down, down.

"Your lot – you men – you destroyed it all," she says as her fingers reach my waistband. They don't stop. I try not to react as her gloved hand gropes my behind.

It's not like it doesn't happen to every boy. A grab here. A grope there. Small belittling moments we're meant to endure, because it's girls being girls. Shouldn't we be grateful? Flattered? And when they don't even know they did anything wrong, what? We're meant to apologize?

Someone behind us coughs. She snatches her hand away to

grip my arm tight enough to snap it off.

"Sorry, Spinny. We … um … need elevator six E," one of the smaller officers squeaks. She points to a bank of gleaming copper doors. "You're the only one with a clearance card for the fast one to the Pent House. Rest aren't working again anyway."

"This fogging place," my guide swears. "It's falling apart." She groans behind her mask and pulls me back towards her swarm of Lice. "Did anyone call Maintenance?"

The squeaking officer won't look at me as we move towards a pair of dirty golden doors.

I've never taken an elevator. Never even seen inside one. They say that the fastest can take you to the top of the Tower in a minute. Spinny swears again, swipes a card at the wall, pushes the button and we wait.

Each time Spinny moves her fingers, my heart jumps back into my throat. I flinch – don't mean to. The Lice respond to weakness. Don't show them you're nervous. Think about something else…

Above, one of the biggest murals is being painted over. I think it once showed the birth of the Foundation's First Daughter, Pallai Dunn, but not any more. Now there's the faceless, unfinished painting of a glowing silver-clad woman as tall as the tenth storey. It's half finished. Around her feet, hundreds of small, smiling women look up at her. Everything in that world is warm. And welcoming. And bright. There isn't one man in it at all.

"Our glorious Chancellor," Spinny says, leaning the snout of her mask close to my ear. Drumming her fingers on my upper arm as the silver figure's unfinished, empty eyes stare down at me.

"Your date."

In one great clunk, the elevator begins to whir behind the doors, a deafening monster of a noise.

Doors shudder open, exposing a small room made of metal. Inside, the lights buzz. My instincts pin me to the ground, but Spinny's pull is strong and soon the grilled floor beneath my slippered toes cuts cold into the pads of my feet.

The Lice fill the space behind me with a wall of black backs, boxing me in behind the stink of well-worn clothes, sweat, dust and grease. As the elevator doors screech closed, my heart thuds. Any one of them could kill me right here, right now, if they knew what I'd been sent to do. Maybe they don't know. Maybe I was wrong. But Romali Vor knew. She had to, right? Why else would she want me arrested? Did she tell her Lice friends, or want to arrest me herself? Her chance for glory in the Chancellor's eyes.

The elevator lurches and groans, knocking me off balance, and we begin to climb.

Spinny hasn't stopped watching me. Her head tilts as she looks me up and down. Taking stock. The circle lenses of her goggles reflect me in their glaze. I try to grin through it, *everything's-fine-nothing-to-worry-about.*

She lifts the glass of her goggles up to get a good look at me. I can only see her eyes. Dark brown, cruel. Maybe she'll stop the machine just high enough to give me a long fall, a quick death.

"Come on!" one of the officers grunts, hitting the old walls to speed up the elevator.

It jolts up so fast my bones rattle like the world is trying to drag me into the floor. Sounds suck into silence and the inside of my head feels as if it might burst.

I'm going to be sick, so I clamp my hands over my ears because my brain is going to leak out if I don't.

Spinny snorts. "It's the air pressure," she says, sharp. "Hold your nose and blow."

For some reason, the whole swarm of Lice find this hilarious.

Outside the elevator the world is rattling, rattling, rattling as we climb ten floors at a time. The world is falling away below us and we're flying.

My ears pop so I crack my jaw until— *Ping*.

We stop, the earth letting me go so fast it's like I might hit the ceiling. But instead the doors open and the Lice shove me into the dark. It feels like for ever before the floor catches me.

Pent House, says the elevator's voice behind me.

Spinny waves her armoured fingers. "See you soon." As the doors close, they're all laughing, leaving me in the darkness.

7

There are stories about how high the Tower is. As my feet cling to the warm stone floor of the Chancellor's apartment, the air tightens in my throat. It feels like there's a million floors below, maybe more.

Top floor, my friend. Top floor! you say.

"That doesn't help," I respond but no one answers.

My eyesight's good in the dark, my senses sharp to sounds, but my ears still feel funny after the elevator. Hands shaking, moving through the pitch-black corridors feels awkward. Can't believe I'm actually up here. How many boys have been in the Pent House? I bet even only a handful of the women have visited.

Rounding the corner, the lights start to blink on as I nearly crash into a man in front of me. Every nerve in my body jumps, but this sentry isn't real. He's made from bones and bleached animal skulls, all twisted up with wires and mirrors, jewels and flowers. He's wearing the same outfit the House of Expression made for us last year: white, collarless, with leaves embroidered on it. The Gardener hosted last year's Reserves, so the theme was hers.

I must be mad because the longer I stare at the figure the more it seems to look like you. I guess this is what they call art but it makes my skin crawl. It even has a pair of shoes, not that we get them.

When you ran, in the atrium, where did you get your shoes from? Replaying the moment in my mind. Slowing it down. Speeding it up. When we were prentice in the kitchens, we only had ugly, slop-covered rags to wear. Nothing to protect aching toes from being stood on, but at least the clothes were *ours*. The dream was to have a pair of shoes. Something sturdy. Heavy soles. Silk slippers are the best us boys can hope for. Soft skin, sweet-smelling feet, that's the mark of care, Father Jai says. Of course boys without shoes don't run either.

Where did you get a pair of shoes?

The Chancellor's white walls glint with mirrors, opening up into a high space with dark windows stretching all around. You could fit every boy I know in this place, up the stairs to the open-sided floors above. Trying to twist open the top button of my collar, to get some air to my throat, I shuffle over the stone floor, keeping my elbows in so as not to break anything, past animal-skin rugs, and ancient paintings of gowned women reaching down to muscular, naked men. Push my nose up against the glass of the windows to try and see the world in the darkness beyond. But all I can make out is my own reflection and the room behind me.

There's a protocol for Reserves. Shower. Get dressed again. Wait. The reserve cost covers from the time the woman arrives to mid-dark, when our House Father is meant to come and collect us. I should find a bathroom and get ready. It'll be hours until the Chancellor arrives. She'll be at the after-party. I'll have time to calm down, prepare myself.

You sure you can do this?

Yes.

Just one little push?

Upstairs, looking for her bathroom, the walls, floor tiles, cushions and tables twinkle with small, mirrored scales. The whole place winks at me with my own face, my own eyes. On the side table near a large bed, three times bigger than anything I've ever slept in, there are small flowers made of folded paper. Did she make them?

You used to hoard paper. You'd put it in your mouth to sneak it away from the cooks. You'd make little men out of the mashed pulp.

Before my heart has slowed, the double doors behind me open and my whole body jumps.

Two high-heeled shoes fly from the Chancellor's feet, kicked off as she glides away from the stairs into her bedroom, her curves as smooth as a sculpture of melting ice. She's dressed head to toe in sparkling fish-scale silver. Behind her diamond-studded mask her large grey eyes are bright, unblinking.

"So…" Her muffled voice is musical as if she's about to burst into song. "Here we are."

"M-Madam Chancellor," I begin. The muscles behind my knee tick as I bow, staring at the floor.

"Shh," she says, putting her finger to her false lips. "I didn't say you could talk yet." Her voice is a whisper. "Presumptuous, going into a lady's bedroom without being invited." She drops herself on to a chaise, starts picking at the moulting fluff, adjusts her dress where it clings to her in the heat and pulls her fingers through her long hair. Her curls are white all the way to the tips, though her roots are black – the colour of charcoal.

She peels off her mask with a sigh and drops it on to the carpet. "Aren't you going to look at me?"

I shake my head, look at my feet fast.

"You got a good gawp at Vor's girl."

The muscles behind my leg pinch.

"Younger, I suppose. Much like when I became Chancellor. Some say she wants my job. What do you think?" I shake my head again. "Over my dead body, of course," she laughs.

Does she really think Romali Vor is a potential successor?

The Chancellor's lost in thought now, her breathing slow. "My predecessor, her grandmother, she'd have tried to have her rivals killed, you see. Even me. Couldn't bear the idea that anyone but her daughter would be Chancellor."

But I'm not here because of Romali Vor. I'm here because of you, Vik.

"Ho-hum. Madam Vor, she's loyal. The most loyal. She'll find the right punishment for her daughter disturbing the peace."

But Romali tried to have me arrested. She was trying to save the Chancellor, wasn't she?

She sighs. "Such a shame, though, that mine wasn't the first face you saw. Can't unbreak *that* window. Not that I'm jealous, just sorry such an ugly little face was the first one you saw."

How am I meant to tell the difference between what's beautiful and what's not?

She's waiting, I think. Is that an invitation to speak? I can't tell. She's talked so much my head hurts more than normal. I've not even tried to look at her.

You're messing this up.

"Fine," she says, so quiet I have to concentrate. "Not even going to have a little peek? Perhaps I'm not worth looking at?"

"We ... we blind ourselves to beauty." Maybe reminding her of our oath will help?

"Oh, come on. Promise I won't tell if you don't." She stands, moves towards me. "Besides, they're my rules. I get to break them."

My spine and neck bones click as I pull myself up straight. My whole body is shaking and it takes clenching all my muscles not to show it.

"You can look me in the face, you know. Not bad, hmm?" she asks, grey eyes flashing.

"I—" I begin, before my mouth dries.

Could I call her beautiful when I've only one face to compare hers to? Are stone grey eyes more beautiful than green? One thing's for sure: I can't read her smile. Wide and calm, it gives nothing away. Playing through Walker's instructions, I try to imagine pushing her, here and now, just enough so she'd fall over, but I can't even move.

"I don't *actually* want to know what you think, sugar." She flicks her hand through the air, waving my words away like a bad smell. Her nails are armoured with intricate, swirling metal, pointed silver claws. "I mean, please, I'm no teenager but I'm holding up OK." She checks her face in the mirrors around us, pulling her skin about as if she's tucking in the fabric of her dress. Her stockinged feet kick the dozen pillows covering the lounger on to the floor.

Reaching for a small bottle waiting for her on ice, she twists its top as if snapping the neck of an animal.

"I'll tell you this, there are serums from the House of Beauty that'll give me another two decades of good skin." Gliding round the room, her toes curling through the animal pelts at her feet, she pours half the fizz into a wine flute and empties the contents of the glass down her throat, tipping her whole head back.

I brush the fabric of my suit down, straightening it the way Walker does, drying the sweat from my hands.

She shakes the bottle, sloshes the liquid from side to side as if someone else might be more interesting to talk to, before yawning, sighing.

"Strange thing for her to do, Ms Vor." She says she's not jealous but she keeps talking about Romali Vor. "Throwing her mask off. You do know she could be arrested for that? Why would someone so privileged risk so much … and for a boy?"

Cold sweat trails down from my brow and catches in the bowl of my ear, drying in the sweet, recycled air.

She pouts. "Unless, of course, she wanted to guarantee my interest in said boy…" She taps her ringed fingers against the empty glass. "I can't think of another reason."

Tink. Tink.

Does she want to know what I think? My throat is dust and

nails when I try to swallow. Even if she gave me permission to speak, it's not like I can say Ms Vor wanted to stop me from killing her.

"Nothing?" she presses. The Chancellor drops to sit on the bed. The springs bounce and squeak. "You're no fun. To business then. I never did hear your speech onstage. Bet Wally gave you some good spin, Jude Grant. Ladies and debutantes…" She claps one hand against her glass. Her diamond rings clink against it.

Tink, tink, tink.

That's the permission I need. And she wants my speech? Remember to breathe. "My name is Jude Grant," I say, no hesitation this time. No distraction. "And I am alive."

Smile nineteen, a *big-old-beamer*. Maximum charm. Full tilt. Ear to ear. It has to hurt, otherwise how does she know you mean it? That's what Walker said.

She rolls the glass between her hands.

Tink.

Tink.

Tink.

"You're *alive*?" Each soft syllable seems to slide along the carpet. Standing, she runs the tip of a finger round the rim of the glass. It sings with a piercing whistle, making my ears ache. She glides closer, unblinking. "Alive, like you should be proud of it? As if it's an achievement?" Her plucked-perfect white eyebrows rise in curling question marks. "And what does that make me?"

"You're alive too," I say. Jokes are charming, Walker said. She doesn't laugh.

"Let's see how tonight pans out, shall we?" She winks.

I catch my breath, feel my heart fall through every single storey of the Tower.

She knows.

I should have guessed the moment she mentioned Walker. "I presume he sent you to try to kill me, like the other one?" she says, so soft.

"O-other one?" I say, before my mouth gets under control. I swallow the warm air, bite my cheeks hard.

"You know anyone would think Wally didn't love me any more. It's things like that that can offend a lady." She gives a half-suppressed laugh. "He's getting unoriginal in his old age. What was the name?" She clicks her fingers in the air as if trying to spark a thought. "Viktor … something."

My eyes widen. There's a pressure building behind my ears like in the elevator, and I want to clap my hands over them and curl up and scream.

"I mean, he was fun. I promised not to break him," she says. "At least not straight away."

The shaking in my knees has reached my throat.

"No, I wanted to see him run a bit first. Always fun when they run."

That's how you got your shoes? The Chancellor gave them to you so you could run. This is it. This is the moment that fight in me comes out. Let it out, Walker said, and I can feel it bubbling.

"I take bets with Madam Vor on how far they'll get."

Madam Vor, Romali Vor's mother, is the most brutal, most

faithful member of the Chancellor's Council. Always at her elbow. Unleashing the Lice.

She moves right in front of me. I can smell the vinegar fumes on her breath. "Do you know how many men vie for my favour, all looking to replace Wally? Too many. But it's no fun when they're willing. A girl wants something to tame."

The Chancellor rubs my shoulders in circles as she leans in close. I'm waiting for her hands to wander, like the officer's did. Instead, she whispers, "You realize you haven't denied it yet, sugar?"

Focus.

One little push, that's what Walker said.

I could still do it.

"I … I need air," I say.

Finally she's stopped smiling. Her face is so different when she drops her mask. Her bared teeth are longer than I expected. Her mouth reminds me of those ancient creatures the House Fathers showed us pictures of in history classes. Tight-lipped, too many teeth – sharks.

When she pulls me close, wraps her arms round me, I think maybe she'll take a bite out of me.

"Don't worry, I've got you. I won't let you go," she whispers softly, as if she cares.

I can feel her heartbeat steady as she pulls her armoured fingers through my hair.

"So now we've agreed that trying to kill me is a really silly idea and you're a good boy, I can tell. This way, let's talk about what you're going to do instead."

8

"Now," whispers the Chancellor from behind me. She pulls her soft palms from my eyes. Her elevator doors are open and the world is too bright. I didn't think the elevators could go any higher.

With her hand pressed between my shoulder blades, pushing me to step beyond the metallic edges into the world. Just one push.

"Enjoy it." Her soft voice makes it sound like a suggestion, but it's an order.

And good boys don't say no.

I'm used to concrete walls, bottled perfumes, light that the House Fathers say is better than Outside and will keep us from going mad.

Kicking off my slippers, I roll my toes through the prickling, uneven green carpet. Except it's not carpet, not like I've known before. It's alive.

The air tastes rich. Drinking down breath after hot breath, my head spins and I have to steady myself but there's nothing within reach except me. So I fold my arms across my chest and squeeze to stop my lungs from filling up too much, my body from floating away.

"Now this is beauty!" the Chancellor hums. "Right?"

Under vast swirling bulbs that plink and sparkle like they're dancing, she leads me, light-headed, into a garden beneath a huge glass dome. The artificial glare almost blinds me from chinks of darkness beyond. The sky? Real and endless and black.

The ladies call their dark-hours the 'night'. In the kitchens, the dorms, our appointments, the dark-hours are when the House Fathers flip a switch. I wonder who turns off the sky. Maybe no one.

My whole life I've felt small – didn't imagine I could ever feel smaller.

For the first time, there's hardly anything between me and all that Outside. All that endless black and space. Thinking about it too long makes my heart hurt.

"If you're really good, I'll show you the balcony." She winks.

One little push, you say.

"You can see right down to the clouds from there."

Hundreds of birds cackle. I recognize 'birdsong' because the house pipes it into the dorms, except this sound makes my head hum. Another me, long ago, would have danced to the sound. Birds, like in pictures, swoop and twitter. Insects crawl through the strange green carpet, over my toes. If I could just touch everything, smell everything, spin and fall and fly, but it'd split me apart, make dust of me. So I keep my arms wrapped round my chest to stop myself from spilling out.

"It's called grass." The Chancellor laughs, like I'm a fool, as if

I had never been taught about the green things in the world. "And that there's called a tree, sugar. These are the last of their kind."

She goes on about how she does love special things, rare things. The rarer the better, she can look after them the best. "On a good day, if you squint, you can see the tops of the skeletal towers outside. All that's left of the Saints, the people of the old city. Eaten by the sand and the fog, of course." She glides past and I follow, open-mouthed, as we pass large glass doors that must open on to the world. Not that we linger.

One little push.

My fingers itch under my elbows as she pushes through arches of dripping greenery, going on about all the things she's protected us from. Everything she's done for High House and how hard she works, so hard, the hardest, you'd think she'd be recognized for that. Saints, if it wasn't for her, the rabid Hysterics would loot the Tower piece by piece, stealing every last mouthful; kidnap and corrupt and rape our precious men, my brothers, and then feed what's left to their animals. They'd replace us, she insists; we're the last hope for civility.

I'd bet even the men in the mines have heard the stories about how our way of life, our safety, our decency are under attack from the Hysterics. It's almost all the women in my appointments talk about. Then there's the stories *we* tell, designed to scare, about mad, banished women in the fog pulling pieces from the outside of the Tower, gnawing through cables, stealing power... But the boys out of maintenance say that our building is too old, that the Chancellor diverted half their budget to the House of Peace to 'maintain law and order'. That any day now everything will just stop working.

I'm never sure of the truth of it. Never sure of the truth of anything. Because there's certainly less and less food, but then there are tales from boys back in the dorm, the ones that come from the Agro – the tunnels the House of Agriculture manage, way below the kitchens. They tell stories all the time about how the Hysterics are to blame, but no one's ever really seen an attack. They *have* seen crops rot with blight and animals die from disease or hunger because there were too many of them to feed…

Am I imagining it? Can I hear barking?

You want to die today? It's kill or be killed, that was what you said. It was the light-hours and the cooks sent us to the dogs, you and me. I thought we'd die that day.

Coward.

Our mouths to feed or theirs, that was what the cooks said.

I swear I can hear barking.

"It's my job to protect life. To protect our Tower," the Chancellor purrs "I do what has to be done."

She doesn't mean protecting boys. She means protecting women who can vote, who can merit her for saving them from the terrors beyond our walls, who don't need to worry about where they'll sleep, about what they look like, about the failures of their namesakes like weights on their ankles, or whether they'll be disappeared if they misbehave.

I try and listen, because somewhere in her speech might be a clue to what she wants from me, but still she goes on about how much she cares, that no one cares more. No one has sacrificed so much.

There's another voice inside my head. Not your voice, not Walker's. It says what if all she wants is someone to look after, someone to see the garden, someone to protect?

Other Chancellors, she tells me, had statues made of them. Glorious celebrations, there was so much love, but what have the people ever done for her? They should be grateful. They're ashamed of where she came from and I must understand that. "Do you know how much it hurts, Jude? To be so misunderstood?"

Did she grow up down in the tunnels like we did? There were history lessons the cooks gave us, all about Madam Hyde, the Chancellor's mother, who ran the Surrogacy beneath the Tower. Madam Hyde was the House Chief who brought in the Mind Absolution Act, pinheading the women sent to her Surrogacy out of 'kindness' they claimed. Our mothers.

"I want someone who understands me, who trusts me without question. Loyalty. That's all I've ever asked for." She shark-smiles again, showing all her teeth, and cups my cheek in her hand. Her skin is so soft, so cold, it feels slippery.

She wants me to show loyalty? Did she ask the same of you? Did you refuse before you ran?

For a moment, I can see myself as the Chancellor's ward. In charge of the House of Boys. Could I make things better? There wouldn't be any more boys dreaming of running. No boys would be disappeared. And we'd never be hungry or desperate or lonely again. If she buys me at auction, if I'm a good boy... If I do everything she wants.

"This way." She turns.

The trickle of water is falling somewhere beyond the towering trees, rustling grass, the crowding flowers and drapes of living green we push through. Things I've only ever seen in picture books, real and here and only a touch away. As we pass through another cluster of leaves into a clearing, she points to the tree with the largest trunk.

"Here we are."

The clearing is small and it's beautiful, except for the bruised and beaten woman kneeling at the roots of the tree. A woman with blood-red hair.

She's not Romali Vor – her hair is shorter, laced with grey. Her multicoloured dress is torn.

My knees collapse on the strange, soft green ground, smack into sweet soil. I've seen boys beaten but not as badly as this. Did the Chancellor do it? Did she have someone do it for her?

She pulls me up, introduces me as if I've come for dinner. "This is Lorri; Lorri, be nice to my guest." She seems excited.

The woman's face is a mask of bruises; one swollen eye looks at me as if pleading for help. I can't help. I don't know how.

I pull back but the Chancellor draws me closer, laughing to herself as a large white shape guarding the woman bounds towards her, its pink tongue lolling, its barking eager, hungry to be at her side.

I wasn't imagining it! I thought all the dogs were dead. Killed during the first food shortages when we were kids, when the crops got sick and there were too many mouths to feed.

I want to run but I'm frozen; memories of snarls and scratching paws glue me to the spot. I'm eleven again. And it's you and me, and nowhere to run to, and I know I'm going to die.

Is this why you didn't kill the Chancellor? Did you see the dog? Did the memories get the better of you too?

"Lorri has been sororitizing with my enemies – making friends with ladies, even men, that she shouldn't have. Isn't that right?" the Chancellor says as she rubs the ears of the creature that's eyeing me up like food.

The Chancellor said she likes rare things. Special things. The dog licks at her face and she laughs as the beaten woman tries to talk.

"No, no, Lorri. I told you, I've heard all the excuses I need to." The Chancellor's voice is still soft, gentle. "I asked you nicely to help."

Help with what?

The dog barks at the woman who scrambles towards the tree, gripping it as if it will help her. Why has the Chancellor brought me here? "One vote my way was all I asked."

"Madam, Madam Chancellor…" I say hurriedly. "You have to get a doctor."

"I don't have to do anything of the sort," the Chancellor says.

The balcony. Walker said I had to get her to the balcony, but I can't. I'm not brave enough. The balcony beyond the garden dome is behind me. How could I even get her there?

"And you have to do what I want, sugar. That's how this works," adds the Chancellor. "It's what I paid for."

One merit. She paid one merit just to show me she's capable of hurting women too? There's a brick in my stomach weighing me down and if I lose control I might sink through the floor, and all the floors below that, until I'm swallowed up by the earth.

"It's clear you're not going to kill me and we don't want to let all that training go to waste like the last time. I've been thinking I was a little – what's the word?" She bites her lip. "Rash? With the other one?" My fists clench whenever she mentions you. "I mean, yes, he was an assassin, but with a little discipline, and a little work, skills like that could really be worth something."

She laughs. "Right, Dee-dee?" Her dog growls protectively, while the Chancellor lifts the hem of her dress and removes something metal that was strapped to her ankle. It's a gun, silvery and beautiful. They're rare too. Only the Lice have them. Walker tried but couldn't get hold of one. I can't take my eyes off it.

"I thought Lorri here was a friend. But she's been voting against me for years while pretending to be my ally. Working with the Hysterics!"

The woman tries to protest but can't get the words out. She's missing a few teeth, her lips swollen.

No one would do what the Chancellor was accusing her of, would they? It's just another lie, right?

"She's meant to protect life but she's been feeding our precious children to madwomen, helping them kidnap boys. Men too, from the mines. I don't know about you, Jude, but I think a few bruises aren't enough."

If the woman was afraid before, there's terror in her eyes now.

The Chancellor continues. "There's this law in our constitution about the women in High House; it says because we can make life we don't deserve death, blah-blah. Based on that, some people would say Lorri here is above the law. I mean, please!"

The Chancellor glides towards me, gun in hand.

Just one push, Walker said. Maybe he wasn't talking about the balcony, but what I needed, to take her life. Except he was wrong. I'm not strong enough, never was.

"When women do terrible things, we simply take their minds and use them to surrogate our boys."

What are you waiting for?

"The lot of you, all birthed by lobotomized murderers and thieves and traitors." She turns and winks as the struggling woman begs for her life.

"I prefer the word the kids use: 'pinhead'. More poetic. But you see –" the birds in the rafters scramble as she clicks open the barrel of the gun – "we'd still have to have a trial and that'd be pretty embarrassing. Not to mention deadly boring. Death is a mercy. I presume Wally showed you how to use one of these?" she asks, holding out the gun. Somehow I have the mind to shake my head. "Oh, it's easy." She closes it up, shows me the trigger and puts it in my hand. So heavy.

Do it, you say but I can't.

The Chancellor lifts my shaking arm until the beaten woman

is within aim.

Kill or be killed!

"So I'm going to give you a choice, because I think *that's* fair. You can shoot Lorri for me, or I'll let you run."

Always fun when they run, she said. You ran.

And now the woman is begging me too. Pulling herself up, dizzy, falling. I think her leg is broken. Her coloured dress is dark with blood.

"What about … Walker?" I manage to say, stalling.

Coward, you say.

"Oh, I'll have Vor arrest him soon enough. His games have been a distraction. Can't blame a lady for getting bored, though, can you? I'll probably have Romali arrested too, for good measure," she says. "Lorri, you should have seen her performance this evening. What a riot. She actually—"

But before the Chancellor finishes the woman has launched herself at her, coughing up swear words, protests and shouts.

"Saints, you're disgusting, Loz," the Chancellor complains as she pushes the woman away with ease. She lands near my feet.

Do it, you say.

My arm isn't shaking any more. I'm pointing the gun at the Chancellor.

"Really?" she laughs. "You know Walker lied to you."

The woman is trying to say something, reaching up, grasping my trousers with broken, bloody hands, trying to pull me away. "You don't have to do this," I think she croaks. "You don't have to do this."

"Your friend's alive," the Chancellor says.

Her words punch my knotted gut but I manage not to drop the gun. "What?"

"Viktor, right? He was your friend?"

How does she know?

Every word, no matter how softly she speaks, cuts through me like a buzz saw. Did you talk about me? My hand shaking, I step back. Could I run? Should I run?

Go on, you say. *Kill or be killed.*

"You're lying!" The words burst out of me, that pressure in my head breaking out.

"He won't live if I'm dead, of course," the Chancellor grins. "Shoot or run, go on."

But there's another choice.

Good boys say yes. Good boys also don't plot to murder people.

I drop the gun.

"No," I say.

My name is Jude Grant. And I am a dead man.

THE HOUSE OF WARDS

I am yours.

All others are sin.

All else is death.

9

LESSONS IN BEING GOOD

The steam and stink of the underground kitchens. The hiss and clank of pipes. My bare feet kicking at the rotten food we hoarded to feed pet mice. Scrubbing and starving. That was life before the House of Boys.

At five I was sent straight from Madam Hyde's Surrogacy to the kitchens for my prenticeship. Three large floors below the dorms, all dented and blackened chrome, dedicated to making food for the ladies Above. The cooks prepared elegant meals, banquets, snacks, anything Above wanted, to order.

For the ladies: tagines and rice, pickled fruits and breads, sweet sauces, melting meat, cheeses and fruits and ice cream.

For us: protein shakes, scraps and peelings. All the nutrients a growing boy needs.

The cooks sent the junior prentice boys to collect ingredients grown in the Agro tunnels further beneath us. Food growing under the huge lamps the Foundations built. There were shelves of plants, caverns of animal pens, grain grinders, rooms that bloomed with salt crystals as big as my head. They treated the food better than us, I thought.

The ladies' orders came down huge pipes. More senior prentice delivered boxes and trays up the backstairs, or via dumb waiters spiralling into the Above. One day I could be a delivery prentice! Maybe I could see the sky! So, whatever the cooks ordered me to do, I tried to be a good boy, not to put a foot out of line, or at least to never get caught. Tried to be like all the rest of the boys, scraping this, packing that, washing and stacking and learning.

You came later, when I was ten.

Viktor Perrault: the boy who broke into the kitchens to steal leftovers and was sent to work for the cooks as punishment. Saints, did they take it out on you! Never known a boy bear so many beatings. Never thought we'd be friends. Never *dreamed* it. A bad boy like you would never bother with a good boy like me. By the time you got to the kitchens, half the boys there had already heard about you.

You arrived on my birthday; the cooks didn't feed me that day but I didn't complain. A new mouth to feed, they gave you my dinner. When they weren't looking, you gave it back.

You didn't want to get fat, you said, but I knew: you were being kind.

Kind.

I'd heard the word but how do you know what it means until you feel it? It made old bread taste softer, warmer; made lumpy protein shakes dance with sweetness (strawberries!); made crusty cheese rind melt, as precious and bitter as chocolate. I tried to make each mouthful last for ever. It was the first time I didn't feel alone.

You were about the same age as me but you'd been kicked out of four prenticeships by then, almost one a year! There are over twenty houses, you explained at dark-hours when we curled up to keep warm in the slop room of the kitchen. Each house had designated floors and ran everything in the Tower. Maybe you'd get to work in them all, you joked. You told us the kitchens were part of the House of Entertainment. You knew so much! You could list all the houses and the women that ran them and the prentice programmes that boys could be in. Even when the other kitchen boys got bored, I stayed up, kept asking questions.

I wanted a prenticeship at the House of Life, I told you once, trying to sound clever. "That's where they make us, you know," I said. "You, me, our brothers, even the women. Like magic."

"The Gardener doesn't take boys into prenticeships," you said.

"Gardener?"

"The Chief of Life, Lorraine Dunn. And it's not magic. She grows people in pots, that's what I heard, like plants. That's why they call her the Gardener."

Your last prenticeship almost stuck: the House of Air, vent maintenance, which is how you got so thin, you said. Had to stretch out like thread to do that job, but, "Oh, the secrets I know."

You leaned in, whispered close. "There are tunnels that can take you to the end of the world! Vents that climb to the moon."

Now that you were in the House of Entertainment I'd said, maybe you'd make it out of the kitchens and be a theatre prentice, or even get into the House of Maintenance and end up cleaning! Cleaning prentice got to visit the Above. "If you're really good, you might even get moved into the House of Expression and work for Madam Cramp; she's the kindest, the cooks say. You could be a muse, a model, maybe even a seamster at Cramp's."

"I've got other plans," you said.

In the dark-hours, the cooks made you sleep on the floor on the far side of the room, near the rag-wrapped heat pipes. After five years, all my good behaviour had earned me a spot by the door, where the air was fresher.

Two weeks into your prenticeship, you stepped over me as you snuck out.

What if you never came back?

Peering from behind the stove, I watched you hunt through the shelves, finding as many pieces of paper as you could – scraps of tickets from orders, notes from the cooks. You pushed them into a piece of cloth you'd stitched to the inside of your trousers. Then you found a large pan that shone so bright you could see your face in it. The cooks had really had a good go at you earlier that day. Your grey skin was almost purple with bruises but still, there you were, practising all thirty of your smiles.

Any day now you'd earn enough merits to make it into the House of Boys. You'd do all the dirty work; you'd take the beatings over the demerits; you'd do whatever favours you had to, to earn the merits you'd need to climb the floors. You were going to show them, you said. And I believed you when you told me that you were going to change the world.

10

There's a memory I'm trying hard to forget ringing in my ears when the lights turn on in the dorm. The morning after the garden, my life before the House of Boys feels a long way away. It's been hours since I gave up on sleep, last night playing over and over, making it harder to pretend it didn't happen. Still, I grunt, pull the sheets over my face and turn in my bunk.

"Mornin'." Stink yawns. He's hanging upside down over the side of his bunk above. Justin Reed; when he arrived in J-dorm ten months ago, he introduced himself as Stinger but we all call him Stink because of his terrible breath. He scratches at his blond shock of hair and tongues his bad molars. "You were shoutin' in your sleep," he says, poking at my shoulder. "Something about a deal?"

"I'm fine," I lie, and roll over, trying to ignore him.

"We all heard you clatter in. Did the Chancellor ride you blind?" Stink ignores me ignoring him. He keeps poking. When I smack his hand away, he drops down on to the floor and pushes himself right into my bunk. "Seriously, the fogging Chancellor, brother! What happened?"

"Nothing." I grit my teeth.

"Come on, 'fess up!" says Stink, pulling the bedclothes away. The cold air stings as I curl up, hug my knees.

Someone on the other side of the room throws a cup at him. Stink does not do quiet. It clanks on the metal frame and lands with a thud at his feet.

"Shut it, will you? Some of us still want to sleep." That sounds like Rodders. Our resident style guru. Thin as a pipe after a year of practically starving himself, he's polished the perfect smouldering look (he says) to bag the best guardian. Half the time he's staring in a mirror, pouting and screwing up his eyes like he's holding an ice cube between his butt cheeks. Rodders' given name is Jarod, but no one calls him that. For most boys, the names that High House give us don't matter; it's the ones we earn that we use. No one has given me a nickname yet, at least not one that's stuck.

"This is important," Stink says, throwing the cup back.

Rodders swears as he dodges it.

"So was she nice? I heard she's *reeeally* beautiful."

Stink doesn't even know what the word means. "You mean rich," I groan.

He grins a wide, crooked-toothed, stop-messing smile. "You stumbled in like a hooch-head at two in the morning. Threw up in Jipper's slippers."

So that's why my mouth tastes as if something died in it.

"We talked," I say. That part's true, after all.

The strip lights flicker, harsh and blue. Every boy in the dorm groans as they pull themselves up from where they lie, stretched out in their bunks like slabs of drying meat. The beat of the morning drums echoes through old speakers. Chattering and whispered conversations start up as the other thirty-three J-dormers drag their feet out of bed, scratch and stretch.

The usual games begin. Jig and his boyfriend Jag roll out of the bottom bunk near the door. Opposite, Joe pulls the covers over his head. Beau, whose given name is Jamaal, in the bunk above Joe, starts to pile as much of his stuff as he can on top of his bunkmate until Joe has had enough and throws it all off. Rodders is doing pull-ups while his bunkmate Woody, the new boy, searches for his clothes as they're thrown from bunk to bunk. Jeb starts folding notes to his latest crush (it changes every week – right now it's a boy in D-dorm; last week it was some girl in his appointments). The air fills with the comforting early-morning fug of hair oil, deodorant and farts.

I reach into the hole under my mattress, out of habit, to check my stuff is still there. I made a cloth bag in the kitchens like you had. Pulling it out, I empty it under the sheets. There are some things for trading, sweets, old pens with most of the ink still working. Then there's the note I never gave you and the little paper man, the one made out of mushed-up pulp. He fits in the palm of my hand and he's always breaking. I stuck him together with some glue from the med-kit in Father Jai's office, so he's not like he was when you first made him, but I've still got him.

Stink punches me in the shoulder through the sheets and swears as I emerge into the light. He throws my clothes at me before Jipper can ambush me and chuck them down the garbage chute for ruining his slippers.

"Pants and shirt. The essentials for any good, hard-working boy," Stink chirps. "Maybe, since the Chancellor reserved you, you think appointments are beneath you?"

"No," I groan, tidying my stuff and waiting for him to look away before I stash it back under my mattress. If it wasn't for the appointments, I'd not have earned a single merit against my debt. I'd have been in the mines long before my first chance at auction. "Give me five, won't you?"

"You mean you're not leaping out of bed with abandon at the thought of waiting hand and foot on our beautiful benefactors? Jude Grant, you shock me!" Stink holds his hand to his breastbone in mock horror. "Why not change the habit of a lifetime and enjoy this?"

"Because I'd rather be in bed, maybe?"

Stink laughs. He turns to shout to the rest of the dorm. "OK, brothers, hand it over!"

"What?" I sit up as they start throwing things into the middle of the room – their most tradable items: scraps of paper, notes from appointments, stolen food, make-up, pills.

Stink winks. "Just took a little bet that you'd be grumpy, even after your night with the Chancellor."

Stink can be kind of annoying. Fifteen, square-faced and naturally blond like you – which is pretty rare – odds are he'll get a buyer this year. He tells me he was rented by some new debutante his own age, a mid-floor girl called Quinn. She's already booked up two of his appointment slots today so they can keep snogging. He *would* get one of the young ones. Lucky sod.

Climbing from my bunk, I stretch. The low ceiling feels lower than ever.

"So I heard this story…" Stink is picking up his haul. He tries to catch my eye.

"Hit the showers, will you? I need a break." I'm walking away but I do sort of like his company, not that I'd tell him. Stink trots behind, talking so fast he might burst. So I listen. I nod. Number seven, *encouraging-but-not-too-much*, as we hop into our shorts and walk past our brothers rolling from metal bunks.

"Fogging hell, you'd think they'd turn the pipes on," swears Rodders, banging the radiator beside his bed. "Don't they know what this does to my pores!"

"The House of Boys will keep you safe!" Stink yells, repeating what the House Fathers say whenever we complain about the cold. It's easier than saying the heating has been diverted to keep the ladies warm. "Like rare wine," he concludes.

"Wine can be kept cold," Rodders sneers. He catches up, cleaning his specs. "I shoulda stayed on working with the boiler prentice; at least it was bloody warm!" He slips on his lopsided glasses and wraps a frayed excuse for a towel round his shoulders, rubbing his hands over his goose-pimpled arms as he heads out to the shower.

Stink is still waffling on with a story about a kid in G-dorm who managed to get his hand stuck down the drain as we dress. We then line up and file out through the low concrete space of the basement, down the dark corridor towards Father Jai's office. There we're meant to collect the keys to our allocated appointment rooms above, on the ground floor.

"*Sooo…*" Stink keeps asking. "What happened?"

Of course I'm not going to tell him.

11

"So it's a run then? Good." That's what the Chancellor said as she picked up the gun.

"No." Double no. By now, she probably thought I was like one of the pinheaded women in the Surrogacy. "You ... you think she's the only one," I stuttered, my mouth stumbling over words as my brain ran too fast. "She betrayed you, didn't she? You think she's the only one?"

That was how I got her to listen.

"You're right, she's not the only one."

"I ... I can help!"

"Help?" She laughed.

My mouth ran faster than I ever thought it could; with every word, the pressure inside my head was getting lighter. "I'm a big earner; my appointments are always popular. And with ... after tonight, more women will book. Every dinner, every tea service, every session, every day, the guests ... they talk." Grasping for something, anything – I had to keep her attention. "You ... you have more enemies, don't you?" I bet my life it'd get her interested if I had something to offer her that no one else could. "I can give you their names. Tell you what they say."

"You think evidence from a *boy* has any weight in a trial? That's sweet."

"You don't want a trial, though, right? You can arrest them, discredit them… You just need names."

"True." She looked at the woman at her feet. The dog snapped at her whenever she attempted to move. "With the vote planned –" the Chancellor was talking to herself now – "she'll inherit her aunt's merits, which makes her dangerous…"

The woman waved her arms. "No, no!" Her throat crackled. But the Chancellor wasn't listening to her any more than the distant water, or the birds cawing above. She turned to me.

"I want Romali Vor exposed. To be specific, I want her out of the way."

I stepped back, the energy inside me collapsing. "You want me to kill her?"

"Now, now, I didn't say that. Unless you could…?"

I pictured the face of Romali Vor, the desperation, the pride, as she looked up at me from the edge of the stage.

"Jude?"

"I—"

Why did I hesitate? Romali Vor tried to get me arrested!

"So I was right, you do know her." The Chancellor grinned like she'd unearthed some brilliant gossip.

"She… She just never said anything about you."

"You know I'm convinced she's been working with Lorri here, helping Hysterics infiltrate our walls … not that my friend would give her up. And I was at my most persuasive. Now, if

Romali showed her true colours, she would reveal her treason. A handsome young man in need of a brave saviour would be just the thing."

"But there are others!" It wasn't a lie. I've heard them. Women who feel trapped like we do, who love men warded to others, who want to climb the floors but who can never be merited, who've gone hungry. Even they can be afraid; even they can lose everything. Not many, maybe one in every ten appointments, but it's happening more often.

"Others?" The Chancellor laughed as if any woman could be unhappy under her care.

Why was I protecting Romali Vor? She's not my friend. Not like you were.

"You think I'll change my mind? You have my terms," the Chancellor insisted, opening the gun, inserting a handful of bullets. Had it even been loaded?

"I need time," I said. I wouldn't promise something I couldn't deliver. If Romali Vor had tried to get me arrested because she wanted to *save* the Chancellor, then there was no threat to expose.

"Two days then, by the talent show." She was thinking fast too, I realized, working out what to do next. "I'll send notice."

"You'll send someone?" I asked. "You'll let Vik go?"

The beaten woman, tears pouring from her swollen eyes, shook her head. Maybe I should have come up with a better idea.

"If you give me what I want, then why not?" The Chancellor shrugged her soft shoulders. Then she clicked the gun and pointed it at the woman. I didn't have time to close my eyes.

The air thumped with the sound.

The woman stopped moving.

My ears were still ringing as the Chancellor strode towards her kill. Her white dog, splattered red, sniffed at the body, before beginning to clean itself. The Chancellor pulled a circular brooch from the woman's dress. The circle is the symbol of the House of Life, I remembered as her blood bloomed, spreading in a dark carpet over the green grass. The Chancellor had just killed the Gardener.

12

It's not just still ringing, that shot. It's getting louder the harder
I try to shut it out, my limbs shaking with the memory of it as
Father Jai starts the morning the same as always, with a lecture.
Eyes popping, his jowly, overly made-up head bobbing at each
boy that passes through his 'office' – a broom cupboard with a
cut-down desk that threatens to be consumed by the piles of
papers, old cleaning equipment and boxes that more important
House Fathers have stashed round him.

We all have our place in the order of things, Walker says.
Father Jai, who hasn't had a decent sale in the auctions for as
long as I've known him, is no exception. But today he seems
to hold himself taller. The bottle of cloudy hooch, normally
unstoppered on his desk, is on top of the cupboard. As I enter, I
swear he actually winks one kohl-lined eye at me.

"Every house has its duty, an oath," Jai recites, looking up as
he searches his desk for… "Aha!" he says, finding the rectangle
of plastic.

"We blind ourselves to beauty. Our speech is sacred. To love
is illusion," I mutter while he spits on and wipes the keycard,
bestowing it on me solemnly. I need to know if Walker's sent a

message summoning me. He said he'd see me in the morning but he's not come. He's Head of House but he doesn't normally visit unless there's been a fight or something really bad. If he had sent a note, Jai would be all aflutter.

Pinching the card with the tips of two fingers at the far edge, I smile your best *thanks-but-no-thanks*. The card is ancient, cracked, with centuries of dirt even a good lick-and-spit can't budge. If we lose or damage the keycard, we're thrown out of the house, into the mines, Jai reminds me, with the usual ominous, wide-eyed dread.

No message. Why wouldn't Walker try to contact me?

"*Aaand…*" Jai encourages, circling a sausagey hand.

What follows is not part of our official oath, just something Jai likes us to say. "I will make my house proud," I add with a roll of my eyes.

"*Aaand…*" Another encouragement, this time with a wobble of his chins and a quirk of his eyebrows.

"Father, are there any messages for me?"

"*Aaaand…*" he presses, ignoring me.

"And our guests –" I swallow, covering the churning in my stomach with a *can-I-get-out-of-here-now?* smile – "satisfied."

"Attaboy!" Jai grins with apple-cheeked glee. As I leave, he ushers in the next boy.

Walker hasn't reached out. I'm on my own.

Next in line is Woody, Rod's new bunk-brother. He joined J-dorm a month ago. At thirteen he came in from his prenticeship in the House of Air, so all the boys are after him for their Collections. Jimmy Wu, that's his real name (it was Rod who dubbed him 'Woody') is the first airer to join the House of Boys since you. And you were only in vent maintenance for a year. Woody was in Air from the age of five.

In the days leading up to this year's Reserves, there were boys queuing outside J-dorm before breakfast, each clutching scraps of paper and sticks of graphite, to get their five minutes with Woody. Each one drawing, fast, on the sheets of paper they'd managed to earn or pilfer – the black market in paper is pretty impressive.

Half the boys who crowded the dorms came just to watch. The House Fathers had to come out and get everyone in bed, even lock the dorms. The Collections were hidden in a scramble and stories about how the new kid had chocolate (not information) were dutifully spread. A few years ago, B-dorm had their Collection discovered and destroyed by Father Bull, every boy made to kneel in salt for a week. No one from B has got involved with the Collections since.

It hasn't stopped the rest of us, though. In fact, since food got cut, since boys started getting sick, since the demerit rules got stricter, since the blackouts started to happen every week, efforts have tripled to collect as much information about the worlds Above, Below, Beyond. Every fact questioned and analyzed and compared. Every rumour tested and challenged. Every bit of info from any boy, man or woman pressed into pages. Each dorm competing with the others. I wonder if the Collections could help me find something that will get Romali Vor to give herself up to the Chancellor? What else have I got?

There are rumours T-dorm has a full chart of every madam's bloodline – all the way back to the Saints. And M-dorm, their speciality is instruction manuals for all of the machines the Foundations left us. They also collect spare parts, broken bits, and will show them to any boy who can trade a good story. P-dorm, they like to collect secrets. They're my best bet.

Apart from B-dorm, the only boys that don't play are V-dorm. They stopped when you left.

But you didn't leave, I remind myself.

And you didn't die.

You were taken.

Are you above me right now? Maybe you're below? After you were arrested, did Madam Vor send you to the mines? Does Walker know you're alive? Maybe he'll come to my appointments. Yes, that's what Walker's waiting for; it has to be. Unless I'm no good to him any more – it's not like I did what I was meant to. Maybe he doesn't think he can trust me?

As we head to our appointments, Rodders swings an arm over Woody's shoulder. Rod looks after J-dorm's Collection and has already quizzed Woody enough to make the kid cringe whenever he appears. He reminds Woody that any other boy from any other dorm has to pay for an interview now.

"What with?" asks Woody, shrinking away. He's only about as tall as my shoulder.

"Info, tips, whatever," Rod answers. "Just don't give 'em anything for free, kid! Everything has a price." He tidies his hair, adjusts his glasses and winks, sticking to Woody like a rash until we get to the top of the stairs and Woody's appointment room. Escaping Rod's grip, the kid swipes his key against the panel on the wall and the door clicks open.

On the way to his appointment, Rod tells us about his latest addition to J-dorm's Collection. A map of the elevator system. He says there's a secret maintenance elevator that goes all the way up to the garden. His description makes my neck cold. I saw it. The Chancellor had me move the Gardener's body…

Don't think about that. I can't help her but I can help you even though there's nothing in J-dorm's Collection of any use. J-dorm collect stories – except Rodders, he's a map man, addicted to knowing what houses occupy each floor, where the chiefs live, which floors are no longer occupied, which elevators get you where. He's certain he'll prove the stories of Outside are lies, that the Last War that trapped us all in the Tower was made up by the Hysterics to drive us mad.

Idiot, you call him.

I try not to laugh.

Maybe all the hair oil he uses has seeped into his brain.

You're one to talk, Slick Vik. That's what your dorm mates called you.

Still, Rod's Collection of notes is impressive. There are even drawings of High House Tower, its eight-pointed, star-shaped footprint a great compass in the desert, Father Jai claims. The first building visible from the moon.

"Space!" Rod laughed after Jai tried to explain, one history lesson. "A big rock floating in nothingness? That's what they want you to believe!"

Should I tell him I've seen it? The vast night sky. The glow of the moon.

He probably wouldn't believe me. I try to remember it but can't. All I remember is the weight of the Gardener. Dead.

After the gunshot, my memories are a blur. *Tell anyone you want but no one will believe you*, the Chancellor said. She left me in the dark, her dog staring at me, sizing me up.

It seemed like hours but can't have been long before someone came to collect me. A dark shape, spidery, dressed from the after-party. Masked like the rest. She kept her hand on my shoulder, her long fingers holding me tight. I couldn't stop thinking about the body, staring at the blood on my hands as the spidery woman bundled me from elevator to elevator until we reached the dorms.

"Jude." Stink nudges me. "You OK?"

Swallowing the bitter burn in my throat, I push away the memory. "Yeah, fine."

"Don't get sick now," Stink jokes. "You get sent to the infirmary and miss auction, and Jai has to cover your reserve," he reminds me.

"One merit?" I roll my eyes. "How *will* he cope?"

Unlike most of the boys here, I do *not* want to go to the infirmary. You want your teeth fixed, your chin a better shape, hair implants or a nose job? If you're lucky, the ladies in your appointments will pay for a treatment. Sure, they can heal you up fast these days but a trip there will waste time.

The Chancellor keeps a room up there for Walker, so he always looks his best. Maybe he's there now, getting something tweaked or trimmed in time for the ball, his big performance. Not like it's important to come and check on me or anything, not like we've been working together all year!

Rod reaches his appointment room, swipes his card with care as if the thing was made of ricepaper and might crumble if held too hard. Then suddenly he's swearing, waving his schedule board. "Four hours foot massage with Old Crusty-bunions!" There's the wafting smell of incense from his room. Crusty is what we all call Madam Swann, who heads up the House of Construction. Her callouses are notoriously tough. "You have to be foggin' kidding me!" Rod yells so loud his door shakes. Half the boys are still laughing as I get to my room and duck inside.

13

Room forty-two. The plinking-plonking music they pipe through the speakers starts up on cue. The usual ache in my head is gone, for now, but it'll return. Once I might have danced when I heard music like that, but not any more. It's meant to be relaxing. It isn't. It always skips in the same damn place.

The same damn place.

Gulping down the sickening incense smell, I get busy.

Checking the appointment bookings, a card with bumps of dark-text: those small raised dots the House Fathers teach us to read with the pads of our fingers. No names or details yet, just notes to say there are five bookings, each an hour long.

There's a card with the details of my first appointment: name, type of service, how to arrange the room. Appointment one is Madam Cramp from the House of Expression: a suit fitting, so moving the furniture around is my first job. The room is medium-sized, with space for no more than four guests. I wrestle the old table to one side.

How do I give the Chancellor Romali Vor? It's impossible but I have to give her *something*. What the fog did I agree to?

Maybe Madam Cramp won't come. Maybe it'll be Walker.

He always books appointments under a different name.

Dragging the golden floor pillows and chaise longue far enough apart, I stand, stretch and imagine all those floors above, the star of the Tower meeting in the point of the garden.

I have to stop. Close my eyes to stop the room from spinning. It's the exertion of moving things. My dorm clothes are sticking to me so I pull off my shirt. I'll need to change soon anyway.

Keep going, you say.

My hands shaking, I collect the ugly trinkets from the surfaces and hide them inside the drawers of a dresser so I don't have to worry about knocking them over. The demerit fines for any damage have gone up again this year.

If I stop moving even for a second, there it is, under the surface, the dog, the blood, the shot, the promise. It shakes through me, trying to burst out. All I want to do is scream into a pillow, throw things and tear at the walls with my hands. It's like I'm a kid again, in the Surrogacy, shut in that dark box, no way out.

Keep going.

A bell rings. In the dumb waiter is my work outfit. A grey jacket buttoned over a white T-shirt. It's high-necked, long-sleeved (Saints forbid we show even an inch of flesh). Hot, itchy, bland. The black trousers aren't much better. Too tight for a start. The high waist comes up to my last rib, with braces clipped under the jacket to lock them in place. I don't like how the trousers cling, I'm always pulling at them, but they're designed to show us off, Walker says.

The women get to wear colours. Bright, swirling, all shapes, all shades. Light, loose cloth. Everything about them moves. We have rigour and rules and restraint. Elastic that holds everything in place. Madam Cramp complained about it to me once. She longs to give us something with shape, with brightness. Not the usual grey, black and white.

And I think of the Gardener in all her colours. How the bright fabric darkened with her blood.

And then Romali, at Reserves.

From my trouser pocket, I dig out a fat strip of thick white ribbon. A blindfold. I'd get more merits docked if I'm reported for breaking my oath – or worse. Being sent to the mines used to be a last resort. Before we're disappeared, there's a menu of punishments they use first in the cells to show penance for oath breaking. Boys are blinded for catching a glimpse of a woman's face before being warded.

Even with the Chancellor's protection, I'm not going to risk another peek so tie the cloth round my eyes tight enough so there's only darkness. Humming to hear how the pitch changes as I turn my head, bouncing the sound off the same old walls, I find the familiar rough path of worn carpet around the room. It's more recognizable in the dark. Safer too somehow.

"The eyes are the windows to our souls," I mutter to myself, doing my best impression of Father Jai. "And no one can sell a house with dirty windows," I say as my shin bumps into the table and I swear. For the first time in a year, I think I can hear you laugh and I smile. A proper smile, not a practised one. I'll call it number thirty-five. The kind that puffs out my chest, makes me stand taller. Makes me hope.

You're alive! ALIVE! And I'm going to find you, whatever it takes.

*

Bzzzz

The blindfold makes the sound of the buzzer stab as it blares above the other door, the one they don't give us a keycard for. The guest entrance clicks open and locks behind the new arrival. The clock on the wall ticks loudly.

Appointment one: Madam Cramp, not Walker, arrives on cue. She smells of glue and fresh linen when she takes my arm, leads me to the chaise longue. The skin of her hand is old, papery. Today she's brought the suits Walker ordered for me for the shows, one for the ball, one for the auction. Just in case, he said. Never pass up a chance to order a good suit. Unlike the outfits from Reserves, they feel good.

The scrape of her pen means she's making notes. The rattle of her tape measure means she's taking measurements. The scratch of her pins, the softness of her apologies when she nicks me.

I wonder what would've happened if I'd been a prentice at the House of Expression. There's peace there, they say. She lets boys create. I could make clothes for the rich, the famous. Top-floor ladies. I could've had my own room. I could earn enough merits to be happy, healthy. That would be a kind of freedom, right?

There's a bag of sweets on the table as a tip after. I can almost taste the sugar but I'll save them to trade with Stink. In the darkness, when Cramp's gone, I don't feel alone any more.

You should give the Chancellor Madam Cramp's name, you say.

Cramp's one of the good ones. Someone else.

You have to give her something.

Walker will come soon, I tell myself.

*

Bzzzz

Appointment two: still no Walker. A brunch. I count four guests, two older voices, two young. The three-course meal I smell, coming up the dumb waiter from the kitchens below: hot chilli jams, sweet lamb, pastry, warm jasmine tea. There's a menu delivered in dark-text. I dance the tips of my fingers over it and announce the courses, my mouth still watering.

They talk about the latest 'mercies': the men who sacrificed their lives in the atrium yesterday. If the mines are full, then there has to be a better way proposed soon to vote on, the ladies say. The mercies are, of course, a kindness, but it's getting too gruesome. Funny, on that last point we agree. Soon there won't be any men left, they say, and who'll do all the men's work then? They change the subject to Reserves and one of the older ones says something about how she thought I'd be thinner.

Don't flinch, you say. *Spit in their tea when it arrives.*

I feel my way across the room, open up the rattling hatch, lean into the dumb waiter. I wait to feel the steam of her tea on my cheeks, before I let out a good glob. Listen to it plop before turning and serving with an *anything-I-can-do-for-you?* grin.

Nice work, you say, laughing in the faces of the women as they slurp.

Small victories. That's what gets me through the day.

∗

Bzzzz

Appointment three: a work lunch plus coffee. Two women, one from the House of Maintenance and another from the House of Air, discussing the impact of blackouts on the upper-floor filtration systems. Worries about top-floor women breathing lower-floor air. Improving vent resilience.

I doze off at one point but manage not to fall over, or snore. Then I'm alerted by whispers, quiet breath, crying so quiet that if my ears weren't sharp I wouldn't notice it.

The woman from the House of Air's ward has been arrested, but no one will tell her what he did. They were together fifteen years – now what? Her friend comforts her, shushes her. Not in front of the boy. Not here. Swallow it down. Don't let anyone know it hurts.

"But he looked so… The cleaners left him all day in the atrium. All twisted. All mess. People just walked past. Like rubbish. He … he was my friend. My best friend. He would never hurt anyone. What am I going to do?"

You'll get another at auction, says the maintenance woman, comforting her tears and snuffles. But the first woman hasn't the merits. If she had, maybe she could've stopped— The second woman tells me to go and get something to eat, give them the room to themselves. I don't argue.

When I get back, they've gone. But I can't get their conversation from my head. It bounces around. Are there women up there who feel like we do about the mercies, about the Chancellor? What if it's not just those two? What if there are more of them?

I push the furniture aside and try to distract myself by practising the steps they taught us for the ball. They feel stiff, uncomfortable, so I stop, kick the couch until my toes hurt.

Where the hell is Walker? I can't do this on my own. This is all his fault!

∗

Bzzzz

Shit!

Appointment four.

"Once moment, please!" I cry, moving the furniture.

Bzzzz

The appointment card delivered under the door doesn't have a name I know but, as I set up the room, the layout is familiar. Like a code to tell me it's her. Rain Girl. Like Walker, she never booked under the same name, maybe bribing the stewards to keep her appointments secret. I never asked her name, and eventually it felt weird to try, but I remembered her voice, the hours of listening to it.

Maybe I imagined it; maybe Romali Vor just sounded like her?

Bzzzz

One time, a few months after she started booking appointments, she just cried. Girls don't cry. The daughter of the Chief of Peace wouldn't cry. So Rain Girl probably isn't Romali Vor.

Before that she'd come a few times, three or four, and not said a word. And then she just turned up and cried.

I thought my only friend was dead and I couldn't tell anyone, didn't want to be accused of being 'emotional' on top of everything else even when the grief ate at me. But here was a stranger who could do everything I wanted to do. She could show her emotions, come and go as she pleased. I had to stand there, be good and quiet and hold it all inside. Something, maybe the passions the House Fathers always warn us about, made me reach out, take her hand, hold it. Her fingers felt rough and hot, her fingernails short. Jagged and torn.

I knew she could have told the stewards. The list of punishments tore through my mind: demeriting wasn't enough. I'd probably lose my hand. Bad thoughts pushed into my mind: the urge to lean into her, find her lips, kiss them. Even if every bone of me knew she wanted the same, or even just wanted to ask, boys can't do that. The Lice don't even send us to the mines if we're caught, just a one-way trip from a high balcony to a hard floor.

The next visit I asked if she was OK and that's when she started talking. It was hard to stop her then. Every other woman that booked an appointment ignored me, or wanted something from me, except her. She just wanted to talk.

She'd tell me about the girls she knew, and how they'd talk about her behind her back, how they thought she didn't know. She'd complain about one of her mothers, and how they'd fight, and how she wanted to move in with her aunt. Then the next day she'd want to listen to the radio, or read. She'd tell jokes, dirty ones. Sometimes I'd ask questions, like what she did all day. School, she said, in the mornings, at the House of Knowledge, then working as a junior. "Is that like a prentice?" I'd ask. Same thing, she guessed, but they got to choose. Anyway, it was dull. She'd wanted to join the House of Exploration, but the Chancellor shut it down. Then she'd go quiet.

Sometimes she'd talk about helping at the House of Amalgam, where they keep all the old stuff – books from the Saints' times and machines, thousands of them, and huge stuffed animals! It's amazing, she'd say, and draw pictures on my hand with kohl. When she'd gone, I'd pore over the scrawls in the minutes between appointments, try to remember them, try to imagine a world where these things were real. But then I had to wash them off before anyone saw.

The next week she'd talk about which girls liked which boys, which wards too, and which girls liked which girls, the last party she'd been to and who was caught flirting when they shouldn't. There were stories about the top-floor girls meeting the older prentice, even though it was illegal. Stories of prank orders to the kitchens; girls who'd had their wards' noses fixed at the infirmary and hated the result.

She'd talk about the Outside. The sun. Vik, she'd talk about the sun! The heat on her skin, the colour of the desert beyond, how it changed in the light. And the storms! Great electrical bolts of white light, the fog, the stars. I should've told the boys in the dorm, put what she told me in our Collection. But I wanted to keep it for myself.

Is that bad?

She'd bring piles of records and play them loudly, and she'd nag me to dance, but I'd said I couldn't. All those knots inside and the ache in my head. I'd say no and she'd dance round me, laughing like an idiot. I never saw her. OK, maybe once I peeked, just at her feet, moving and jumping until she fell over, out of breath.

Sometimes we'd move the furniture out of the way and lie on the floor and she'd read aloud. Long books about great adventures and stories of warrior women rescuing handsome princes, of other planets, ancient cities made of glass, of monsters and magic. And I'd curl up and listen, and sometimes I'd fall sleep, not because I was bored but because it was safe. She wasn't a girl really. She was like a brother… A kind of crazy, really talkative, better-smelling brother.

So you thought you were friends?

Well, she wasn't like you, of course, because even the times she and I were just quiet you were always there, in a corner of my head, to remind me.

She just wants one thing.

It's not like she wanted to buy me; she said she didn't want a ward. She never tried to touch me, not like that.

Maybe you wanted her to?
It wasn't like that.
Girls like that don't need a ward; they just want some fun.
Maybe.
She tried to get you arrested.

*

When did the buzzing stop? My heart thumping. After everything, after Reserves, I didn't think she'd risk coming.

14

The door closes. I can't hear any other people, only her breath, her footsteps.

Say something!

I want to ask her about last night.

Go on, you say. *Coward. You can't even break one rule.*

"It's you, isn't it?" I ask, not waiting for permission. "Romali?"

"Just … give me a minute," she says, still pacing.

I was right. That brittle, bristling voice. Full of energy.

I reach behind my head to take off my blindfold, struggling with the knot, like she did with her mask at Reserves. I need to see her again, to look her in the eye.

"Don't," she says. She won't stop pacing. The perfume of rainwater makes me shiver; my brain rattles with it.

"But I've already seen—"

"I don't want you to see me like … like this," she interrupts, sniffing.

"Like what?"

"I just … I need a fogging moment, Jude, OK?" she snaps. There's the slap of a thick wad of paper landing on the table. "I … I needed somewhere safe."

Safe.

She feels safe with me? Like I did with her – before. Before I knew who she was. Before Reserves. Before the garden.

"Don't freak out," her voice shaking like she's cold.

"What about?" I ask as something flies against the wall and smashes.

Romali Vor really likes to break things. Here she is again, doing everything I want to do.

I duck, covering my head as something breaks opposite me, then to my left, my right.

"What the fog?" I shout. "Are you trying to kill me?"

She stops. "What do you think?"

The hairs at the nape of my neck stand up. I can feel her looking at me.

"You … you tried to get me arrested!" I remind her.

"No, you idiot. Of course I'm not trying to kill you. I'm trying to save your ass!"

"Don't call me an idiot," I say. "Please." Always that need to be nice.

"They could've got you out!"

"Who?"

There's the scratching sound of a drawer opening. She's found the trinkets I hid in the cupboard.

My teeth press together so hard my head pounds as things crash and smash all around me. I have to stop her. I'm the one who'll be punished for this. Maybe the House Fathers will lock me in the store cupboard for days like the last boy who damaged his appointment room, a freshman N-dormer who came out mop-thin, stinking and dry-retching. He was never the same.

The sounds get closer to me, like walls closing in. That boy inside, the one who danced until they squashed it out of him, starts kicking at my bones. I let him kick. They trained me well.

When everything breakable is in pieces, the soft sound of thuds follows as she punches and yells into the pillows.

My hands are shaking with anger, nerves. The room feels too small and too big at the same time.

"The Hysterics!" She throws something again. "They've been breaking people out of the cells for years." So the Chancellor was right: she *is* working with the Hysterics. Is that all I need to get you out? No. I have to get her to admit it publicly. "All you had to do was play along!" Air puffs as she flops down on the nearest couch.

"Maybe if you'd warned me," I say.

"There wasn't time. And I didn't know you'd be up there … not till I saw the docket. I had to act fast."

I ask if I can sit.

"Of course, do what you want," she says, like she's surprised I even asked. She doesn't get what it's like to need permission to do everything, even going to the bathroom.

Feeling my way to the couch, careful as my slippered feet crunch through broken shards, I try to slow my breath, before pulling down the blindfold ribbon until it hangs around my neck. Can I trust her?

"You'll get in trouble," Romali says, rolling her puffy, mascara-smeared eyes. She's slumped in the cushions. She's real. Really real. Her green eyes lock on to mine.

"You going to tell?"

I think she laughs, even though she doesn't want me to see. "I could have you arrested," she jokes.

"Not funny," I say.

"Sorry."

I rub at my eyes where they burn with the salt that's built up under my lids. It's hard to blink after a day of wearing a blindfold. Takes an hour or two to see straight. Her face is a little blurry but I don't care.

"Anyway, I wouldn't. Not now. Try to get you arrested, I mean. They can't get you out now you're under her protection. The police wouldn't lock you up without her consent."

"So you knew the Chancellor would reserve me?" Does she know I was meant to kill the Chancellor?

She laughs with a snort, sits up and looks at me like I'm fresh out of the Surrogacy. "Do you even look in the mirror?"

We have one mirror in our dorm so it's a fight to get to it. I'm not sure what she's trying to say. I did my best this morning to get smart for my appointments.

"The hair, the dimples. Those eyes?" Her eyebrows shoot up as she waves her hands up and down.

Maybe if the couch cushions would swallow me up I wouldn't be so aware of my body, and how gangly and weird it is compared to hers. "What's wrong with them?"

She laughs. "Saints, Jude, there's being coy and then there's

98

being obtuse. Don't pretend you don't know how cute you are. It's not ... cute." She rolls her eyes. "Anyway, yes, everyone knew. And maybe it's not even about how you look. She's been looking to replace Walker and you're the most expensive boy on the docket. She likes rare things."

"Expensive? But no one had reserved me yet."

"'Expensive' as in you have the highest debt. Nearly a million demerits, right? That's what the docket said. Super rare. Most boys are between five and three hundred thousand."

Last year you were the only boy onstage with a debt higher than mine. I've never met any boy with a higher debt than you. Is that all Walker needed to get the Chancellor to bite?

Me, you, my brothers, the boys before us, we spend our whole lives trying to erase the debts we inherit, to give ourselves, or the boys that take our name after we're dead, even a distant chance of freedom. It's drilled into us that it's our duty to erase our forefathers' sins. When you have nothing, it's something to hold on to, that hope. That maybe, one day, one of us might do it.

"So are you going to tell me?" Romali asks, not looking at me.

"Tell you what?"

"How you're still here." She sits up straight. "You know what happened to the boy she reserved last year?"

That boy has a name, I want to say.

"If she knew we were friends..." She reaches out, puts her hand on mine. I pull it back. "I couldn't let that happen to you."

We're friends?

"I guess she liked me," I say, tugging at my ears as if they're on fire. Maybe Romali can tell I'm lying but how can I explain what really happened? If she doesn't know I was meant to kill the Chancellor, I'm not going to tell her. I'm still not sure if I can trust her.

"You know I shouldn't be here. She's crazy, thinks I want to be Chancellor, has people watching me, makes up stories in the news. I wish I'd been able to put my name on our appointments but … whatever she learns about me she spins and manipulates, turns against me. She's obsessed and getting worse. You have to know, coming to see you today, I'm taking a risk. You're hers now."

"I'm not her property," I say.

"Not yet."

True.

"But … I had to come," she says, tensing. "We promised we wouldn't lie to each other, right?" She can tell I'm hiding something.

"Why didn't you tell me Walker was training you?" she asks.

So she does know. And she knows about Walker too? Months ago she told me there was no one she could trust; she told me not to trust anyone either. Was she warning me about Walker? This place twists everything good, she said. If she was right, can I even trust her?

My words trip over themselves. "It was a secret, not a lie. Like how you didn't tell me who you were all year. You didn't need to book under a name, you still could've told me," I say. "I wouldn't have said anything."

"Don't change the subject," she groans, before taking a deep breath. "Saints, what did you expect me to do? Sit down and give you the whole saga? Like, 'Hi, I'm Romali Dunn Vor. You know, last of the Dunn bloodline; they ran the Tower for centuries. My grandmother *did* go crazy but don't worry, I'm a totally normal girl really.' Yeah, that wouldn't have been weird and we'd totally have been able to keep seeing each other."

"You're trying to be funny again," I say.

"I guess. Anyway, maybe I enjoyed being anonymous; maybe I wanted you to like me for who I am not who you assumed I might be." She raises both her eyebrows up high. "You think we don't know you guys have lists – the best girls to get bids from?"

There are lists, bets, but I never—

"Now your turn. Walker?"

"Why do you assume I'm working with Walker?" I ask.

"I have my sources," she says. "There's something else you're not telling me."

The words are building in my chest like a boulder I have to choke out. I'll tell her about the Chancellor, about the Gardener and Walker's plan, and how you're alive and I'm going to find you. Maybe Romali will help if Walker won't. Maybe she'll give herself up and no one else will have to get hurt.

But then I see what Romali's left on the table: a news pamphlet from the House of Information. I search for words I understand. Boy. Dignity. I get those. Grace and auction too. I'm getting better but it's still full of hundreds of words I don't understand. I screw up my eyes to try to read the three at the top.

"Madam Dunn missing," Romali reads aloud, then goes quiet.

I think about what she said about her family. Romali Vor is a Dunn. And then I remember the Collections from T-dorm. Those family trees.

Not missing, dead. The Gardener was Romali's aunt.

"I told you everything," Romali says. "I've risked *everything*."

"I know." That stone still sits in my throat. I could tell her about what happened – she'll go after the Chancellor, expose herself, and then I can save you.

"What aren't you telling me?"

I shake my head, try to smile. That *butter-wouldn't-melt* smile. I can't – I'm a coward. Why aren't you screaming at me? Help me. Why can't I just tell her?

She stands, snatches up the paper and looks down at me. Maybe the stories we hear of Romali Vor aren't true, maybe they come from the Chancellor's lies. But for a moment there's the Romali Vor we hear tales about, in the way she stands, the strength, the certainty. She tries to clean up the mess she's made, kicking stuff under the couches. I want to tell her it won't be enough; the cleaning prentice will find it, report it and I'll be the one that's punished for it.

"Are you in the talent show tomorrow?" she asks.

I shake my head. Walker never planned for me to get that far.

"Look, the Hysterics can maybe still get you out during the show." Romali heads for the door. "Unless you'd prefer to be the Chancellor's new ward."

"Tomorrow?" I say. Of course I want to get out: it was our

dream. But I can't leave the Tower yet, not without you. And the Hysterics, aren't they dangerous? And if I leave without giving Romali to the Chancellor then you're a dead man. Maybe we could all escape. I want to ask if she's going to leave too...

But Romali Vor has already gone.

15

Another dark-hours without sleep and the Chancellor expects Romali to give herself up today! I thought maybe Walker would send for me after my appointments, but still nothing. If the Chancellor had had him arrested, everyone would be talking about it. There's only one conclusion: I'm on my own. I need to stop hoping he'll come.

This year's talent event is swimwear, so it's the prime topic of conversation in the line to get our appointment keys. Shaving vs trimming. Oiling vs tanning. Sticking vs spraying. Starving vs sweating.

Prep started early this year: half the boys in J-dorm fasting months ago even though only over-sixteens compete. Doesn't stop everyone being caught up in it, though.

Only the boys with the right measurements get to take part. The list went up on the board before Reserves. Rodders is in – after spending every free second in the gym this year, that's no surprise. As soon as he wakes up, he's preening in front of the dorm mirror, practising his routine for the show. He has to do it exactly right, doesn't want to get marked down by the judges for non-regulation footwork. Two other boys in J had the measurements to make the cut too, but neither of them got through Reserves. Walker never planned for me to make it into Swims. As far as he was concerned, the whole auction process would be cancelled after the Chancellor turned up dead, so I never even tried to get on the list.

*

Bzzzz

"I really can't do this right if you move, Jude," she sighs.

Appointment one today: posing for a painting with Madam Strand, who heads the House of Media. Another regular. She tips with a kohl pencil every time. Normally I slip it under my mattress with Stink's sweets.

I keep thinking about the Gardener. If I'd killed the Chancellor, the Gardener would still be here but then I'd never have learned you were alive. You'd think the women would be talking about it, the Gardener going missing? Maybe they're used to their wards disappearing. Not one of them has mentioned it. Are they too afraid to talk?

The Chancellor can do anything she wants. In the dark of my blindfold, the idea of you pokes at me.

Stop worrying. You're going to expose Romali; we both know it.

*

Bzzzz

Appointment two: a meal, three ladies. The women talk politics, ask my opinion and laugh because I can't answer.

They didn't pay for me to speak.

"Opinions?" says Ms Harry. "Their brains are too small. And I read they're shrinking. It's the hormones the House of Life puts them on to stop them jerking off until their brains melt."

I think she sort of said something less than nice about the Chancellor once. Am I kidding myself, or could I still persuade the Chancellor to accept someone else's name instead of Romali's?

The loudest of the guests, Ms Joy, has her upcoming Insem – the appointment at the House of Life when the women get their babies. "You know, talking about hormones," she says, "I heard that there was a woman on the fifty-second floor who thought she had been Insemed with a girl – like everyone else – except when they did a scan it turned out to be a boy!"

"Ugh, fifty-second, no surprise there. They don't wash," says the third woman, Ms Box.

"Lies," says Ms Harry, with chewable disgust. "The Gardener only puts boys in the – you know –" her voice drops to a whisper – "the Meritless."

"Like I said," continues Ms Joy, "she was on fifty-two. Bet her merits were only in the double digits. Can't afford soap, see. Infections."

Ms Box laughs.

"Nonsense," Ms Harry sighs. "Don't you remember science class? History? The Mathematical Repopulation Act."

Ms Box swears. "You're such a swot, Leah. Science is for nerds."

Ms Harry sighs. "All 'bryos are female at first, that's just fact.

You have to afford the treatments to keep it that way, though. It's the hormones, the balance, the pills the Gardener prescribes. Read the literature, Su. Saints, all the reading, thought I'd go blind. And the pills. So fogging many."

Her friends throw things at her and laugh like it's funny.

"Seriously, it's a delicate process the Insem: one germ and you end up with a boy. Nobody wants that."

Ms Harry I remember. Her name is Ms Leah Harry.

*

Bzzzz

Appointment three: auction tea. Paid for by the House of Entertainment as a 'perk' for helping with the swimwear show later. I'm meant to serve tea, perform a traditional dance, listen and laugh and be my most attentive. But all three guests arrive already drunk, I think, still debating the opportunities we boys are so grateful to receive.

"Education is entirely irrelevant to the life they have to lead," says a woman with a sharp voice, slumping down on the cushions with a burp.

There's something about the way they talk over each other, in a garble, that makes me guess that they're younger than most of my guests, nearer my age. Three guests, no names on the appointment list, so I name them by how they sound: Sharpie, Squeaky and Crackly.

Barking their food orders, they try to outdo each other with how crude their meat orders can sound. I fumble to open the hatch of the dumb waiter and carry hot plate after cold plate through as obstacles, pillows and legs are moved into my path. They snicker as I count steps, hoping my instincts find the table before my shins.

Sharpie sits near the door, based on the draught. The smoke from the spiced hookah she ordered makes me cough as she blows it towards me. Fruit-and-spice blasts hot. Holding your breath when blindly serving tea isn't easy.

"Pour," she snips as I cough.

Cradling her cup in my hand, I slip my thumb over the edge and pour the tea. Listen for the sound of the liquid; the note of it landing gets higher as the liquid reaches the top. The steam rises up until the tip of my thumb feels the heat; the note hits the right pitch to stop pouring before the liquid touches my skin.

The cup is snatched away from me. As her friends laugh, Sharpie carries on between slurps. "It's a fact that they can't think out matters coolly and calmly."

"Yasmin on one oh nine said reason isn't possible," says Squeaky, her voice high like a whistle. "You wouldn't try and make a fish waltz; why waste time teaching a boy to read?" Squeaky doesn't sound convinced, more like she's trying to make her friends laugh.

"Please," Crackly protests. "Think calmly? They can't think *at all*." Crackly's contempt oozes as she stands. There's a fume of alcohol.

"Only good for eye candy," Sharpie laughs with a snort.

That snort... Sharpie, the woman sitting nearest to the

hatch, is the tall officer that pulled me aside on the way to the Chancellor. The one hell-bent on telling me the histories I already knew. The one with the wandering hands.

My fingers tighten round the handle of the teapot. The room is full of Lice!

Slow as I can, I turn and move away from them, hoping they don't notice everything in me tense.

See you soon. That's what she said before my 'date' with the Chancellor. Did the Lice know about the Chancellor's plans? About the Gardener? The Chancellor murdered her but it seems as if I'm the only one who knows. Maybe the Chancellor changed her mind; she can do that. Maybe the Lice are here to arrest me for the Gardener's murder?

I make it a few steps to the door but Sharpie is up on her feet fast, blocking my way. I bump into her wall of cold armour.

"Where are you going, gorgeous?"

Her breath warms my nose. The remnants of her dinner caught in her teeth. Something meaty.

She's about my height but she's got the advantage.

Sharpie's voice drops to a whisper. "You have something for me, don't you?"

Did the Chancellor send her?

It's too soon! And how do I answer if they didn't pay me to talk? I try to step to the side.

Sharpie's hot hand slips between my legs and everything in my stomach jumps into my throat. My whole body goes cold. My teeth clamp together so firm my jaw aches. "Tea," she orders and rattles her cup between us. "Pour."

"What are you doing?" protests Squeaky behind her.

"Sit down, Trood! I said pour, pretty boy."

Crackly giggles and hiccups into her teacup.

Nodding deferentially (the way the house teaches us) – slow, respectful, graceful – I offer up a *gracious-without-being-smarmy* smile, lift up the teapot and wait.

Sharpie lets go of my groin and pushes her rattling cup in between us.

So I pour. Listening as the hot liquid lands, not to the deep note of liquid landing in cup but to the splash of it scalding the officer's wrist.

Sharpie screams as she knocks the pot from my hand. It smashes on the floor. I tighten every muscle in my body, preparing myself for a beating.

Maybe this time you'll hit back?

Her friends are laughing. Splashes of boiling water hit my hands as I hear the officer swipe at her clothes.

I could say it was an accident, but I won't. It wasn't. Inside my head, I'm waiting for you to laugh, or clap, to tell me I'm smart and brave and you're proud I'm your friend.

"I think I'll bid on this one come auction. Teach him some manners," Sharpie says.

They're not here to arrest me? She thinks I'll make it to auction.

Smack! Something flat and hard hits the side of my head. It sings through my skull and my eyes water.

110

"He's the Chancellor's boy, Spinny!" her friend squeaks in protest.

That's what they called her before. When I hear her name, the tightness in my chest goes. Could I give the Chancellor *her* name? It's not like she's said anything bad about the Chancellor, but I have to do something. I won't be just another boy who takes it. Not any more.

"Not yet." Spinny dismisses her friend. "She'll go off this one like the one last year. There are *always* ways to lower the reserve. Even hers."

I need something more than a nickname. She's not just going to give me her full name and I can't ask, can I?

Rule Two: don't talk unless they pay you, you remind me.

But I'm under the Chancellor's protection, at least for now.

"One merit?" I say. Turning to face her, hot saltwater sweat itches at my eyelashes. It seeps into the white cotton around my eyes. I notice every breath as it heaves in and out of me. "Good luck lowering that."

"No," her friend squeakily answers me. "She upped it this morning. Half a million."

"What?" I say, holding on to the wall to stop from falling. Half a million merits. That's over half the debt I owe the house. About twice that and I'd be the first free man in the Tower. No one's ever reserved a boy for so much.

"Shut up, Trood!" Spinny shouts.

"He deserves to know," adds 'Trood' with a defensive squeak.

"He doesn't *deserve* anything. They're not even meant to talk,

111

dumbclot," the groper says.

I clear my throat. This is it: this is how I'll get her full name. "The House of Boys regrets you feel you've had a less than satisfactory service, Officer—"

"Olive Aspiner, pretty boy, and don't you forget it."

With my best *butter-wouldn't-melt* smile, I store the name away to give to the Chancellor.

"Officer Aspiner, you're welcome to tell the Appointment Steward," I say, reeling off the usual disclaimer. "Or maybe the Chancellor?"

The laughs of her friends are muffled behind me.

Something cold and metallic rests against my cheek. I don't need my sight to know it's a knife. I catch my breath, freeze as she grasps my neck with her other hand. Her palm damp where I soaked her. She pulls me so close I can almost see her features blurred beyond the blindfold.

"I've cut the tongues out of higher-floor wards that speak when they're not spoken to," she says. "Who do you think ordered that? Madam Vor? No, it was your future guardian. You're no more above the law than any of the rest of your kind, not in my eyes, not in hers. I don't care what you're worth. Remember that."

16

LESSONS IN WORTH

Every so often, down in the kitchens, the House of Knowledge would send a lesson for the cooks to teach. Maybe they felt sorry for us up Above? Everyone would crowd in to listen.

"They call it a meritocracy," the head cook droned as he wrote the word merit on the orders board in dark-text dots.

"Yes, Cook," we replied, all sitting between the ovens in a line, picking at the grit between the tiles.

"Merit," he said.

⠰⠍ ⠄⠑⠐⠗ ⠂⠞⠦

All us boys copied the dots down on our papers. You scribbled in the furthest corner, saving as much of the paper as you could for your sculptures.

Every woman Above, Cook explained, is born with a thousand merits to their name as well as any inheritance officially sanctioned by the House of Merit. On top of their birthday gifts, girls would be credited merits for doing good works, helping others and passing exams. This is what they call 'showing your worth'. Although I'd heard stories that some girls got merits from the house fairy when they lost their teeth, I never got merits when I lost mine, no matter how many I pulled free.

Cook said that girls got to choose which house they'd work in. At fourteen, girls could apply to three houses and, depending on their skills, they'd be assigned a job at the most suitable one, where they'd study and work. The girls could change houses after they turned eighteen, based on application.

Every house paid the same merits for a job, no matter the rank, but the girls – now women – could earn more from their colleagues, friends and family for hard work, deeds that supported the community or bettered the success of their house. After the age of eighteen, Cook said, by law all women had to pay at least a quarter of their earnings to others within the year. The House of Merit, run by Madam Glassey, monitored the transfers in vast ledgers.

It's not like that for us.

We already knew that boys get a thousand merits at birth too, but that's used up fast to pay the Surrogacy to take care of us. It's enough for the first five years and that's it. It's all debt after that, the debt of our forefathers, the men of our name who went before, all the way back to the first of our name.

"Meritocracy," Cook continued, "means that the best people in the Tower are in charge. The kindest. The smartest. The most selfless."

"But—" I raised my hand, the other hand itching at the tattooed number on my ankle – my starting debt.

"I know what you'll want to know." Cook ignored me. "Any woman, or boy, can be demerited, of course, by anyone. Papers of demerit, with a reason, are written and submitted. If the reason for a demerit is considered just, then the individual's account is demerited according to the amount dictated by the House of Merit's rules."

⠆⠄⠢⠆ ⠶⠆

Rules.

He wrote the word on the orders board in dots and all the boys copied.

"But—" I raised my hand again. I was trying to be a good boy, I was. You tried not to laugh.

"The system is designed to elevate the most worthy person in the Tower –" most worthy woman he meant, because there was no way one of us would ever make it into credit – "to the position of most power. Based on this, we know that our Chancellor will be the most kind, most selfless, most respected—"

Most most everything ever? "But—"

"But WHAT, prentice?"

"But ... but what if it doesn't work?"

"If *what* doesn't work?"

"The meritogracy."

"*Meh-ree-toh-krah-see*. And I think you're missing the point – it does work."

"But what if it doesn't?"

115

The boys around me laughed like I was an idiot. You actually threw something at my head.

"It does," Cook insisted.

"Yes, but—"

He pulled the demerit book and a stamp from out of the drawer and waved it in the air. "You want to continue to question the Foundations? How much is it worth to you?"

"I just think—"

"Don't," Cook interrupted as he stamped a demerit on the slip he ripped from the book – only boys get the stamp for a demerit. Of course he couldn't use the women's letters, the ones that aren't made of dots and bumps. No boy could ever demerit a lady. We can't. They don't give us the tools.

"Don't *think*." Cook sighed and looked at me like I was a lost cause. "Trust me," he said. "It's not worth it."

"But—"

"One more word and you're down for kennel cleaning. Since merits mean so little to you, perhaps scraping up dog crap will learn you."

"Teach," you corrected him, and winked at me. My friend.

That's how we both ended up with the dogs.

On the board Cook wrote a third word:

⠺⠕⠗⠞⠓

Worth.

And all the boys copied.

17

I stood up to the Lice! I can do this. I can save you. There's a small nick on my cheek from Aspiner's knife. But it's no worse than a shaving cut, which is how I'll explain it if anyone asks. Heading down to the dorm dining room, I join the queue for food, my chest lifted up high.

Half a million merits? Is that what I'm worth to the Chancellor now? For a second, it feels good to know what she's willing to pay for me. Doubt drips into my ear. Maybe her reserve will go down if I don't give her Romali. Maybe she's decided not to let you go. Maybe it's all a game, giving me hope, before snatching it away. Or is it a promise: I give her Romali, she lets you go? If I stay, maybe, just maybe, she'll pay enough to erase my debt and give me my freedom. There's that hope itching away. What if both of us could be free?

The weight of the hundreds of floors above seems too heavy for the concrete dining-room ceiling. The pipes, looping in a rusting metal maze, creak. Even the air feels thick, weighted with the stink of dishwater, kitchen crud and old vegetables. Breathing through my mouth so the stuffy air doesn't ruin my appetite, I move through the queue.

How do I get the Chancellor to accept Aspiner's name instead? She wanted Romali to give herself up by this evening. If Walker could get me to see the Chancellor, if I could give her a different name … maybe I could buy some time. But Walker's not going to come to me either, it seems. Not unless he has to.

Under the grease-caked yellow light, the House Fathers at the doors check for any trouble, but I keep catching them looking away from me. Groups of boys stop practising dance moves for the ball as I pass. Even the kitchen prentice peer at me through the long hatch as they slop out our late meal.

By the time my tray's loaded up (the usual brown protein-powder stew), the pressure inside my head is back.

Maybe I can make Walker come to me. He'll be rehearsing the boys who got into Swims.

I'm weaving through the tables to reach the brothers from my dorm when Stink limps in, dripping wet, nursing a black eye.

He didn't have that shiner this morning. It could be from his appointments, but as he shuffles into line his eyes are everywhere *but* on the hulks sitting at the table right beside me. Vinnie and the rest of your old gang, busy running through all seven of the compulsory poses for this evening's show. They can't even squeeze on to one table there's so much meat on them.

You want Walker's attention, right?

It needs to be a big enough brawl for the House Fathers to send for Walker, but not so bad I risk a hefty demeriting. With a reserve of half a mil I can afford the dink.

Do it! Hit them.

Aye-Aye isn't smiling. He's flexing a full-front double biceps to compete with Toll's rear lateral spread. Did they go for Stink instead of me? They dunk half the kids in here when they can, so that they miss appointments. It's been getting worse as we get closer to auction; they haze other boys daily, scare the rest out of the running for the better women.

"Muh-muh-muh name is Jood Grru-gru-grunt," Aye-Aye snorts.

My grip on my tray tightens as if I could snap it.

Then there's a cough, barely covering the word "slut" underneath it.

Laughter ripples from the Roids to the boys on the tables nearby.

Viñnie shakes a grin away. He's one to talk: there are plenty of rumours of what he gets up to in his appointments. He's changed since you left V-dorm, all hair and knuckles now.

I turn. "I heard that the roids your appointment ladies give you made your nads shrink down so small that you talk as high as a top-floor madam."

His fist hits my tray, sending it clattering to the ground; my stew spills on to the floor. There's a wafting scent of gym deodorant and chalk from Vinnie's pits as he casually lifts his arms, finishing a yawn.

I told Walker about them months ago – how I'd be fair game if I failed to kill the Chancellor, if I ended up back in the dorms.

So don't fail, kid, Walker had said. *Besides, a gentleman knows how to defend himself. When they hit, hit back, hit harder.*

Until now, ignoring them was my plan. Because how stupid is it to pick a fight with Vinnie, the six-foot fist?

Hit harder? You laugh. *Hit FIRST!*

The nick on my cheek feels warm, burning through my skin. If I can take on Officer Aspiner, the Chancellor … a bunch of Roids are nothing.

The anger is easy to find when I want it; it tastes of metal in my throat. Everything gets loose in my head as it crunches, gritty in my muscles, climbs up my legs and wakes up my bones. It's the thought of every time I've wanted to lash out that clenches my fists. The whispers in appointments, the accidental way the guests touch, and how many times I've looked in the mirror and felt small, it all pushes through my knuckles into his cheek with a jarring *THWACK!*

And damn it hurts!

My knuckles swell as Vinnie falls. In an intake of thick breath, the hall becomes a squall of smacks and cries. Everything slows down as I'm hit – uppercut by Toll. My teeth crack into each other, the taste of blood. By the time I get the chance to fight back, there are four bodies on me. Sharp, blade-like feet hit my ribs, hot sweat and hair and grunts and grabbing, thudding, heart-pounding, shirt-grabbing.

"Not before Swims, you idiots!" I hear Aye-Aye yell. He dodges out of the way, covering his face. Knuckles smack, louder than the barking crowd.

Stink roars as he runs in to my defence, landing on the mass. The rest of my friends in J-dorm too. Even Rodders piles in, after handing his glasses to a kid from T-dorm. They all plough forwards, blunt sporks held high.

"Don't!" I grunt from inside the ball of bodies.

I may not be onstage this evening, but Rod is. I don't want to share my bruises – they're all mine.

Two boys from R-dorm, Rene and Ramah, catch hold of me. I blink the sweat out of my swollen eyes. They grip me tight as Vinnie launches a round kick into my stomach and I think I cough up a lung.

Shit.

When the Roids turn to move the fight to my brothers, nothing matters. I twist quickly, land my knee in Rene's stomach. Pull my arms free. Adrenaline pounding, muscles shaking, I launch myself at Vinnie. His foot jams into my thighs and – crunch – the bones in my knees hit the stone floor, the nerves up my spine spasm and my teeth jam together over my tongue. It feels like dancing for the first time in ages. The blood I spit up is as thick as custard. There's sweat and spit and dignity and grace all over the fogging floor.

A high-pitched whistle stabs through my head.

The second the Roids drop me, they're running. I look upside down as they disperse into the crowd. I try to get up, get away, but my head weighs a solid ton. After the third attempt to roll over, I see Father Jai looming above me, sweating in his button-bursting brown uniform. His whistle swings round his neck as he shakes his head.

"Afternoon," he sighs. "Making my life easy again, I see."

By now, the other House Fathers have begun dragging their dorm boys from the dining hall.

Father Van, who is roughly the size of two Vinnies, tuts. "Training up fist-fodder as usual, Jaipur? Will you notify Mr Walker or shall I?"

"No need, Van." Jai wobbles with deference. "Already done."

"Enough demerits to cover the costs to V-dorm, right?" Father Van confirms.

Jai is all nods as I swallow a wad of blood. He grabs my tenderized shoulder, yanks me up. "Fighting is undignified," he mutters in my ear. "Gentlemen don't fight."

"But they—" I croak, my lips sticky on the inside with blood I try to tongue away.

"*They* are their Fathers' business. *You* are mine. And I've still got a business to run here. Let's get you cleaned up before Mr Walker arrives."

18

Jai spends five minutes slapping make-up on me, hoping to cover the bruises, before he gets to the threats. If I don't start to 'play the game', he'll put me on rations, saltwater showers, blah-blah, the usual. Normally I'd apologize. But not today, not after last night. On his desk, the hooch bottle is unstoppered again. He offers me a shot, for the aches, he says. I knock back the cloudy brown liquid. Bitter, the fermented taste of honey and orange peel shivers through me.

When I see Walker, I'm going to tell him I know he lied about what happened to you. I want him to see me strong.

Father Jai scrabbles in boxes for every anti-inflam, cold pack and painkiller he's stored up – being House Father, he's got a good stock for these kinds of incidents.

"Right, off you go to the Auction Hall," he says when he thinks he's done enough.

"Go? But what about the demerits? What about Walker?"

"You're to get yourself over there now," Jai explains, squinting to read a note left on his desk by a prentice halfway through my lecture. The kid had the little stitched '!' on his shirt so I know he was from the House of Entertainment. Walker must be angry if he won't even leave the rehearsal.

As I limp up the stairs to the backstage door of the Auction Hall, I can hear Walker shouting, counting beats.

You never did Talents before you were taken. It's not Reserves: one in, one out, do a spin, say your piece. There's a whole fogging dance routine. All the boys in the show have had weeks to practise but, as I move through backstage to the wings, I can tell Walker's frustrated. Rod's looking stressed, nursing bruises under his clothes. Aye-Aye, the only Roid in Swims, seems to have escaped the fight unharmed but then he was doing most of the kicking. He's swearing under his breath that the old man has lost it.

None of them are turning to acknowledge the Lice standing at the back of the theatre, by the doors.

Of the twenty-four lucky boys whose measurements have made them eligible, only one will win an auction discount. Ten per cent of their final bid gets covered by the House of Entertainment – as if that's the reason for the talent show and it isn't *just* an excuse to gawk and leer. It's a nice incentive for the ladies and a huge honour for the boy who wins, I guess.

With the lights up, exposing every crack and crevice, every worn velvet seat cushion and peeling corner of carpet, the hall really does seem 500 years old. Walker leaps up on to the empty stage, mid-speech, raging about how he's been training them for weeks and none of them seem to have been listening. It's not just about knowing the steps – it's about owning the space, demanding attention. It's about moving those gangling teenage limbs with actual intent.

He tugs his waistcoat straight and grabs his jacket, sliding it over his shoulders like a second skin – the one that turns him into a showman. I've seen him dance, a showy step here, an instructive move there, but I've never seen him perform. Walker's first dance at the ball with the Chancellor has been the highlight of the season every year since I was a kid. People talked about it for months. But the last few years the gossip changed. *He's looking tired*, say the women in appointments. *She can do better.*

Classical music kicks in over the speakers. It's all snares and drums. I catch myself tapping my foot and curl up my toes tight to stop myself as the prentice boys in the booth flip off the main lights. My brothers stop grumbling and fall silent as Walker shows them how it's done. Small movements to start, like he's shrugging off the urge to perform, they get bigger as he moves round the stage, his feet fast as he leans, taps, switches, rolls.

He sees me in the wings – I know he does. Walker always knows where his audience is. There's a cheer from one of the boys in the stalls as the beat kicks in. Every part of his performance rehearsed but it seems as though he's making it up on the spot. He's playing. The boys watch, transfixed, wishing they could be him.

When it's done, Walker isn't out of breath at all. There's nothing tired about him. He seems alive. My brothers applaud, throwing their slippers on the stage to show their appreciation.

"When I get back, anyone who has not got the routine down gets a fine so large their forefather's molars will squeak with shame." Groans erupt. "And you'll be out of the show too.

This is important," he says.

He leaves them to practise and meets me in the wings, grabbing a towel as he walks past. "With me, kid."

As I follow him, two of the Lice aren't far behind.

Walker's dressing room is three times the size of Jai's office. The sparking filaments of yellow bulbs hum. He sits me on the stool by his dressing table.

He raises his perfect eyebrows to their full arch. "I take it your scrap with the Muscles wasn't just to let off steam."

I shuffle in my seat, move some of the bottles and brushes and blusher around on the counter as anger bubbles in my stomach.

"Sorry they went to town on you," he says with a sigh. "I should've been there."

I shrug.

"I told you—"

"Hit back. I remember," I say, picking at the scab forming on my lip.

"No." He pulls my hand away. "I told you I'd take care of you. I just needed time, a plan. Get round the police watching me."

It's been two days, I want to yell, but I don't want to show him I care. I sniff, wincing as my nose burns with bruises. Don't need his excuses. Walker puts his hand on my shoulder. I shrug it off, puff out my chest. "I can handle the Roids."

He leans forwards, waits, desperate to ask what happened with the Chancellor. I'll let him bring it up. Let him ask. He waited this long to show his face, I want him to be the one who goes first. It's not like I get to be stubborn with the women.

"Clearly." He raises an eyebrow. "You know what, go and wash that slap off. Jai has the beauty skills of a drunk toddler – I'll do a proper job." He hands me a cloth and some cream to clean my face. "So what happened? Nerves get to you?" He's trying to play it down as if we don't know how screwed we are because I failed.

I shake my head, trying to be cool as I tell him. "She knew."

Walker sits up straight, his blue eyes widening. Lips pursed and breathing heavily, both long-fingered hands scrub at his face, trying to hide how afraid he is. And then he's thinking, pulling at his lip, rubbing his moustache, scratching the slight stubble on his cheek. Maybe he doesn't believe me. As he stands, paces, he shakes his head.

"She knew?" he keeps asking. "How could she? I was careful."

"She knew."

But he's not listening. "Bloody Romali! I knew her stunt would—"

He's talking like he knows her.

He kicks at a stool, swears some more. I've never seen him this angry before. But a second later he's in control, laughing it off and pinching the bridge of his nose. "Not very gentlemanly." He picks up the stool. "And they call me a role model." He laughs as if I don't know he's panicking underneath, that he's thinking of all the things she'll have done to him, that's he's wondering exactly when those Lice following him are going to strike.

"I'm glad you're OK, kid," he says. And I believe him, even if I know what's underneath those words – that we're not OK, either of us. That he's wondering why I'm alive. "Don't worry about the bruises. I'll send a note to the infirmary, get you something to help. Hell, at least you still have all your teeth." Walker's normally so in control but the way he's looking now I guess he's wondering if he can trust me. What did I do to survive, he's asking himself? There's something like power in not telling him.

An announcement crackles over the speakers. One hour until the show.

He's had too much work done up in the infirmary to frown but he's trying. "You didn't sleep with her? I told you—"

"Er, no." I screw up my face in disgust.

"Good. You're too young. I'm not a prude, just … you need to keep some dignity." He's a traditionalist, of course, thinks boys should wait until after they're warded. The Chancellor's paid for him to look good, so it's easy to forget how old he is. Nearly fifty, I heard, but I never asked. You don't ask a man his age. He rakes his hand through his hair, pulls the stool over to sit on.

"Are you going to make me keep guessing or tell me why you weren't arrested?"

I drink, fill my mouth with water to keep my cool. The dog. The shot. The blood. The body. Maybe he won't notice I'm shaking all over. "We talked – she liked me," I say.

"Talked? Hell, she doesn't talk. She plays with her food."

"She let me go."

"Guess you would think that's what happened."

"I persuaded her." It's the truth but he rolls his eyes like I'm lying.

"Maybe you're right. She must like you." He's being sarcastic.

"So you talked, huh? What, pray tell, did you converse about, kid?"

"Stuff."

"I heard she upped her reserve."

He won't believe me. There's a bottle on the surface: painkillers. I'd drink poison to get rid of the feeling my head is being stamped on. "Can I have this? Jai's stash was out of date."

"Not until you tell me what's going on." Walker snatches it away. "You need a clear head to get through tonight. Maybe if we both survive, maybe if she really does like you, then we'll … I don't know … have another chance with the Chancellor come auction. Thirteen days." He says it like neither of us will live past tomorrow.

Should I tell him you're alive, tell him about the deal?

"So can I go back to the dorms now?" If Romali and the Hysterics are going to try and get me out, maybe I can persuade them to get you out too.

"No, you're joining the understudies." There's a glint in his eye. "I'm not letting you out of my sight."

✳

Rehearsal is exhausting. Everything, I mean *everything*, aches. From my inside out. My bruised body keeps giving up on me.

Two hours of, "Stand there, stop that, in time, hips-hips-hips, lips-lips-lips," from Walker in the stalls. He took my measurements, said I was a bit underweight, but I'd pass. The four of us that nail the routine become official understudies for tonight's show.

Every step makes the bruises harder to hide.

"SMILE!" Walker groans. "You're meant to be enjoying it." He turns his gaze to me, grinning as usual. It's between a *you-should-have-let-them-finish-the-job* and an *I'm-hungry-and-need-a-sandwich* smile. Whatever's going through that slick head of his, he's picking on me the most.

"Try harder, gentlemen. What if this was the last-ever auction? You want to go down in history as the most flat-footed fools who ever danced?" And, "Move, damn it, move. Jude! You have to feel it while you can," he shouts. He seems more frustrated than before, as if our lives are on the line if we screw up his show. It could be him just being a diva, but it feels like more.

There's a part of me that's enjoying being able to dance with actual permission. It's all regulation moves and old music, my bruises are burning and I have to think hard to keep up, but it's still dancing.

During break, the boys whisper in corners, about the fight, about special treatment. I limp to the refreshment station. I need water and to avoid my brothers as best I can. It's not going to work.

"You don't need the discount." Rod shoves me in the arm. "Some of us worked all year for this."

"I'm not in the show, brother. Don't worry."

"So Walker just put you in the understudies at random?"

I shrug, can't really explain. "Maybe it's a punishment for fighting," I joke. As an understudy, I get to wait backstage in case one of my brothers collapses, or twists an ankle or throws up. Chances are I won't even go onstage. I wonder if Romali is with the Hysterics now, looking for me in the dorms, disappointed, angry that I'm not there.

✳

Two minutes to Swims.

Twenty-eight of us wait behind the curtain. The main group and the four understudies. This was a stupid idea. I didn't know I'd have to wait around in shorts smaller than something I'd cough up with the flu. I've never even been in a swimming pool. Saints alive, they probably don't even exist.

The air is thick and hot but my skin prickles all over with cold. I itch as my brothers huddle round me, their shoulders folded inward in protective wings. I tuck myself in again, downstairs, check for decency as the Senior Theatre Prentice, a tall man with terrible skin called Fry, counts us into position. There's a prentice boy at his side; on his perfectly creased shirt is a smiling-face symbol stitched into the collar. I don't know which house it's for. The prentice looks at each boy as Fry calls out the names in each of the four groups of six, each in different-coloured shorts, and the boys answer. The blue, yellow and green shorts, then the seven of us in red. We're all from different dorms: Mo, Orin, Keane, Raffi, Blake, Nate, Aye-Aye and… "Name?" asks Fry.

"Jude Grant, understudy." As he ticks off my name and turns away, the prentice reaches up and hands me a piece of paper. Walker said he'd get the infirmary to send down more painkillers.

But there's nothing – just the note. A small piece of torn paper folded into the shape of a man.

"Aw, a love note from Mr Walker?" Aye-Aye laughs.

It's not from Walker. It's from you. I know. I watched you teach yourself to fold paper this way. My hands shake as I unfold it.

⠠⠃⠑⠀⠎⠞⠗⠕⠝⠛⠂⠀⠎⠊⠎⠞⠑⠗⠲

The other boys in red shorts laugh and make kissing noises as Aye-Aye barks and humps the air. "Maybe after the Chancellor's done with you, Squinty, Mr Walker will give you a sympathy bone?"

No time to think. I crunch up the paper in my fist. Bite down hard and throw my knuckles firmly into Aye-Aye's nose.

19

Tonight. Onstage, your note said. I didn't have time to think. The Chancellor made you send the note. I had to get onstage.

But she wants Romali. How am I going to deliver what she wants?

Excitable squealing drills through the heavy curtains until the audience is hushed by the shadows of Walker and Madam Glassey, Chief of Merit, spinning their welcome speeches on the other side. Aye-Aye is in the wings, holding wads of paper to his bleeding nose.

The other red-shorts stare at me. Taking a boy's place in Swims isn't going to win me any points with my brothers. Rod, in the green group ahead of me, widens his eyes, mouths, *What the fog?* at me. I shake the ache from my swelling knuckles. I'm doing it for you, I remind myself. Maybe Romali is in the audience so that no one can tie her to the Hysterics when they get to the dorms. I'm suddenly cold and very aware of how little I'm wearing.

Distorted laughter from the audience. More applause.

The make-up Walker pasted over the bruises on my stomach smears when I drag my thumb over it. The chalk paint grinds between my fingers as it mixes muddily in the sweat of my palm. I can feel my heart pounding in my knuckles, in the bruises.

Onstage.

Did she make you send the note? Or does she just want me to think it's from you? *She plays with her food*, Walker said. Is this a game to her? Maybe she already has Romali, without my help. Maybe she'll never let you go.

The curtains fly apart. Shadows move slower than they should against the searing light. My brothers dancing. The music is wild and happy but it drags through my head like wet cloth.

You're late, you say, as clear as if you're in the front row. Shit!

The world speeds up as my brothers explode forwards in a flood of clapping and cheering and flesh.

My mind's playing tricks. In the blue worklight of backstage, I think I see you in the wings. Tanned to the max, just like the last time I saw you, except you're missing the scars on your face and sporting this big *come-on-you-can-do-better* smile, number twenty-three, rolling your eyes as if I'm making an idiot out of myself. I'm imagining it, I have to be.

Smile, said Walker. So I smile.

What beat is this?

Listen for the lyrics.

It all sounds a mess!

Watching the feet of the boy in front of me is all that saves me from complete failure. Slide to the left. Clap, clap. Slide to the right. Clap, clap. Bounce and turn. Up on toes. Turn.

Everything is clearer now. All I can think is you're alive:

that note had to be from you!

First the blue shorts take the front of the stage, then the yellow, the green, then it's us. The boys walk round the circling catwalk as Walker and Madam Glassey read out their measurements.

What did the Chancellor do to you to get you to write that note?

The boys in my group are posing like crazy: lats, quads, glutes. They let the masked women in the audience reach out from the dark and touch their feet, grab their hands. There's a bit more crotch-thrusting than in Walker's choreography.

When my beat comes, I step up to do my turn at the front. Try not to fidget, scratch or mess with myself. Don't think about what they're looking at. It's not me. Not really. It's not me, only an idea of what they might make of me.

Did she hurt you?

We're meant to move fast round the podium and only pause at the judges' table. Maybe I could say something then, something to accuse Romali? I search the box above for the Chancellor.

I should be worried about you so why can't I stop remembering the Gardener, her face swollen, her voice shouting.

You don't have to do this, she begged.

My head is still swimming, bruised from the fight; everything seems slow. My brothers, dancing around, half dressed for the hungry crowd. Rod's desperate for the discount, for their merits. Grinning and twisting and trying so hard. He's right. I didn't earn my place on the stage, not like him. I've seen how he earned the spot: eat, throw up, eat, throw up, pushing himself at the gym until he can't move any more.

He's not the only one. I've counted three new noses among the dancers, two with freshly sculpted abs from the infirmary – paid for by women in the audience, probably excited to show off their prizes to their friends. Not a hair in sight either, except on their heads. Aye-Aye and some others popping the pills their favours feed them like sweets. Fighting so hard for their future. For a life Above. We tell stories of the mines and how terrifying they are but is it really worth this?

You wanted a future, that's all. You wanted it so much. How did Walker get you to try to kill the Chancellor? Did he promise you freedom? Power? Did you try to say no? The next Chancellor could be worse. All I want to do is find Walker and ask him why. Why now, why her, what if? I never asked before. I had my reasons; they were enough. You were dead. But now…

You don't have to do this!

I know. There's got to be another way.

When I reach the judging table, my muscles are twitching with all those hours spent practising podium poses with the House Fathers.

You don't have to! the voice yells.

So what the Saints am I meant to do? Give the Chancellor Romali, or another name? Stay and save you, or escape and … and what if she never lets you go anyway? Every part of me wants to collapse into a ball, but I can't. I have to keep moving, surviving.

From the edge of the stage, I can see their masks. The

Chancellor's not here, her box is empty, but as I sway someone else is in the crowd. Green-faced, silent among the sea of empty mouths, eyes, making all the noise in the world behind porcelain. Her skin loose on her face. Madam Dunn, the Gardener, waits among the mass, cloudy-eyed and watching me, mouthing, gasping for life while her peers whoop and whistle and cheer. I blink and the swelling around my eyes throbs.

I'm not moving.

There's that noise, that ache in my head, and it's fused me to the spot.

I could give the Chancellor what she wants right now. But then what next? She's messing with me, I know. She's not even here. What if, instead, I show her I can play too. For one moment, even if it never happens again, maybe I could play by my own rules. Buy more time for us both?

Behind me, on the stage, the rest of the red-shorts stop dancing too; they stop clapping to the music. I'm still at the judges' table, beneath the dust burning on the lights above. My stomach aches with bruises that I want them to see. I push my sweating palm through the paint and let the purple-blue-yellow-green blotches bleed through. Dragging my arm across to wipe my lips, show the split Vinnie made. Pulling at my hot, swollen eye. I straighten up with pride. My heart thuds in a slow, distant drum.

There's confusion onstage behind me.

Rodders is whispering, "Jude! Jude!"

Madam Glassey, at the end of the row of judges, squirms in

her chair until it squeaks. Her golden mask looks plastic in this light. The skinny one in the blue mask rifles through her notes. The oldest in the red mask blinks fast when I look her in the eye.

And everything else is quiet.

And no one is standing up to stop me.

Now I move. Now I walk. Let the theatre echo with the sound of my bare feet creaking on the stage as I return to my mark. Walker will be furious but I don't care.

When the sweeping light stops, the music slows. Deep notes rumble in my stomach as Walker brings the results to the stage. He encourages the audience to cheer, thanks us for our performance and catches every single eye but mine.

"Ladies and debutantes, with a resounding six point zero across the board…" Even I can tell he's trying not to stutter through his speech. He coughs. "Jude Grant."

I won?

How could I have actually won?

The flowers the masked judges bring me are yellow and green. They must've been pulled up from the garden. Is the Chancellor sending me a message? She wanted me onstage to win. Why?

Madam Glassey brings the crown from the wings on a plush cushion. A golden ring glinting in the stage lights. Walker rests his hand on my shoulder and for a single moment of terror I wonder if he's going to hit me but there's something else behind the mask of his face, a little tic in the corner of his right eye. He's worried.

"A few words?" Madam Glassey offers, pushing a microphone

towards me. I stutter. *Tonight. Onstage*, your note said. The Chancellor fixed the results; what does she want me to do? Do I tell them all Romali has been helping the Hysterics? But they won't believe me, right? Maybe she's changed her mind and I could just name someone else.

She made sure I'd win so I'd have this moment. Why? Just so I could look like an idiot? Maybe she's just playing with me.

"I…" I look around, at my stunned brothers, at Rod cheering. I thought he'd be upset but he seems happy for me.

I can take control of this moment. I could do anything right now.

"I … I want to thank Ms Vor for her special support at Reserves." The audience laughs, a second before catching themselves. "And the Chancellor, of course, for her faith that I will live up to my potential." Will it be enough? Will she understand, wait for me to find a way? If I'm going to give anything to the Chancellor, it'll be on my terms. "And I … I want to pass the discount to my … my brother Rod … er, Jarod Katz," I garble into the mic. Applause rings in my ears; red-coloured paper flutters from the rafters. If you were here, you'd be stuffing handfuls of it into your socks. You'll be safe, right? She wants Romali badly enough to keep you alive until I deliver. She has to.

20

Wrapped in warm dressing gowns, Rod helps me push through the doors to the dorm. At first I think I'm imagining my brothers singing my name, arm in arm, belting out a song loud and proud. But this is real. If it was a dream, they'd be in tune. It hurts when they crowd round me. If their cheers didn't feel so good, I'd have told them to shut up.

I spend my life smiling. Right now I actually want to.

Stink leads the cheers. "You're Swimwear King! Be thee forever crowned, he of the spectacular package! All hail!"

"Hail!" they cry and drum their feet. Bang their cups against the metal of our bunks.

Rodders bows in a huge and over-the-top way, and the others copy. Some keep a straight face for longer than I'd expect, before the circle of bowing boys collapses into snorts and guffaws and whispers.

"Jai says we can stay up past lights out, to celebrate," Stink announces.

"Who knew? Jai has a heart!" I scratch at my bruises as I stumble through my brothers towards the comfort of my bunk. Some of the boys from my dorm have left me things to celebrate my win. Even boys from the other dorms have dropped stuff off, real prizes, the best tradables. Things from Outside – stones and little bottles of brown dust called 'sand', strange oils. Things from Above – soaps and perfume, fabric and make-up. I check my old stuff is safe before taking the folded note out from the belt of my shorts and tucking it away. Romali never came, but I've bought some time, I hope, and even if the Chancellor is trying to drive me mad *at least* I know you're alive. For now.

I can't get Stink to shut up. As I tidy my bunk, change into my dorm clothes and start to wipe away Walker's make-up, he's on a roll, telling stories about how he worked as a prentice in Madam Bocharov's Agro tunnels, pulling potatoes. Apparently it's an art. "That was till they started burning the crops," he says.

"Who? The farmers?" I ask, trying not to remember my own failed reserve with Madam Bocharov last year.

"No, the mad ones, the Hysterics. They sent their hordes."

I wondered how long it would be until the stories about the Hysterics would start. To some boys the Hysterics are heroes and will save us all. They're sent to calm and soothe them when they cry. To others they are witches, or creatures who eat boys whole. To the Lice they're terrorists. To me? I'm not sure anything could really be *all* of those things.

"The Hysterics broke into the tunnels, set the lot on fire—"

"You actually saw it?" I interrupt.

"Well, I'd left by then, but that's why there were shortages, they say. Bocharov had every boy in the tunnels sent to the mines after the fires, on account of how the Hysterics used the tunnels. She said the Head Prentice, Eli—"

"Eli Han? Isn't he one of the rebels on the mines deadlist from last month?" The next Eli is going to have it tough – they'll have upped his debt for that."

"He was in league with the Hysterics before that. Madam Bocharov had him..."

"Don't tell me!" I cringe, imagining the things Bocharov might have done to me last year had she not been stinking drunk.

"She scarecrowed him, they say – took one of his legs! I'd earned enough new merits to interview for the House of Boys, seemed safest to get out of there."

The hum of the lights dies. The whole dorm groans as everything goes red. "Another blackout," grumbles John.

"Won't last long," I tell him.

But the lights are still burning red after mid-dark. By then, half the dorm are snoring in their bunks, while the rest are still up, telling tales about the mythical swimming pool somewhere high above us.

My eyes are tiring but I have a plan. When the boys are asleep, I'm going to sneak out of J-dorm. I'm going to walk straight up to the Lice that guard the elevator doors and tell them the Chancellor wants to see me. Can hardly keep awake, but I need to get to the Chancellor before she gets to me.

"Your turn for a story, Swimmer King," says Rodders,

propelling a pair of pants at me via the elastic. He's still made up that I gave him the discount.

"How about the one about the boy who was really tired and wanted to go to sleep but was ambushed by a crowd of mad prats who tortured him all dark-hours with terrible stories? So he cursed them to Hysteria and they all woke up the next morning turned into goats," I joke.

"Heard it," Stink laughs and everyone joins in.

"Come on!" Someone chucks a sock. "You know the one we want."

"Fine. OK." I stretch out my fingers, crick my aching neck. They lean forwards and I begin.

"The kitchen tunnels are stinking, damp and steamy, a dozen floors beneath the dorms. They spread under the Tower in rat runs. One year the cooks brought in a glut of piglets from the House of Life. They took two kitchen boys to the dog pens to help 'make room' for the new meat. We kept dogs to eat the trash, you see? Pigs eat rubbish too, the cooks told us, and taste better to eat when they're grown. A necessity. Dogs were an affectionate luxury, Cook said. They'd been sent their orders, no room in the Tower for luxuries and they needed two boys to help dispose of the dogs since they were too busy. So who did they send? Well, we'd been on pen-cleaning duty for weeks so it was yours truly and my best friend, with two large hammers.

"We took the darkest stairs down to the darkest room. And there were the dogs, half blind without light but they knew our smell, and wagged their tails when we arrived. Smacked their fat black gums. Bouncing on their hind legs for us to give them a good rub behind the ears. Now I won't lie, we argued. See, Cook said one of us should hold the dogs still and the other, whoever was stronger, should … you know."

Too right, we argued, you say.

"Finally it was settled. I'd hold. He'd… Well, so we coax the smallest out of the pen and he's my favourite, see, always happy to see me. We called him Switch because he had different coloured eyes, right? And I won't lie, I don't think I've ever felt the way I did that day. I said my goodbyes, I held him tight, let him nuzzle me half to death and I rubbed his belly and said, like we'd trained them, 'Stay!'

"Brothers, there never was a more obedient animal, I swear it. He looked at me with such trust, such hope for a treat. I held his gaze, braced myself, looked up to give my friend the nod and…

"He'd gone. Gone out of the door, left it open. Next thing I hear his voice saying…" I point into the darkness.

"Open the pen!" Stink hollers from halfway down the dorm where he had snuck during the telling of the tale. I've told this story a few times; it's well rehearsed now.

"Then…"

Stink's sharp whistle pierces the dorm so loudly every boy jolts upright.

We all laugh.

"And OUT they follow, every dog! Switch and Bluey and Shag and, well, you don't need all their names, but there were twenty of them. Barking and chomping and running with glee, out into the kitchens, out into the halls, out into the tunnels and out, out until no one ever heard from a dog in the Tower again. Some say, to this day, if you put your ears to the walls, you can hear them Outside, howling at the moon."

The applause for that story is always my favourite. It rings in my ears as my brothers crawl into their bunks, as I fake sleep and wait, wait for the snores so I can save you. You'll be safe by auction. You'll see.

That's not what happened, you say. The story is still going round in my head. The truth of it. *You folded, creased up in the corner and cried. And then when the dogs turned on you…*

I know.

So I had to…

I know.

All of them.

I know.

You took my face.

The cooks came before the attack finished and there's not much I remember after you killed the first animal, but your scars were deep from the dogs that tried to stop you. The cooks stitched you up but what handsomeness you had was gone. You'd have to work hard to get a buyer if you ever got into the House of Boys.

I owed you. When you got it into your head that you had to get out of the kitchens and into the House of Boys, I thought if I came too it'd be enough. But as soon as we arrived I knew

I still owed you. I'll always owe you. You changed, after the dogs. It was my fault.

By the time I applied for the House of Boys the year after, *we* were the only affectionate luxuries left in the Tower. Or so I thought. It's still bothering me. All those animals were killed, used for meat, sent into the desert. But she kept one for herself, up in that garden.

The light is still an eerie red. This blackout is longer than normal. Stink's snoring up a storm above. Every fibre of me wants to sleep, but I can't.

You wouldn't be here if it wasn't for me, you remind me. The dogs would've killed me, I know.

I scratch at my bruises, the ache of them returning, until my finger finds the cut on my cheek. Turning over and over the voices in my head. Why didn't I just give up Aspiner's name in my speech? Or Romali? Or anyone!

Coward.

When I let the dogs attack, I told myself after that I was being brave refusing to hurt them, but I was putting your life at risk, for what? Who would it have harmed if you'd let the dogs kill me? Was tonight the same? What about the night of Reserves? I thought I was being brave then, clever even. But I had another choice. When the Chancellor gave me the gun, I could've turned it on myself. The idea doesn't seem new. There's a peace to the thought, an old friend saying hello. When I told Walker I'd help him, I knew his plan wouldn't work but I was tired of fighting the ache inside. Part of me hoped it'd get me killed too. I was always too afraid to do it myself.

Coward, it says.

But of course she didn't even load the gun.

*

Hours pass, it feels like decades, and I don't move. This time the Chancellor will kill you and it'll be my fault. When I close my eyes, we're still in that dark, stinking room, a bright white dog at the Chancellor's side, and when she orders her to attack you I just watch.

21

Someone grabs my arms and I'm awake!

A half-dozen hands hold me down, forcing me into the creaking springs of my mattress.

"Get off!" I shout and kick as the gang turn me on my front and hold my arms. There's that gym deo smell, chalk. The Roids.

A knee pushes between my shoulder blades. A sweating palm crushes my ear. The whole bunk creaks under the weight of them and me. When I kick again, I catch one in the thigh. He shouts. I know that's Aye-Aye. I can smell Vinnie too. When he speaks, getting down close to my ear, his voice is a lot less soft than I thought it'd be. "You think she'll buy you after we've lopped off your balls?"

Stink tries to get down from the bunk above, but Toll threatens him with the same torture.

"Don't," I shout up, but he tries again and Aye-Aye throws a swift punch. I hear his nose crunch. Stink cries out and writhes around as I squirm below.

"Get Jai, get Walker, anyone…" I protest. I keep calling out until one of the Roids pushes something between my teeth. It tastes of old cotton. I cough but he keeps pushing until the fabric scrapes my throat.

"Shouldn't wake the House Fathers," Vinnie says, his voice slow. "That wouldn't be nice."

There's a half-digested swell coming up from my stomach. I try to swallow it down without choking on the cotton, while they tie my hands behind my back.

Can't spit, but I can still kick. Railing and pushing and pulling as they wrestle me from my bunk.

The women say all boys are born to be killers, that we need protecting from ourselves, and I can't stop thinking about that as we squall. I wanted the stories to be wrong but I didn't think twice about knocking Aye-Aye out of Swims. It's his last auction, he might not get a buyer – then what? I may as well have killed him.

I pull short breaths through my nose. My eyes hurt where they're still bruised and swollen. It's the struggle to breathe that makes them water. Just that.

It's me and the muscles now: the ones in my legs, the ones in their arms as the Roids drag me up the stairs, slamming their way into the red glow of the dining room.

Toll and Aye-Aye congratulate themselves as they shove me forwards and press my head against one of the dining tables. There's still a blackout but there's some light flickering from the green exit signs and emergency floor lights around the walls.

Vinnie jumps up, grabs hold of the pipes above. He swings from one, does a few pull-ups. Is he showing off? He drops, landing with a thud, before climbing up to test another.

A tall, triangular-chested boy who I think is from B-dorm hands Vinnie a long, twisted sheet.

"Vin?" says Aye-Aye. "I thought we were just going to bruise him up a bit?"

"It's our turn to show a little mercy," Vinnie says.

The end of the sheet is looped in a noose. Inside my skin, everything goes cold. I thought they were just planning a beating too. Vinnie loops the knotted sheet over his favoured pipe, twists the sheet round a few times, knots it and tugs.

They wouldn't? No, they can't.

I heave and push up my body, try to get away, try to shift against the weight of Toll and Aye-Aye, but they slam me down so firmly that everything jars inside my skull. This is a joke, right? Vinnie, Aye-Aye, Toll, the lesser grunts … they're trying to scare me. That's all. Focus on the knot at my wrists, on tearing the fabric, anything. If I have my hands, I can fight!

Stink must've gone to fetch Father Jai. He'll stop them. Maybe he's already heading to the dining room. The Fathers have ways of watching us, they tell us, everywhere. Watching. Even in here, right? Someone has to… The blackout! The cameras are dead. Fear pulls through me. What if no one's coming?

"Come on then," Vinnie orders, gesturing for Aye-Aye and Toll to bring me to him.

No. Wait, I try to shout.

"Look, Vin…" Aye-Aye hesitates. "Maybe he's scared enough?"

"What?" Vinnie snaps. "This is why I'm in charge."

My teeth bite down at the grating sound as Vinnie drags a

150

chair across the stone floor. Toll doesn't stall. He isn't afraid of what they're planning. Fighting me to the chair, he pushes me up until Vinnie grabs me by the hair, the shoulders, whatever he can get hold of. I try to kick, knocking the chair away as I go. Aye-Aye follows orders, brings it back. Toll plants my feet firmly as Vinnie pulls the noose over my ears, my chin. He pulls it tight until I'm choking.

There's another boy fighting them, in another world. But not this me, not here, not now.

This boy, this boy I am, is trying to breathe.

"Hang on," says Aye-Aye. "I thought I heard something," he whispers to Vinnie, then runs out of the dining hall so fast I hear him slip and fall.

Coward.

My head feels funny and I can't stop my eyes blinking enough to focus. Everything is a mess of shadows. My lungs rattle.

Just breathe. Count.

One…

Breathe.

Two…

Breathe.

Three…

Toll, laughing, nudges the leg of the chair and I close my eyes. Bite down. Screw my stomach tight. The flinch before the fall. The chair shifts. The muscles in my neck stretch as I reach, try to keep steady. Want to exhale but can't.

"Hey!" Vinnie shouts up at me.

Cold water hits my cheeks. My toes fumble to grip the chair. I cough as sparks of white light flash across my eyes.

"Not a good idea to pass out, Superstar." I hate that nickname. I preferred Squinty. My head burns.

Vinnie clicks his fingers near my face and gestures with the glass of water as if he's about to throw the rest. I try to turn away to keep it from going up my nose. He doesn't throw. He laughs and pushes me in the chest with his flat palms. The cotton stretches tight.

"Idiot," Vinnie says.

The knot of my throat rubs against the sodden, tightening cotton. Twisting my neck, I feel the fabric pull my skin.

They're not going to do it. They're not.

Why am I disappointed? There's a sudden distant bang and I imagine the Chancellor's gun.

"Get him down!" shouts Aye-Aye, slamming into the dining room. "Get him down NOW!"

After, there are voices. I can't tell whose.

I should have been braver. I should have helped the Gardener. Why was I so selfish?

"What?" Someone drags over another chair.

"Police!" someone else shouts. "FOGGING LICE. I saw them! In the dorms."

"WHAT?"

"They're looking for *him*."

The tightness around my throat loosens as one of the Roids tries to undo the knot. But he can't. The wet noose has fused tight. The lightness fills my head as they untwist the fabric. The world is pulled out from under me. Someone, swearing, catches me as I fall, holds me up on the chair. The sound of the noose clicks in my ears as it stretches and the fabric tightens again round my throat.

"Stand up, will you?" Aye-Aye means me, I think. It's him holding me up. His voice is quick, quiet. "You want to die?"

Behind me, Vinnie is working at the knot at my hairline. He shouts back, "TOLL! Will you at least help?"

You want to die?

Vinnie tears at the cotton they pushed in my mouth and I throw it up. I want to smack my lips together but my jaw won't work, neither will my tongue.

So tired.

You want to die?

"He's not breathing in!" Aye-Aye yells, still pulling at the noose. It won't come free. "I told you this was a stupid idea!"

"The note said to put him in the infirmary."

"Yeah, not kill him, though," Aye-Aye mutters. A note from the Chancellor? Because I didn't do what she wanted? Or just from one of the Fathers, trying to get me out of the auction?

Perhaps Romali's Hysterics have come to take me away, to hold me and calm my fears. The boys run, scattering, thudding steps between shouts, squeaks, the sound of kicks, thumps.

You want her to see you like this? says your voice.

Blood is pumping in my ears.

Pathetic.

I smell flowers. It makes my eyes water.

Weak.

Everything is so green and the air is a wind, and I can smell gunpowder and blood and dust. And rain.

You don't deserve her, you say.

"OUT." A voice. "OUT!"

Her voice. Romali Vor.

No, I'm dreaming. I'm on my own. Hoping. Dreaming. Lying to myself as always. I can hear the Gardener dying. Or maybe that's me. My head, packed tight with fog and pounding blood, is burst by the sound of a gunshot. Freedom. That's all I wanted once. Maybe there's another way.

My name is Jude Grant and I am alive, I said. Alive, like I should be proud of it. As if it's an achievement, but it's the only thing in the whole world that I can control, that I have any power over. My life. The idea settles, that old friend, and it feels good. Air filling me up. I'll never give the Chancellor a name. Fighting this world can't save you. I'm sorry.

I kick the chair behind me and pray for a snap.

THE HOUSE OF BEAUTY

Be the best you.

Be the better you.

Be the beautiful you.

22

LESSONS IN DEBT

"Is it really that bad?" you asked.

It was your twelfth birthday. The cooks celebrated it by making you clean the bathroom drains. I heard you didn't argue. You used to argue.

I'd not seen you for weeks. I had to. To get out of duties I dropped all the pans while carrying them to the head cook, took the smacks round my ear, was sent to the bathrooms as punishment.

Seeing you, the first time since the dogs, was hard. I nearly fell over when I saw your face, the mess of stitches and swollen skin that once gave you the best chance out of any of us to get into the House of Boys.

"No, no," I lied, stumbling over my story that the cooks had sent me to help, skipping the part about me making it happen.

"Liar."

You'd been working hard since they explained the merit system, doubly hard, trying to be a good boy, the best. Compensating, the cooks called it. They called you a steamer, since you started shovelling the steaming waste at the House of Death; thought it was funny, fixing your face themselves rather than paying to put you in the infirmary. All you had was that face, they said, better you look like where you came from.

"I heard you can spend against your debt to get in," I say, trying to get you to talk. You loved to tell us all about the rules to get into the House of Boys.

"Only new earnings. Besides, you think I've earned enough to make up for this?" you said, pointing at your face. "I still have to audition." Were you joking? You didn't laugh any more like you used to. "Maybe I should escape into the desert. Fight monsters. Survive on my wits."

I laughed but I liked the idea. It took root.

"You still going to try for it?"

You shrugged.

The auditions would be next month and it was the first year we could put our names forward. There were criteria to get in, not just merits: the way we looked, how well we could lay a table, sew, perform, smile, things like that. There were rumours that Mr Walker, who managed the House of Boys, had a new set of criteria this year; everyone was trying to find out what.

"What about you?" you asked. "You got enough?"

"I don't keep a record. No point." I didn't think for a second I could be in the House of Boys, no matter how good I was.

"Breaktime. Let's see those sins," you said and stuck your toothbrush, which they told you to clean with, behind your ear. Taking a wad of paper from the side, you soaked it, tore it up and started to mash the pieces into a shape.

With one eye on the door, I rolled up my trouser cuff and showed you the number. It was tattooed on my ankle like every other boy. Never shown anyone before. My debt was stupid-big: 942,621 demerits.

"Impressive," you said, sticking out your scarred lip, nodding with respect. The paper man you were making was taking shape.

"Airman Jude Grant. They say he dropped a bomb. Two million killed."

The first Chancellor took the names of the men they say led the Last War, gave the first of us their names, and their debt. Each demerit a sin. In five hundred years, every merit the Judes before me earned had hardly eroded our sins.

You started to make another figure with the paper, four-legged.

"Viktor Perrault," you said, and showed me the number on your own ankle. "He was a spy. But my forefathers have been doing a good job earning it off so it's come down a bit."

One million exactly.

"Wow," I said. I'd never met anyone with a bigger debt than me.

I started to imagine both us high-debts, Jude Grant and Viktor Perrault, together, winning the hearts of the top-floor ladies. We'd earn so many merits we'd give the boys they named after us a debt so small they'd be sure to be free men in a generation.

Later I snuck back to the bathrooms, found the little dried paper man and kept it. I'd put my name in for the auditions too. The next Jude, the next Vik, they'd pick new names.

The next Jude Grant would pick the name Vik. And the next Viktor Perrault would pick the name Jude, because we'd been more than friends. We'd been brothers.

23

Air explodes in my lungs. Then again. A burst of heat. Salty lips on mine. Pounding on my chest, pushing me into the ground over and over and over and over. My stomach spasms. Pushing all my insides up, up, up, until they're a stone against the ache in my throat. It can't get the air out through my mouth. *Don't you dare die.* Your voice or hers? The spasm from the depths of me. I roll over. Fear and air and liquid come out in a gush until I'm empty.

Roll back.

The cold concrete against my shoulders.

Breathe.

Breathe.

Breathe.

24

Soft pillows swallow my head whole. Pressing my hand to my throat makes me flinch. The skin is swollen. Alive with heat.

Alive.

I bury my face in fabric folds, fresh, washed, white. When I search for the familiar sounds of the dorms, I can't find them. Twisting the heel of my palm against my dry eyes, I blink myself awake. The room is lined with paintings of long-dead places, ancient photos of perfect men. It smells medical, overly clean. There's something strange about the light. Rolling over, I clutch my bruised ribs. The pain passes fast when I see it.

A real window.

I must be dead. I'm out of the bed before I know it, one hand holding my broken body, the other reaching to touch glass, cold and thick. Spots of water on the other side of the window blur the light, red and blue and golden. My whole head might collapse at the sight of it, or my heart, and all the parts inside until I'm made of light and I can float through the glass.

A real view. Saints, *real* light.

The world Outside is an endless room.

Looking down, the sides of the building sheer away. I must

be on the top floors somewhere. There's nothing below but a looming, mucky green cloud clawing up the walls of High House with soupy fingers. Is that the fog?

"We changed your shirt," says a voice behind me. Everything tenses as I turn.

Romali leans against the open door. No mask. Her braided red hair bright, green eyes smiling.

"You coughed up half your stomach before you passed out," she adds. "It suits you, the shirt." She points. I clutch the fabric against my chest as a shield. I check to see if I'm still wearing my dorm trousers. I am, so I peer under the waistband. Still wearing my shorts too.

"Yeesh! You think a lot of yourself, man."

I try to answer. I don't have the protection of the Appointment Steward, or Father Jai, anyone. She changed my clothes! They're not meant to touch, not without paying the house.

"I mean ... you were unconscious," she says, raising both eyebrows.

My cheeks burn hot. How could I let this happen? She saw me naked... I'm meant to stay pure. Doesn't she know what her mother's Lice do to impure boys, the things they take?

Romali steps back, her expression switching to concern as she sees my panic. "Jude, the *nurses* got you changed."

My chest is actually on fire; I rub at it to cool it down. "Nurses?" I croak.

"Guys like you. I guess you'd call them prentice? Anyway, the Chancellor keeps this room for Walker." Romali shrugs.

My heart is still drumming in my ears. "It was the best option. Look, we tried to get you out, but…" When she steps away, that fug of disinfectant and cleaning fluid swells between us. "We had to bring you to the House of Beauty," Romali says. "You almost died."

Everyone Below calls it the infirmary as a joke. Above, they use its proper name, I guess: the House of Beauty.

"We?" I try to say.

Romali crosses the wide floor; she puts her hand on my arm and my throat tightens. From the neck down, she's dressed in a Lice's uniform. She never told me which house she got into back when she was fourteen. Of course Romali Vor would get into the House of Peace with her mother. I picture her laughing with Officer Aspiner and pull my arm away.

"Look, there's something I need you to…" She clutches her throat and rubs it. "I just need something from you then we can get you out. Somehow…"

She's never wanted anything from me before.

A cold wave hits me. I start trying to explain that I have to see the Chancellor but it comes out as a crackle. Madam Vor is about to burst in with Aspiner and a swarm of Lice. She'll arrest me, pull out my tongue for speaking without permission.

Romali frowns. "It's safe here. We can talk," she says, leaning forwards. "You don't have to pretend."

How do I tell her that I'm not pretending, that I need to see the Chancellor, that I made a deal for your life?

"Maybe you should rest that apple of yours." Her eyes are on my neck like I'm a delicate thing that might break.

I put my hand to my throat, feel the heat, remember taking that step.

"I'm making it worse, aren't I? Sorry. Changing the subject now." She laughs. "So do you like the view?" In this light, she doesn't seem as sharp as she did at Reserves, or as open as in our appointments. Something in between, more real. "The fog always closes in after the rain." She's right beside me now. She knocks on the glass. A dull, deep *clonk-clonk*. "The glass is thicker than you think. Clever people, the Saints, low-emissivity, self-cleaning solar glass with enhanced thermal insulation."

Now it's my turn to raise my eyebrows. "Sm-ar-t –" I croak out, one syllable at a time – "ass."

"You should count yourself lucky they don't force you boys to learn this stuff." She's blushing too, I think. Maybe I'd like the chance to learn, maybe I'd like to tell my brothers, fill up our Collections with all their big words and facts. But I won't tell her that today.

"Mum said it's lasted half a century." She puts on an epic voice, puffing out her chest. "Architectural triumph, the beauty of the ancient desert, the comfort of the future!" She sniffs. "Not that they lived to see it. You ever wonder if they knew?" My blank face tells all. "Knew what'd happen after they abandoned it, I mean," she says. "After the Foundations moved in and the Last War…"

Squinting at the crumbling tops of buildings peeking through the fog cloud below, I can almost make out the city around the

Tower. G-dorm's Collection said it was abandoned years before the war. Beyond that I even think I can see the ancient city, the one from long before, the Melts, thousands of years old. The rain Outside melted the salt stone. Romali watches me trace the world in the glass.

"The fog clears up for a few hours most nights, you'll see. That's when the view gets good. Guess even now it's sort of beautiful." She screws up her face. "I'm talking too much, sorry."

"No," I croak. "It is."

"The edge of the city's over there." She presses herself against the glass. "See the old hospital the Saints built? That's the edge – after that, it's desert for hundreds of miles."

"Hysterics?" I manage to ask. They're out there somewhere.

"They move around. You know, some think there are tribes out there too, descendants of the Saints that survived the centuries, but if they do exist no one's ever come here. Nice idea, right? We could go and find them, what do you say?"

Trying to make out shapes beyond the glass hurts. I'm not used to this much light. I close my eyes. The brightness of the sun leaves dots and lines of blue and yellow dancing in the warming red of my lids. Here I am, with a girl, standing in front of the whole world.

"You've really never seen it before, have you?" she says after a while.

I shake my head.

"I forgot they don't let you."

"Because it's beautiful," I explain. She knows our oath – that we're not allowed to see beautiful things.

"Yeah, like a view is going to turn you into some sort of sex-crazed death machine." Romali swears. "I mean seriously, the things they teach us about you. By the House of Minds' reckoning, your average guy should be humping the window by now."

Planting my hands on the window, I lean into the view like I'm about to lick the glass.

She punches me on the arm. "Stop it!"

I look at the deep black roots of her blood-red hair. The curls of sleep in the corner of her eyes. How her whole body laughs when she does. She said she needed something from me. I try to ask what, but it comes out as a scratch.

"Look, I could get you some paper. It'll save your voice. They teach you to write down below?"

Dark-text yes, her letters, no. But she's out of the door before I can stop her.

I sink into the bouncing hold of the bed. This must be a dream. With the sheets to my face, I inhale, even though it burns. Reality doesn't smell this good. It doesn't have fresh fruit and clean floors and that twist of hope in my chest, sharp like lime.

I can hear you laughing at me.

But no. I know this is real. Like the memories from last night of red lights, shouting, the smell of elevator grease and lips on mine and pressure on my chest, the taste of bile. Did she bring me up in the elevator? Was it Romali in the dining hall?

It couldn't have been. Romali Vor's certainly strong and she's fast. The idea of her chasing away a pack of Roids makes me smile. I don't think I'll give this one a number. It's too big a feeling. I'll call it my *I'm-alive* smile.

I'm still grinning when a streak of striped, smart suit appears in the doorway. Walker.

He looks older. His hair greyer, his skin shining with sweat, eyes red-rimmed. He strides over to me in three paces and pulls me to my feet. Holds me tight against his chest like he'll never let go.

"Don't you ever do that to me again," he says.

25

"I can come back later," says Romali, returning with a glass of water instead of the paper she went for.

"No, stay," Walker says. "Jude, you remember Romali?" I try to croak out a yes, but it comes out bitter, deep. "My lady is playing games, pulling you into Swims like that, forcing a win. Until I know why I needed you out of the dorms. Couldn't have got you out on my own, see. Not without this little firecracker and—"

Romali interrupts. "Hey, I'm not so little any more and only Vor calls me by my full name," she tells me. "Call me Ro. When you can talk, of course." She winks as if we've never met before, and my stomach flips as I wonder when she and Walker started working together. "I ... I put some aspirin in," she says as I stare into the bubbling glass she hands me. "It'll help."

The water is warm and fizzes, and tastes of the bottom of a cooking pan.

"Drink it slow, kid, it'll hurt," Walker says. I glug it down in one go, to show him I can. But he's right – it hurts, so now I'm coughing, and he's laughing and ruffling my hair like I'm a child.

"Told you," Walker says to Ro. "Stubborn. It'll take more than

169

a few jealous jocks to take out our Jude. Right?" He throws a few fake air punches.

"Wally, this is serious." Ro sighs, sitting on the bed. She's so familiar with him, not following protocol, not ladylike. She pulls up her feet and tucks them under her body. She explains fast that she came to get me out of the dorms but the Hysterics wouldn't come, wouldn't risk helping, not now. So Walker knows she's working with the Hysterics? He doesn't even blink. She kicks off her heavy police boots. "Since I'd had my peace training and I've still got the uniform."

"You're not—"

"In the House of Peace? Quit last year. Anyway, I thought maybe I could get you Outside but I couldn't. Not after you—"

"Stop," I interrupt. I don't want Walker to know I jumped.

She pauses, realizing. "Yeah, so." She shrugs. "Like I said. You needed a doctor, I knew Walker's room would be free so ... that's that."

Ro starts to take off the police jacket, revealing a light top underneath, shoulders, freckles, so little effort or care for her skin. I try not to stare as she gets up and moves round me to speak to Walker, her arms folded. "I did my part. You said you'd ask him – that it'd be better coming from you."

Walker shakes his head. "He can barely talk."

"Well, that's no use. I'll get that paper," she says, disappearing at speed.

Walker is staring at me.

"What?" I croak and try to stand up straight.

"I knew she'd like you." He smiles, his best proud smile. It makes me angry. What's he got to be proud of me for?

"Ask me then," I tell him and his grin drops. It feels good, somehow, to know I did that.

Walker looks away. "They still teach you about families down there, right?"

Of course, I want to tell him. We get lessons, not a lot, only what's safe to teach us. And one word they spend a lot of time explaining is family. The House Fathers show us drawings of happy women and their good wards working hard to support the perfect family. The men are always smiling, holding plates of food, dusters, or looking with smouldering, half-closed eyes at their guardians.

Walker tries to explain. "You know Ro is the last daughter of the Dunn family?" he says. I nod.

Walker takes a deep breath. "Lorraine Dunn – everyone calls her the Gardener. She was last seen before Reserves, heading up to see the Chancellor."

"I know the Gardener was Ro's aunt," I interrupt, wanting him to get to the point, every part of me cold as I remember the Gardener's body, how her blood bloomed.

"Was?" Ro says, appearing in the doorway, paper and pencil in her hand. She's staring at me, her mouth open, green eyes blazing with horror. "What do you mean 'was'?"

I need air. "The Chanc—" I choke on the word, lean on my thighs to help suck air down my swollen throat.

"Aunt Lorri went up to confront the Chancellor about the

vote," she says. "When I read the news, I hoped she'd left, that she got out herself with the Hysterics, but she never did."

I can't breathe. I'm on that dining-room chair again, the air tight round my throat.

"Romali, give him space. Let him rest," Walker says.

"He owes me," Ro snaps. "She was there, wasn't she, at the Chancellor's, my aunt?"

"I'm not... I—"

"You must have seen her. You don't have to protect the Chancellor."

"No one'd believe me—"

"Believe what?"

Concentrate on my breathing. "It'd be a mercy, she said."

Ro looks at Walker then at me. Searching my face for a moment. She shakes her head. "No, not—"

I interrupt. "The Chancellor. She..."

Tell her, you say.

"She shot..." Every breath is like swallowing stone.

Ro's green eyes grow wide.

"She shot her."

Ro freezes. Her body goes tense and her green eyes widen.

"I couldn't help."

Liar.

"In front of you?" Walker asks.

"Tried. I..." I just have to explain. "I tried to help, I..."

No, you didn't.

Walker takes my shoulders. "She killed her in front of you?"

172

I nod. Ro is silent.

Walker starts talking to himself about what he could have done to prevent it; maybe he could have sent a message, warned Lorri, something. He wouldn't have let me go up there if he'd known.

All I know is that he believes me.

"Fog it. She has to go," Ro says, jaw set.

Walker reaches out to her. "Please. I can fix this."

Ro pushes his hands away. "You said that last year!" she snarls. "You promised!"

"Please, Romali," Walker begs.

"She wants to get rid of my whole family, Walker! Sending Mum into the desert, now Lorri, murdered? My family kept High House going for hundreds of years and she's almost wiped us out." She slams her fist against the wall. "Almost every woman in this place will vote her way. The ones who don't like her are afraid, and the ones who aren't afraid are in her pocket, and the rest don't even think their vote counts!"

There's a look in her eye like she's going to go and strangle the Chancellor right now. And I'm certain she'll do it too.

"Ro, you need to keep your nose clean. Once she's gone, you could be Chancellor. Let someone else risk it."

"You think I *want* to be Chancellor? Why, because of my family?" Ro is shorter than Walker but when she stands up to him he recoils. "There's a reason Mum left when the Chancellor asked. There's a whole world out there!" Her palm hits the glass and I swear it shakes.

"Jude, I'm sorry," Walker apologizes. "A gentleman shouldn't have to listen to scandal and—"

Ro laughs. "He can deal with it! He can deal with anything! After last night – you didn't see. He… Oh, screw the both of you. I'm going to do it my way! She can't hide up in the Pent House forever."

Ro turns, whipping her red ropes of hair as she heads for the door. "If you can't kill her, see if I don't!"

26

"You're not going to the ball," Walker insists, after getting me into bed.

I've heard the stories about boys not allowed to go to the ball. Our fairy godfathers fix it. I tell Walker he's doing a terrible job living up to the fairy tales.

I reckon the only time Romali will be able to get to the Chancellor is at the ball and that maybe we should help her. Walker disagrees. "We're done. I made a mistake. I can keep you safe here. Let Ro get herself killed. Stupid, headstrong girl."

"What about Vik?"

"What about him?" Walker's eyes move from mine. "You need to forget about him. He's gone. It's not safe—"

"I'm not made of glass!" I shout, wheezing out every drop of anger. The words are coming easier now, if deeper and scratchier than before. Anger boiling over, hot and ungentlemanly, and I don't care, because it feels good. It all comes out: what happened the night of Reserves, the deal, the garden, what the Chancellor wanted me to do.

He puts his head in his hands. "Jude, my boy. She's playing with you." He pours a sour-smelling sort of drink from the flask in his pocket as I catch my breath. "You have to believe me. Do you think I would have risked sending anyone to kill her if I knew another way? You have such promise... I had no choice."

"No." I won't let him take you away again.

"The Chancellor must have seen how Romali reacted to you onstage. Exposing herself like that, how she'd risk her honour and your safety to keep you from her. You think she doesn't know Romali's been visiting you all year?"

"You knew?"

"I arranged it. You needed something to hope for. Something good. Besides, there was nothing better to get the Chancellor interested in you than making it seem as if Romali Vor wanted you too."

He sits down on the edge of the bed, rubbing at the nape of his neck. Everything about him is tired.

"All I know is Vik's alive," I say. "And you gave up on him."

Walker sighs and massages the muscles of his neck. "I never said he was dead, kid."

"No, I remember you said..." Do I? "You said you couldn't help! After the Lice took him, you said you couldn't help. That ... that ... that he was gone."

"Gone," Walker says. "Not dead."

"What the fog does that mean?"

"Language! I've told you about that temper."

"You wanted to USE my temper. She'll kill him like she killed the Gardener. Don't you care?"

Walker locks his blue eyes firmly on mine. "There are worse

things than death," he says. "Death really is a mercy."

The Chancellor said that too. I bite my cheeks; take a deep breath; slow my heart.

"Right now you need to get well," Walker says, and for the first time his face relaxes into something unpractised, honest. "Trust me, if Vik's alive, I'll find him, and then you'll understand."

27

FURTHER LESSONS IN DEBT

The cooks' bullying hadn't let up since your birthday. No matter how good you tried to be, they had you doing all the worst jobs. Scratches up your arms from the rats they made you catch. They always picked on you the most. I tried to help, get myself on the same duties as you. My hands were sore from a day bleaching plates, red from the chemicals, but it didn't stop me chewing the dead, soap-tasting skin around my nails as we waited for our auditions.

Punishments wouldn't stop you trying to get into the House of Boys. We were outside the head cook's office for hours waiting to audition. Scowling prentice pushed by, the clatter of plates and shouts around us, swearing at us to shift out of the way.

There were four of us who'd put ourselves up to audition: you, me, Berna and Sal. For Berna, it was his third try for the House of Boys and he was turning pale as if he was going to heave. Sal had been moved to the kitchens not that long ago from maintenance. He wanted a day off and was enjoying the opportunity to sleep, spread out on the bench. You had your head in your hands and shrank into the corner, pulling your collar up over your nose to avoid stares from the passing prentice who'd not yet seen your scars.

When I tried to make conversation, you turned away. You were worried too, I thought. Wondering what would happen if you were still stuck here tomorrow and if they'd give you extra work like they did to the boys who failed last year, whether they'd hold food back until you got sick, whether you'd have to go through that alone.

"We'll get through," I said. "You'll see."

The old clock flicked through the light-hours and one by one we auditioned – first Berna, then Sal. They came out, deflated. It was too dark to tell what time it was when you were finished. You strutted past me, head high, and I knew you'd done it. I just had to get through too.

Cook led me down the tunnel corridors, shuffling barefoot through the dark. That's the sound that sticks with me. And how cold it was when the cook's arm left my shoulder and I waited, alone, in the big room.

The cooks called it the Mirror Room. It was one of the storage spaces on the floor above the kitchens. They kept all these old mirrors in there, mottled with age, stacked up against the boxes.

Weaving between them, I thought there was no one there. But eventually the storage space opened up, boxes pushed to the sides to make a large room with a table in the middle. The man waiting there was smartly suited in black, his hair dyed blond, too blond. It was parted on one side and flattened with oil so

I could see his roots. The moustache on his top lip gave him a permanent smile. I'd never met a man over thirty and figured he was older than that but I wasn't sure how old. It was hard to tell because of the bandage over his nose. His eyes looked bruised underneath the make-up he'd applied. My whole body was rigid, every muscle tense like stone. *This* was Mr Walker.

The ache in my head had started. That whispering tightness behind my eyes. It whistled like a voice telling me I was stupid for putting myself up for this. I thought there'd be instructions, what to do, what to say. We're meant to show our skills, right? Mr Walker had a file, his fingers running over the dark-text as he read. He wouldn't look at me, not even when I moved closer.

It was cold in the Mirror Room but he didn't care, buttoned warm into layers of clean cloth. I eyed the flask of water on the table, the plates cleared of food. My stomach felt emptier then under my unwashed shirt than it ever had.

The questions came thick and fast without him even looking up: age – I'm twelve; background – I live in the kitchens in High House; something I've done that I'll never do again – I once ate something I found under a unit – I thought was a berry; it wasn't; what part of my body don't I like – my feet; what makes a boy desirable – what does desirable mean?; what have I learned from life in the kitchens – don't eat everything you find; who inspires me – my friend; what am I most ashamed of – what am I most ashamed of?

Mr Walker's eyes fixed on my foot jigging on the dusty floor, until I stopped.

"Do you *want* to join the House of Boys?" His voice was tired. He was twisting a silver ring round the knuckle of his left hand.

"Yes, sir," I said.

"Why?" he asked, taking a swig from his flask.

I sucked at my dry lips, tried to say everything I thought he'd want to hear. "To serve, to support, to learn, to better—"

"Why?" he interrupted. I started to repeat myself, didn't get to the third word. "No. Why?" he asked again. I wasn't giving the right answer. "Give me something human, kid. Do you know how many of these I've done today?"

"I…" I didn't know what to say.

He sighed, stood and began to walk away.

"Stop," I said.

What? Boys don't make demands. Even the cooks were afraid of Mr Walker.

His tall shoulders stretched in the darkness. I could hear him breathe. "Yes?"

"Did … did he get in?" I asked. "The boy before me?"

Mr Walker turned into the light, lifting one perfectly groomed brow. "*He* gave me something human. We can only take one boy from each house this year. You knew that, right?"

I shook my head. Did you know?

"I guess the spot's his." Mr Walker turned to leave again and I didn't stop him. My head circled round what this meant as his steps faded into the dark.

He was lying. Just one boy? We were supposed to join the House of Boys and we'd be safe and happy, and they'd fix your face and we'd never be hungry and we'd always be friends. Finally we'd escape into the desert and have adventures. My body was shaking – we had to join the House of Boys together. It wasn't fair!

It was bubbling up, that fight. It grabbed at the knots of my hair, yelled anger into the ceiling until the light bulbs shook.

Alone now, there was a spark from deep inside, right in my empty gut, a raging burst as I kicked the table, the chair, then hurled them towards the boxes, the mirrors, sending the glass spinning.

In the silence, I waited for the cooks to come. You break it, you pay for it. I expected them to pile in, merits docked, bruises, isolation. And maybe they'd beat me worse than you, and I'd get sick and die and the boy after me would start exactly where I did. It would be like I was never even here.

But no one came. My breath heaved in and out. I shouted again. Still no one.

We were never alone. In all my life, I'd never been alone. At first my body pricked with nerves, thinking I heard sounds, people, then a voice. *Go on*, said the voice. *Let go*. For the first time in a long time, I started to move, to dance.

I don't remember the moves but I'll never forget that feeling of flying.

Maybe Mr Walker was there all along. I don't know – I didn't see him until I heard his applause.

"Don't stop," he said.

I was out of breath, trying to apologize, to explain.

"Forgot my flask," he said, picking it up from the floor. Walker tidied his hair, then pointed at my hand. "You're bleeding, kid."

The white cuff of my shirt was sopping and sticky, and there was more on my sleeve from the gash in my palm. Must've cut it on the broken glass. It didn't hurt, not yet.

He pulled a cloth from his jacket sleeve, tied it round my hand. "Who'd have thought there was all that fire in a scrawny kid like you, huh?" He handed me his flask. "Drink up."

He picked up the chair, dusted it off and told me to sit. My heart was still pounding. I could feel it in my hands as my hands gripped the chair tightly as if they might snap it. He pulled something from his finger and gave it to me.

"What's this for?" I stared at the silver ring. He rubbed at the finger he'd taken it from; where he'd taken it off was the black tattooed mark to remind everyone he was a ward. Only the Chancellor's ward has a ring too.

"Something Glassey's accountants will know came from me. You can have the spot and save your hard-earned merits, get in for free. Your friend can try again next year."

"Wait, no." That wasn't right. We had to go together. "Give … give it to Vik." I pushed the ring back to him.

"The place is yours."

I shook my head. As much as I wanted to get in, I couldn't go alone. I didn't deserve to take your spot. I got you hurt. I let you down.

"Can you give it to Vik?"

"Fine," said Mr Walker after some time, sliding the ring back on to his finger. "But under one condition. I'm not letting that talent go to waste. You're joining too. I take it you have the merits?"

I nodded.

"Then I can make an exception and accept two of you. The House of Merit will come to take payment from you tomorrow. It's not only our ladies who can offer protection."

He didn't need to tell me I owed him. I was old enough to know everything had a price.

28

There are too many differences to the dorm: the smells, the sounds, the air. Walker's infirmary bed may be the single most comfortable thing ever, but I can't sleep. I roll and twist in the sheets, turn the pillows over and over to get the cold side.

The Roids wanted to put me in the infirmary. There was a note...

Eventually, I drag the sheets down and curl up on the floor, leaving the curtains open to watch the moon rise, the hot orange sun drop from the edge of the world into the dark green setting light. If I could watch it again, a thousand times over, it'd never get dull.

After dark-hours, it's not the night sky that keeps me awake. I've never slept alone before and when I close my eyes there's nothing familiar to silence your voice. If it wasn't for me, you say, you'd be alive, out there. And maybe you'd see those ancient cities. Maybe you'd meet men and women living their lives, people who've never heard of High House, or the Chancellor, or the Last War.

There, the men don't carry the debts of their forefathers, the boys don't have to choose between dignity, grace and chastity

– all those qualities they say boys like you and me should have – and toiling in the guts of the earth. If you can even call it a choice! The women Outside don't care about who lives below them, who lives above. If they keep the company of men, it's not because of how much they're worth, or how tall they are, or thin, or muscled, or hairy, or what shade they are. There's a world out there where people dance because they want to, not because they have to, and that's where you could be right now. Alive.

But you're not out there.

I think I've worked out where to find you.

The nurses that come and go from my room, checking on me, have the same stitched smiling face on their collars as the prentice boy who brought me that note just before Swims. If the note came from you, it came from *here*.

I climb up on to the mattress to press my ear against the vents, listening for noises through the pipes. The air tastes sweet. They pull it from above the fog – you taught me that. They treat it and pump it through the Tower, the tunnels, but by the time it gets to Below there's a staleness even the House of Air can't remove. Height, you said, it means everything. Cleaner air, better views, more protection, more merit.

My eyes closed, pushing my forehead against the cold metal of the grille, I try to think. According to Rod's maps in our Collection, the infirmary is about halfway up the Tower and covers a few floors. Woody said air prentice weren't allowed on certain floors; the vents were too narrow for them to fit. He told a story once of an area around the hundredth floor, where he and

186

the other boys heard noises that kept them up at night. Screams, shouts…

Probably just a story. But what if it wasn't? And what if I'm right and you're here?

Who knows how long I'm here for? Walker could send me back to the dorm any time. He won't let me go to the ball or try to kill the Chancellor again. What have I got to lose?

Through the vents there's a noise. It sounds like barking – no, a scuffle. Shouts. Swearing, panic, tears.

My heart in my mouth, I scramble off the mattress, grab a gown. A strip of light is cast into the room through the gap beneath the door. My sweating hands slip on the handle as I push it open, holding my breath.

Walker's curled up asleep in an armchair. Arms folded. Some guard, I laugh to myself.

The air is cold. Long looping corridors, clean-scented squeak beneath my bare feet. Gritting my teeth, I sneak past dimmed lights. There's never darkness here, I guess, peering round corners.

My ears prick at every sound as I search for you, imagining nurses, doctors, Lice. I open door after door to see women with their faces wrapped in fabric, swollen-eyed, groaning in their sleep.

The shouts aren't from a woman. Louder now, nearer, twisting fear into my chest, tearing through my veins, they come from a boy screaming, fighting for his life.

They're killing you! The Chancellor wanted me here to show

me what happens when you defy her instructions and now…
Running towards the sound, ignoring the smack of my feet,
until a gang of doctors appears, laughing. Catching my breath,
I dive behind a counter, curl up tight, pray to the Foundations
they don't see me. I wait for their laughter to pass. Silence.

The shouts are gone.

I run through room after room, rattling locked doors,
searching for something to prove you're here.

There's a paper flower on one of the desks in the corridor. I
never saw you make anything that detailed but there it is, a knot
of red paper. It looks almost real, like the ones in the garden.

Behind me the shouts start again, louder. A door swings open.
Slams shut. I duck behind another counter.

The nearest door smacks open against the wall. Footsteps run
through, dizzy, uneven. The breathing is panicked, hot, swearing
through tears and gasps, searching the doors, trying every one.
Looking for a way out, a place to hide. There's a thud as the
runner trips, hits the ground. I'm on my feet straight away,
expecting to see you.

"Aye-Aye?" I say as he pulls himself up, naked, shivering. I
fight my dressing gown from my shoulders to try to cover him.

The Roid is long gone and in his place is the kid that joined
from the House of Construction. "Jude! You're alive." He claps
his hand over his mouth, shakes his head. The doors behind
open. "Hide! Hide, dammit!" Aye-Aye drops his voice to a
whisper, trying to force me back behind the counter.

"What?"

"Don't let them see you!"

Run, you say.

I can't.

"Did you see Vik? Is he here?"

Aye-Aye steps away from me, jerking his head. He stutters, stammers and I can't understand. He's slurring.

"Calm down," I say. "Aysel? What happened?"

"The others, they… I'm sorry. We're sorry. We didn't mean to." He's crying now, rubbing at the marks on his wrists. Jumpy, he looks back.

Could I help him to my room? Walker would hide him, wouldn't he? But what from?

He's shivering head to foot.

"Get them out," Aye-Aye says. "You can persuade the Chancellor, right? Get them out."

"Who? Vinnie? Toll?"

Aye-Aye's dark eyes are as wide as plates. "All of them!"

He's swaying, trying to shake his head clear, but his knees give up on him. I try to drag him behind the counter. His body's heavy, skin clammy, hands fighting me away like I'm the enemy. Confusion sets in. He starts to babble. "All of them," he slurs, the only words I can make out clearly. "Promise!"

"Promise," I say.

The nearest doors slam open. I dart for the light switch. In the darkness, I can hide him, maybe. *Shh. Shh!*

A swarm of Lice leads the way, their batons spitting green light that illuminates their armour, a dozen doctors following behind. The doctors aren't like the ones I've seen before. There are flashes of white smocks that reach to their ankles, surgical masks stretched over their mouths, noses, the fabric moving in and out with each breath. Smiling faces beaming at me from where they've been sewn on the breast pockets of their smocks.

From the barked orders, I know the woman heading up the Lice is Aspiner.

Maybe if I stop trying to move, if I get low, in the darkness, the Lice won't find us.

But we're both a hot mess of heartbeats, loud in the dark. Then Aye-Aye groans. I try to cover his mouth as the source of the green lights get nearer. A blast of electricity fires and Aye-Aye begins shaking at my feet.

"We're going to make you better," says one of the doctors, reaching for me. Her voice is bright, cheerful as the Lice wrestle Aye-Aye's jerking body on to a stretcher, its squeaky wheels disappearing into the dark.

"I'm… I'll go to my room," I say, backing away. Then I hear Walker's voice. He must have followed the sounds. He starts to protest, talking about how I'm injured, not myself, fragile, special, as Aspiner and the Lice stride towards him.

"That's OK," says another doctor, soft, gentle. I didn't even hear her appear beside me. Then the needle bites sharp at my neck. "We can make you better."

29

Bzzzz.

The hum is in my head, like the buzzer in the appointment rooms, except it doesn't stop.

I try to shake the sound away, move my jaw, pop that bubble of noise. Everything is dark shadows, silhouettes against bright light.

"Nice evening, isn't it?" the shape in black says, her voice precise with every breath. I try to answer but choke on the smell of her, a cloud of smoke and salt that sticks in my throat. The kind of smell I remember from the kitchen, from when we threw bones in the fire. The kind of smell to take the skin off things.

"I think we should be friends. After all, it seems you have our Chancellor's ear. Who knows, you could be the next Head Ward?"

Is she saying something happened to Walker? Is she a doctor? "I'll be good," I say. "A good boy. Just let Vik go, Walker too."

"I could do that," the shape says. "The Chancellor says she's waiting for something from you. She's not used to being disappointed."

There was a name I was going to give. "Aspiner," I say. Over and over.

"Not Romali? Are you sure? The Chancellor is very keen to speak to her."

I try to shake my head. Everything hurts.

"Do you know where Romali is?"

So they can't find her? She's alive.

"You know where Romali is."

"No."

"You don't know what she has planned?"

"No."

"Maybe tomorrow then."

∗

Bzzzz

Bzzzz

It's not just me here. The other beds are occupied. I think Vinnie, Toll, Aye-Aye ... but I can't be sure. It's early when the doctors pull the green curtains across, hiding the bed where Aye-Aye is. He hasn't moved since they brought him back; they keep putting needles in him. There's a tray shining in the light. I blink it away, slow. Everything in my head is slow.

"Don't." My voice sounds slurred. They pat my head like I'm a pup. Fingers stroke my cheek. *Shh now*, they say, *we're making him better*. The needle on the tray is as long as my forearm. There's blood on it when they take the tray away and bandages around Aye-Aye's eyes when they pull open the curtain, the metal rings scraping on metal. And I think I'm shouting but the noise seems to come from so far away.

✳

Bzzzz

"The nose is OK," says the doctor. "But those ears. A few stitches maybe." Cold, gloved fingers tilt my head to the side. Aye-Aye isn't there any more, his bed freshly made. When was that – yesterday? Did I dream it?

"A stronger chin maybe? She likes that. It would heal fast enough."

"Do we have a peel for the acne scars?"

There's sensation somewhere, down in my elbows, my knees, I could fight my way out before they stick a pin in my head.

"Definitely need to fix the teeth, bit stained," says one of them as I wrestle my way out of bed. I try to get up but my legs are funny and I smash into the cold tiles.

"Needs a trim – that mop won't work. Blond?" says another, fighting me back on to the bed. "Like the other one?"

"No, she wants to keep this one dark."

✳

Bzzzzzzzz

I'm dreaming of the dorms. But they're in these dark, sticky spiders' webs so old and clogged with dust that they've turned into wheels of tarred black spokes. I want to scratch for web strands in my hair but when I try to move nothing happens.

"So we were talking about Romali," the woman says, spidery black too, all elbows and eyes.

"Aspiner," I slur. What if Romali hasn't gone for the Chancellor yet? What if Walker's safe and has found you? How long have I been here?

"Now, now, no one in the whole of High House will believe any of the Aspiner family would work with the Hysterics. I heard you promised a name."

"Aspiner," I repeat. My face feels different, like it's made of a stranger's skin.

"You think you're being strong? Do you want to find out what happens if you don't give her what she wants?"

The beds are empty now. They were all here, the Roids, but now they're gone. Not dead. Gone.

Death is a mercy, the Chancellor said. She pinheaded them. Their minds 'absolved' like the Surrogates under her mother's care. Why wouldn't she kill them like the rest? Or send them to the mines?

"Walker?" I ask.

"Where's my daughter? I know she visited you."

"Madam Vor?" I try to focus on her, but she moves away. This is the woman who leads the Lice. Every boy that's lost their life, every woman their mind, it's been down to her house. She has dark hair, shorter than mine, a stiff dark suit. Every edge of her could cut paper.

"Maybe tomorrow then?"

"No, wait, don't go, please."

*

It has to be a dream, right?

The hands round my neck. Your hands.

Is it a nightmare? Drugs? Memories of the night of the blackout, the sheets creaking, fingers holding fast round my neck.

"No," I croak. "I don't want to die, not today, not any more."

Or it's a memory? Not your hands at all but the feeling of falling. The remembered ache in my throat scratching against my neck bones, that's all.

Or it's madness, thinking I can hear you swearing at me, calling me an imposter, telling me you deserve to succeed. You came from nothing. I don't know what you had to do, sacrifice, to survive. I had everything, you say! You press down with all your strength. But it's insanity, that's all.

Or it must be your ghost.

No, you're alive and I'm going to find you. And I'm going to save you, I say. It's my fault, I say, my fault. The ghost hesitates, but only for a second.

Consciousness comes and goes, from black to swirling faces in grey. I can't shake the vision of the Roids' faces, hollow like the women's masks. A crowd of them. All my brothers. Expressionless, with empty eyes, gaping mouths. And you, bright and burning with your brown eyes wide, and your teeth gritted and tears down your cheeks. Maybe you can still help, you say. Help who?

It's the drugs.

Because it can't be you, because you had scars and this boy has none. Besides, if you were here and you were alive and you did try to kill me, we both know you'd never give in. Not until I was dead. That's the kind of boy you were. Walker thinks I'm a fighter, but I never was, not like you.

Bzzzz

Coward.

Bzzzz

*

"The ball," I tell Madam Vor when she comes again, before she even asks. There's not a part of me that isn't wrapped up, tweaked, bettered. Only one last procedure to make me perfect, the doctors say, the one that the Roids didn't come back from. I thought I could hold on, but you're gone – like the Roids – and I can't, can't justify fighting. Maybe I'm protecting a ghost, falling for the Chancellor's game, and Romali doesn't need a stupid boy trying to help. "Ro – she was angry, about the Gardener," I say. Can't fight any more. "She's going to kill the Chancellor."

Madam Vor's hand grips my wrist.

"Enough," she says. "Enough, Jude." She sits. Black grit and grime cling underneath the chipped edges of her blunt nails. "I burned my sister-in-law's body today." A shot rings in my ears, but it's not really there. My jaw hurts as I bite down; it clicks when I push my bleach-burned teeth together. "We'll find a time to honour her sacrifice. Until then let's talk about nice things." Madam Vor leans close, grips my wrist tighter, her voice falling to the kind of quiet that makes your hairs stand on end.

"The ball, for example. It's our Chancellor's favourite night of the year. We wouldn't want to ruin that, would we? We're going to do everything we can to make it a success, aren't we? Now you're going to ask how you can help," Vor says. I don't answer. "You can't. All you can do is say goodbye to your friends."

Air floods out of my body as Vor moves away and the doctors move in. I didn't even notice I was holding my breath.

30

"I don't know, he looks weird," says Stink, poking me.

They find me in the stairwell.

Father Jai was sent up to collect me. He helped me put on my suit and as the drugs wore off he helped me walk. There was kindness, I think. That was a few hours ago, before he sat me in the stairwell, told me to wait. It's like someone has scraped inside my head with a spoon. Nightmares drift in and out of my mind as I wait, numb. I gave Ro up. I'm a killer; right in that moment I killed her. It should feel good. If you're alive, I saved you, didn't I? Except you're quiet now. That voice, silent. You've never felt further away.

"He's been staring into space since we got here," says Rodders.

"I'm fine," I say. My voice sounds different, deeper somehow. When I touch my throat, it feels like it belongs to someone else.

She'll let you go now she has what she wants, what I promised, right?

"You've been gone five days, Superstar," Rodders says. He's not wearing his specs. The only time he normally takes them off is in appointments and on event days. He says everything onstage is easier if it's blurry. Rod comes close enough for me to smell the fresh perfume of the deo, the bitter tang of aftershave. "You actually look pretty good."

"You're blind, Rod," Stink sighs.

"Five days?" I ask.

They're too close and I feel like I'm going to scream so I move to get away. The chatter of my brothers getting ready echoes up from below. "The ball?" I tug at the dark cotton of my jacket. The suit Walker had made for me. Black, smart, striped. The lining inside red, his favourite shade. The silk tie at my throat feels like a noose.

"You're home just in time." Stink smacks my shoulder. "Just-in, get it?" he laughs, because that's his name. There's a badly covered-up scar on the bridge of his nose where the Roids lamped him. "Though maybe you shouldn't dance too much? Looks like you're going to chuck."

"I'm fine," I manage to say.

"You've got a mirror, right, Rod?" Stink asks.

Before I know it there's a glass in front of my face. The man looking out from the mirror is hardly Jude Grant. I don't know who this man is. He hasn't got a single mark, not one bruise, or spot, or scar. His eyes seem bigger, brighter than mine, bluer than before, his eyelashes darker. No spots, no stray hairs between his eyebrows or in his nose.

This isn't me.

"You sure you're fine?" Stink asks. "Are you sure you didn't get your head rattled by the Muscles?"

The inside of my mouth is burning; my teeth are too white.

My hair's shorter, darker, neater, perfect. Perfect body, perfect smile.

"Promise," says the man in the mirror. My eyes prickle as I remember how they dragged Aye-Aye away. There's the ghost of you as I tug my tie loose, push the mirror away. I don't want to look at what they've made out of me.

"Jai said he had to get you from the infirmary." Rod seems impressed. "Look, sorry we didn't, you know, when the Roids came. But seriously they've done you a favour. You look kinda hot. On trend and everything."

Stink smacks Rodders round the top of his head. "Stop flirting!"

"What? The Toppers won't keep their hands to themselves later. Though we need to sort that hair out, the side parting is way too last century. Hang on." He starts searching his pockets. "I got some decent gel as a tip in an appointment last week. Just the thing."

I'm always surprised at how he manages to carry so much in his home-made pockets without ruining the lines of his suit. Wasn't Rod taller than me when I last saw him? I can't have grown three inches since Swims, can I?

Stink pokes at my neck again like I'm made of jelly. I snatch his hand hard, an instinct. Stink yelps and rubs at his wrist, "Saints, someone's jumpy!"

"Yeah," my new voice creaks, "you would be too."

"Honestly, though, you're actually glowing. What the fog did the Roids do to you? They've turned you into one of them!"

I shake my head and lie. "I don't know."

Medicine, serums, cold presses, injections. That's how Walker stayed so young all these years; she sent him to the infirmary every time he looked tired. I can't count the times he came to my appointments with bandages, or new hair, fewer lines. But when Walker tried to stop them taking me it didn't matter how good he looked. Aspiner drove his perfect head into the ground. Her large palm pressing down on his cheek, the other on his shoulder. Then she flipped a switch and ploughed so much juice into him that I can still smell the cotton of his suit sizzling.

Whatever the doctors did, there's still damage underneath my buffed-up skin. My muscles ache, my throat too. There are parts that hurt that didn't hurt before: my knuckles, the tops of my feet. And there's that dream of you again. *She'll never love you*, you said. Of course not, there's no such thing. Isn't that what they teach us? Even the imaginary you warned me away from Ro. As if Ro ever would – I mean I'm not even sure she likes me, not after she learned about her aunt.

I told Vor that Ro would be at the ball. I'll have to warn her, then we'll find you together and we'll leave together. It'll be all right. It'll be all right.

"Jude, are you sure you're OK?" Stink keeps asking as we make our way with the rest of the dorms up to the front of house.

"Nervous," I say, my mouth dry. My teeth tingle, too big for my face, too straight. I paw at my palm, searching for the scar from when Walker auditioned me. Never thought I'd be so pleased to see that broken part of me.

"I don't need twenty-twenty vision to know you're acting like you left your brain in your bunk," Rodders says, blinking a lot without his glasses on. "Look sharp, Superstar, will you? The debs will eat you alive if you don't snap your wits on." He leans in. "Or I will." He winks.

Stink hits him again.

"What?"

"Rod, you're so shallow," Stink sighs. "I'm surprised you don't trip over your own forehead when you walk."

"Hold!" Father Van calls down.

We're to wait in the upper stairwell. We're to come out at the first-floor balcony to the atrium, be announced and walk down the grand staircase, round the fountain. Then it starts.

"You're nervous. At least you can bloody dance. I get all elbows," Stink sighs. "Never know where they might put their hands!"

"I can't dance," I say.

"Oh, come on! I was at Swims. Besides, you think we don't know about those lessons Walker's been giving you all year! We're not stupid." And I think of Walker and I have this twisting feeling in my guts that I might never see him again.

"He didn't make me a better dancer," I say.

"Yeah, I bet. He's always got his favourites. It was that kid Vik last year," says Rod.

Everyone goes quiet at Vik's name.

Stink laughs to break the weirdness. "I get a lump just thinking about one of them touching me. I'll be throwing ice down my pants all night."

Some boy near us laughs so much he sneezes on the boy in front.

"Toss them Superstar's way," shouts another from above. "He'll distract them for the night. Hey, it's not like they've a chance bidding on him with the Chancellor's reserve. He's not going to steal away your guardians."

"True, and with Vinnie and that lot out of the way," Stink adds.

"Don't," I snap, feeling that twist in my guts again when I think of them. "They're gone."

"Gone?" Stink repeats. "Like to the mines?"

I want to tell them what happened. But I can't even find the words.

"Just gone," I say.

31

Beneath the finished mural of the Chancellor, looking down on us and smiling, the ball is steaming food, hot hooch and warm skin pushing past. Satins and silks brush my arm. Too real. Too fast. I don't know where to look.

Saints, I wish you were here to see this! Never thought I'd be here, not in a million dreams. Am I allowed to be here because I gave up Ro?

Above, the vast internal spire of the atrium drips with lights that crawl down the swirling pillars. Women and girls look down and point from the endless balconies. Against the golden pillars, wax mountains of candles weep.

They call it the Unmasked Ball, but the women still wear half-masks over their eyes, their noses. My brothers wonder and point and whisper about their strange mouths under those large eyes. Pink, red, blue, black, golden, silver lips. Fat lips, thin lips. Old, chattering, laughing lips. Skin of every shade, hair of every colour, perfect teeth and soft pink chattering tongues.

Dressed in an explosion of gold fabric, Madam Glassey catches my arm at the top of the stairs and announces me. There's applause but it's mute. I keep thinking of how you scrambled in a run across this floor, how you fell, how you called my name. But when I picture it now it's not you falling but Aye-Aye. Then it's the others: the Roids, Walker. Gone. Just gone.

I survived. I'm alive and they're gone.

Because of you.

For all I know, you might have been pinheaded like the Roids: alive but gone too, like Walker told me. If I can't help you, then please, tonight, let me save Ro.

My brothers disappear into the crowd of dresses, girls cooing over them, asking for their dance cards. Stink winks, encouraging me down into the mass, but when I look back his eyes seem cloudy, hollow. I jump, shake the nightmare away.

"Jude?" He laughs. "You can do this." He seems certain, smiling with his screwed-up teeth.

As I hook a finger into the knot of my tie because it feels too tight, a woman crashes into my ribs and apologizes. Not an accident. Her hands are all over me until I smile Walker's special number ten *this-is-the-best-thing-ever-and-it's-even-better-because-I'm-pure-charm-doesn't-it-make-you-squirm?* smile, excusing myself, holding tight to the hidden bruises that are locked beneath my suit. Loosening the tie even further, I stretch my neck, my lower jaw until I can feel the air enter my throat.

Crowding women start asking for spaces on my card. I fumble inside the cotton bag Father Jai gave me, grabbing the small book. The women scrawl their names in letters I'll never understand.

Only the music lifts the ache inside. An explosion of sounds

205

that slices through the crowd, through me. Happy drumming bounces from the furthest corner and shakes the candle flames. My foot taps and I stop it, push my toes into the floor until they feel numb as hundreds of women, and the probably less than a hundred boys that made it through Reserves, applaud with joy. The whole floor erupts into dancing as I scan the swirling mass for the glow of her red hair.

"Sorry," I say, colliding with a strange woman as I search my way through. "Sorry. Excuse me. Sorry, ma'am." I swear she wasn't wearing a mask like the others, more like a white painted line across her eyes. She was gone before I could check. I'm seeing things again, the nightmares from the infirmary still swirling in my system.

A spotlight shines from the centre of the Tower, then descends, drawing a perfect white circle in the dark. The crowd whispers and mutters with prowling excitement as everyone moves off the dance floor, pointing to the Chancellor, who stands, glorious, on the silver-clad stage in front of the falling fountain.

Last time I saw her she murdered the Gardener.

One shot. Done. She didn't even look back.

Clad in a sleek, mirrored gown, the Chancellor waves at her people, smiling like she's pure goodness. She swims down, all grace, all light.

Any second now Walker will come out to join her. He's all right. He has to be. They'll have fixed him up and put him back in service.

The Chancellor's skirt is made of shards that slice the light as she spins. Applause echoes in an explosion from the crowd. And I wonder what suit Walker will be wearing. Will his be mirrored too?

He'll come onstage. Any second now…

I'm holding my breath, waiting for Walker, when a few of the women guide me towards the dance floor. Their hot hands push me in a gentle wave.

"Wait," I try and say. "No, but—"

"Jude?" says the Chancellor, right in front me now, all charm. "May I have this dance?" It's not a request.

What about Walker?

"Jude." Her soft voice is insistent. She holds out her hand, bows to me, grey eyes burning.

No choice. I bow like I'm meant to. The crowd squeals, cheers, *oohs* and *aahs*.

"A pleasure," I say under my breath, like we're taught. Maybe this is when she'll tell me she's let you go, that you're safe. I gave up Ro so now we're square.

When the Chancellor takes my hand, she squeezes it so tight my knuckles ache as she leads me to the open floor. In the shadows, the fog-masked Lice surround the clapping, whistling audience. Is Aspiner among them? The Lice have moved from the doors. Why? To protect the Chancellor or to keep an eye on me?

"No need to be nervous," the Chancellor says, my hand shaking in hers.

Don't let them see you sweat, Walker said. Boys sweat. Men smoulder. Thanks to the infirmary, there's no chance.

"I'm not," I say. "Where's Vik?"

She shark-smiles under her diamond eye-mask. "Confidence, I love it."

My shoulders pull tight like Walker taught me. That's it, perfect poise. Chest out. Jaw set, that's what Walker says. When the music starts again, I follow. Trumpeters toot. Clarinets echo the trumpets. A woman warbles and scats to a brassy chorus. Everyone cheers as the Chancellor whirls me round and round.

My feet move as if they belong to someone else, link step, rock step, chassé, link.

You're meant to be enjoying it, Walker said.

Dancing was my freedom once.

Link step, rock step, chassé, link.

This isn't dancing. Maybe to her, but there's nothing inside me. Just movements. My body wants to stop, but I can't let it.

Link step, rock step, chassé, link.

There's that boy somewhere, the boy who danced, the one they told not to, the one they locked away until he stopped. And he's been such a good boy.

Out of breath, we bow to each other, to the audience. My body is numb and I want to be sick. There's victory in the Chancellor's eyes and I know – right then – she's never going to just let you go.

When I look up, there's Ro. Right at the edge of the crowd. My chest hurts to think she saw me dance with the Chancellor. Saints, I want to disappear.

Ro's half-mask is white, her dress as red as her hair, green eyes staring at me, blank with horror. Doesn't she know that I don't get a choice in what I do, unlike her? The most powerful woman alive asks you to dance and – even if your life doesn't depend on it – you dance. Girls like Romali, they get to say no. They get to blame us for choices we're never allowed to make.

I should be angry at her, but it just hurts.

32

The festivities don't stop. Hours, dancing. Hours, stepping on toes. Apologizing, over and over. The women sigh as if it doesn't matter. Dancing doesn't feel like it should. I should be sweating but whatever the doctors pumped me with has stopped that. Should be free to move but everything hurts. Should be able to shake my head loose but there's this shouting inside – how dare she be angry? Doesn't she understand? What, does she think I'd ever want to be with the Chancellor? All I wanted to do was help my friend! I keep looking for Ro but I'm not sure why. To explain? To warn her? To say goodbye…

The music changes but it always sounds the same.

It always sounds the same.

Masked women and girls scratch their name from my card when their turn comes. They swoop me up in their arms, spin me, step in, step out. Again. And again.

Gasping for breath, trying to avoid the queue of women searching for me, I hide behind a pillar. The cold stone helps my aching bones relax when I press my spine against it.

Someone's watching. I can feel it. Maybe it's Ro.

The next girl on my card appears. We dance, we skip and spin, in the same damn place.

The same damn place.

After every turn round the dance floor, my overused muscles judder. I rub at my arms to stop them shaking, or maybe it's that feeling that someone in the crowd is watching me that's making me shiver. I search through the hundreds of eyes on me. But, instead of Ro, I find the fixed dark gaze of Madam Vor. Of the whole room, she's the only woman in black.

A gaggle of women are talking across her, but she's not listening. She's watching me from behind her black half-mask. She nods her head when I see her. Cold.

She told me to say goodbye to my friends.

The music grows so loud it makes my teeth ache. My brothers speed past with their partners, but the whoosh of fabric, the scrabble of feet and laughter might as well be silence. Again, I'm certain one of the women isn't wearing a mask, her face painted instead. That one had no hair.

Turning away from Vor's cold stare, I shove through the crowd.

"'Scuse me," I say, squeezing through. "'Scuse me."

If I'd have done what Walker wanted, then I'd have been dead before Swims and so would the Chancellor. Idiot! Idiot! The Roids would be here, dancing with their potential guardians, not pinheaded somewhere Above. It's all my fault. Like it's my fault that you've gone, Vik. Maybe you wouldn't have run if—

I was angry because you'd not spoken to me all year. We were friends before, but I didn't know you any more.

Something red flashes. There it is again.

Ro? She's heading in the direction of the Chancellor. I push past the girl. It's not just me that's seen her. Lice, dozens of them, have started to shoulder through the crowd. Away from the sides of the hall, away from the doors.

Calm down, you say.

Picking up speed, I make my way towards Ro, through slick fabric, sticky flesh; through the smack of hairspray, hooch and perfume. Fighting to find her face, until her strong shoulders and the twists of her hair are in reach.

My hand, hot, rests on her skin as candlelight flickers with whispers. We're not meant to touch them.

Not how a boy should behave, they whisper.

Not dignified.

I don't care. Angry or not, whatever her reasons, she's still my friend. When Ro turns, I've forgotten what I was going to say.

The whole room is silent now.

I'm not going to say goodbye to her today, not to the boys, not to you.

It's hard to tell where on her body she might be hiding a weapon to attack the Chancellor. She must have one, right? Behind Ro's silk mask her wide green eyes are locked on mine.

"Why don't you go and dance with the Chancellor," she says with sarcasm. Her voice drops to a whisper. "What are you doing? You're going to ruin everything!"

One thing I learned from Walker: if you need a distraction, put on a show. If I get Ro to the dance floor, the Lice won't want to make a scene, right? Maybe they won't arrest her yet. I can warn her and she can get away.

"May I have this dance?" I try not to stutter.

Boys do NOT ask girls to dance.

The crowd prickles and mutters as I take her hand.

"You can't do this," she says, shaking her head.

I let go after we're separated from the crowd, on the dance floor. The Lice don't follow us here. I was right: they won't disrupt the show.

Everything's too bright. I can't think. The idea hits and I pull the handkerchief from my pocket, twisting it. I close my eyes and tie the cloth round them. Tight until the bridge of my nose throbs. In the dark, everything seems easier.

"Jude, you can't fogging see!" Ro whispers closer.

"Trust me, please." I hold out my hand.

The air is heavy, but nothing moves.

Finally she relaxes. "Fine," she says, and we begin.

In the darkness, I can pretend. Pretend she's the girl from my appointments and we're alone.

Beyond the dark weave of the blindfold there's still colour. The red from her dress. The turn of her face to check on the gathering crowd. A movement of light. It's distracting so I close my eyes tighter.

When the muttering voices of the women swell, the sound of their gossip is music. I can do this: their voices give me the walls of the dance floor.

Pressing my right palm against Ro's shoulder blade, her skin is so real. She must know how many rules I'm breaking

213

but she doesn't flinch. I struggle at first to find her other hand. My fingers walk along the length of her arm, over soft hairs, scuffing the roughness of her elbow. She helps me, twisting her fingers into mine. Her hands are smaller than I remember.

"Ready?" I ask.

"OK." Her voice is higher than normal, her breath caught in her chest.

The band doesn't play a note. But I can hear music. Walker used to clap out the rhythm for me.

One step in.

Dum-da-da.

One breath out.

Dum-da-da, gliding, waltzing.

Dum-da-da, dum-da-da, dum-da-da, dum-da-da.

My steps sure, hers slow, hold on tightly, don't let go.

Dum-da-da, dum-da-da.

The band joins in, longing violins sweep. Cellos skip. Snare drums pat. There are shuffles and skips and we mess up. She laughs, catching herself when she does. Her bones and muscles curl under my hand. She's so alive. Sticky skin, pumping blood. The mutter of anger as she fumbles with a step. The hesitation before we spin. She's the girl who saved my life, really saved it.

"You can't kill her yet," I whisper as we dance.

"Yes, I can," Ro says.

Dum-da-da, dum-da-da.

I picture the world beyond the infirmary window. The dusty green fog piling in against High House. As we spin, the doors open on to that world. It's so easy to imagine there's nothing left but us. Is this what they were afraid I'd feel when I was a kid in the Surrogacy?

"She said Vik's alive," I remind her. "Now she has Walker too."

Dum-da-da, dum-da-da.

"When we stop, you need to run. They're coming for you."

The music sounds like the Gardener's pleading, the knuckles of the Roids in the dorm, but none of it seems to hurt any more. Everything before now is beneath our feet, so small. The drums are the gunshot. The snare, cold water crashing into my aching face. The violins are the sound of air bursting in my chest as I struggle for breath. The clarinets are Stink crying in the dorm; they are you shouting my name.

When we stop, everything is quiet again.

The crowd has stopped talking. The band has stopped playing. Ro's body is pressed against mine, her cheek resting against my ear.

I pull my body from hers, tear the blindfold down and blink until the light brings her face to me. Her smile, her *trust-me* smile. The gleam in her eyes. As she comes into focus, so too does the ring of Lice around us. She leans in, then past me. There's a little voice, right deep down that says she's going to kiss me, but she doesn't. Her mouth is right by my ear, a whisper.

"I don't need to run," Ro says as she pulls away. "It's OK."

I'm not fast enough. Strange fists grab at me, pull me backwards. Another fist of fingers yanks my head by my newly cropped hair.

Five huge Lice pull Ro away. She tries to break free, but they won't let go.

"Wait!" I shout, try to twist my arms free, my head too. And I can tell, even though I can't see her face, that among the officers holding me tight is Aspiner. It's not just that smell, it's her hands. Always in places they shouldn't be.

"You can't!" I cry.

A stick crashes into my stomach and I buckle over, spluttering on to the stone. I remember how they shot you with electricity, remember how they dragged you away. Right here, on this floor.

"Wait!" I try to choke out. I want to scream that I was the one who broke the rules. I was the one who wanted to dance.

"STOP!" the Chancellor orders.

As she gets closer, it seems the whole world is retreating into the murals. The Foundations' eyes look away.

My reflection in the folds of her mirrored dress is a collection of colours, splitting into more pieces as she gets closer. The red of Ro, the shock of her hair that disappears into a cloud of black Lice.

"Get off!" Ro shouts as Madam Vor approaches her.

The Chancellor nods at Vor.

Vor waves her hand so that more of her officers scuttle on to the dance floor, locking arms, sealing the crowd away from us. My brothers are fighting to get through to see.

As Vor reaches her daughter, she sighs, loud enough to make the balconies creak.

"Romali Dunn Vor, you are under arrest for crimes against survival and for the murder of Madam Lorraine Dunn, Chief of Life."

33

The crowd surges forwards. Noise and hot faces and drunken shouting. They didn't know the Gardener was dead. Not missing. Not Outside. Murdered.

"No. No, you can't!" I shout but no one listens. It's a struggle to keep sight of Ro in the mass ahead as she wrestles with the Lice. "It wasn't her!"

"Jude, be quiet!" the Chancellor spits. Her grey eyes burn almost white.

I'll never do what she says again. "You can't."

"This is MY House!" the Chancellor snaps. "I can do ANYTHING I want."

The officers take hold of me again. But my arms tear free and my legs are full of fuel as I leap forwards, scramble across the stone, anger swirling in my stomach. I have to stop this.

There are shouts in the crowd, screams. Boys shouting too. A gunshot into the ceiling that shatters glass. It rains down and guests scatter, a whirlwind of colour. Another shot from behind us. Another from the side.

There are women in the crowd with ugly-looking guns, knives, their eyes smeared with raw bands of white paint.

Their cries are wild. I can't count how many there are. They grab for my brothers. All but the Lice holding back the crowd start to scramble, some to protect the Chancellor, some to try to stop the wild women. Hysterics? There are Hysterics at the ball!

Vor barks orders, forgetting her daughter, making sure the Chancellor is safe. "Get them out!" she yells. "Now! Before—"

The Tower is plunged into darkness, the blackout burns red and the Hysterics warble into the void.

"Now!" Vor yells.

Aspiner is swearing as she and her Lice push me through a door. As we reach the front stairs, every candle blows out as the doors to the Outside fly open. Another dozen wild Hysterics in brightly painted fog masks burst inside. I hold my breath, expecting swells of fog, but nothing comes – there's a smell, though, like rancid rat guts. Behind us the screams of the women and boys are so loud they shake the mirrors in the ceiling, the glass high above, the sky and the stars beyond.

In the red light of the stairwell, raging against the dark cloud of Lice, my body hits the metal banisters, then the rough concrete walls. I kick out. Aspiner's gun spins out ahead of her as she falls forwards and lands with an awkward thud on the steps. Some of the officers laugh as she groans.

"Hold him, dammit!" her sharp voice shouts as she limps up the steps. "Bloody Hysterics attack and I have to babysit!"

There are a dozen officers. A surge of bodies slams me against a wall so hard I bite my tongue, swallow down a mouthful of sticky blood.

"The fun we could be having," she sighs. I push against the weight of her officers but they pin my arms, hold my legs when I try to kick out again. "Protective manoeuvres, girls. We have dangerous resistance here," she orders. Laughing, her friends begin to twist off my dancing slippers, pulling at my socks.

The concrete, cold under my toes, grazes my heels in the scramble.

"Hold still, will you?" says Aspiner, dusting herself down. She pulls off her fog mask, shakes out her blond hair, blinks her deep brown eyes and steps up so close that I can taste her breath. She's all muscle and by the Chancellor's standards they'd probably call her beautiful.

She still looks like a monster to me.

"You remember me?" she asks.

I don't even want to say her name.

"I heard you tried to turn the Chancellor against me," she says. "What did I ever do to you?"

There's an ache of shame in me. Your voice telling me not to be upset that she grabbed me before, to deal with it, get over it.

Why should I be ashamed? I should be angry.

"There are a dozen boys that'd be grateful to dance with me," she snarls. "You think you're above it, because of the Chancellor?"

"You never asked," I say through my teeth.

Aspiner lifts up her gloved hands, runs her fingers down the lapels of my jacket, then undoes my top button. "Maybe you should do the asking?"

"Don't," I tell her, the anger boiling over, salted with fear.

It's hard to forget how little she cares about consent.

"Sorry?" she says like she can't hear me.

I wriggle as she twists the next button. "Don't," I say. And the next. "Stop." It pops open, exposing my shirt beneath.

"Pardon? I thought boys were meant to be polite?"

"Please," I say.

"Now you're getting it. Say please again," Aspiner laughs with a snort.

She turns to her group to bark another order.

There's a wad of blood in my mouth. It tastes like a hot dollar of chewed meat. I spit it out, sending the mess right into her ear. After wiping it away, Aspiner brings her knee up into my groin.

Explosions go off all over. I fold in two. Bite down.

The others are laughing again as if I'm on the auction stage, telling a joke. Breathe through it. Locking my jaw tight, I push the agony so hard into my teeth they should splinter into dust.

Did I tell you the one about the boy that said no?

"So sensitive, these boys," Aspiner mumbles. "All the soft bits on the outside. It'll be so much easier after the auction, when the vote's passed. So much better. No more worries in those heads."

I want to ask 'what vote?' but the pain rolls up through my chest, twisting as it travels down.

She leans in close. "She told me I could have you after. I'll take care of you, promise."

My protests slur as I heave breath into my lungs. My calls for Walker, for anyone, echo up the stairwell.

"No one's listening," Aspiner says. My suit jacket undone, she starts unbuttoning my shirt. "Walker's gone."

Four of her officers pin my arms against the wall. Can't fight them off. Can't stop her from doing anything.

You remember that skinny boy? The one who asked all those questions before they made him stop? He's still there somewhere under this armour Walker fashioned for him. A boy who still hopes the House of Boys will keep the nightmares under the bed away. Who wants to believe that women are kind and beautiful, full of love.

That boy wants to cry. But they want him to keep quiet. He can be quiet.

She pulls her hand through his hair. Good boy, her gesture says, good boy.

I can count every ache inside me. One day I'll tell someone. One day they'll believe me. Then what?

My breath fills me up, burning in my chest. With my stomach exposed to her, I think how loose my belt is, how I'm too thin for the world.

"This is for the hot tea you poured on me," Aspiner says as she moves her hands to my belt.

I won't close my eyes. I'm not afraid of her.

Aspiner wields her baton in front of me. I try to knot my tired body together. Close it down, become the plaster of the wall. Twist up my tongue, before she jabs me in the stomach with the end of her baton. I think she's smiling.

A switch flips. Click.

Electricity drills into my stomach, up into my ribs, down

through my fingers, into my aching groin. There's the smell of fabric and hair burning, and the stab of the pins in my skin as I shake against them. Jolt and bolt my neck. Lights stripe past my eyes. Then – hands touching my skin that I can't shake off. The Lice flop my body around on the cold floor. Laughing.

Can't even open my eyes. Am I still in the stairwell? I should scream and shout but the sounds bounce around inside my shell.

There's no boy under the armour any more.

A croaky officer – I remember her voice from the appointment – nudges my foot with hers. "He's not going to fight." Silence. "She won't know. The Chancellor. She won't. Not with the Hysterics back there. Besides, who'd believe him?"

"Olive, please," one of them begs her friend. "He's not worth it!"

Is that what I am now? Worthless.

"It's OK. I can wait," Aspiner says.

34

LESSONS IN POWER

"It's really simple," Kier said. "The more merits, the more their vote's worth."

Worth. I knew that word.

I'd been in the dorms for a month and, by my count, had just turned thirteen. Kier, the oldest boy from K-dorm, had offered to talk the new boys through some of the more interesting parts of his dorm's Collection in exchange for news of which women were popular in the various prenticeships we had come from.

We sat on the tables in the dining room in the green half-light of the emergency-exit signs. You were there, so I was there.

"And a vote means?" you asked, twisting the ring Walker had given you round your thumb.

That ring had got you in, and me. When the prentice came from the House of Merit, they approached you straight away. "Scholarship," they said. "Mr Walker's choice." Never seen you so puffed up but I knew it was because of the ring. When they asked if there was anyone with the buy-in that passed the audition, I stepped up. Thought you'd be happy but you were too excited to notice.

Kier sighed. "Saints, I swear each intake gets more stupid. It's the hormones in the food. Don't eat the sweet stuff, I swear. Every so often, the Council – that's the madams who head the houses – bring the people in the Tower together for a vote. To make decisions … like, I don't know, where to split the workforce between Maintenance and Entertainment, what to do with a glut of potatoes, or population control. Like how many boys get born each year – they voted on that one a couple of months back but the Gardener stopped it getting lowered again. Whatever gets the most votes wins."

Everyone talking, except you until…

"And the more merits they have, like the Chancellor, or the madams—" you say.

"You guessed it: the more merits, the more powerful their vote."

"And they get merits by being good, right?"

Kier shrugged. "Yeah, I guess that's the big one. Compliment a top-floor madam and a few extra merits might fly in their direction, but there are always other ways. Cronyism, blackmail, oh and then there's inheritance. That's a big one – that's why most of the madams are from the old Foundation families. There are massive limits on how many merits each house member has to give to the Council every year and how many they have to give away to others for services rendered."

Meritocracy, Cook told us, means that the best people in the Tower are in charge. The kindest. The smartest. The most selfless.

"Toppers can't get demerited so much now; that went to a

vote years ago. Here's the trick, lads: get one of the top madams in your auction and maybe you can sway a vote."

"How?" You again.

Kier grabbed his crotch and everyone laughed except you.

"But we don't get a vote," you said. Everyone was still laughing.

"Can't vote if you're in debt, mate," Kier said. "But seriously the love of a good man in a woman's ear can work wonders. Who knows, maybe one day we can change the world?"

35

Smoke, sharp. A noise. It sounds like you in the stairwell; you calling my name. You saying it'll be all right. Except it isn't you and it won't be all right. It's a crowd of wild creatures, painted faces swarming, smoking out the Lice around me. Arms pull me up. Strong arms.

"No!" I fight them off.

I don't want to be helpless. Not now, not ever. Never again. I don't want to be saved by them, any of them. I can do this.

Rolling on to my front, my body smacks against the floor. I suck in my aching stomach and pull myself up, dragging my skin along the concrete, hand over hand over hand, until I'm on my feet.

Hello? says my brain but my mouth doesn't move. It can't.

"You really want to be stubborn *now*?" says Ro, catching me as I fall. Blackout lights burning red behind her, making her hair seem white.

But she was arrested. I'm imagining that she's here, right? I'm imagining she's here, and I'm shaking and half naked! Hardly dignity. Hardly grace.

"I can't get you out on my own – you need to run. The others will hold back the Lice."

"Others?"

Ro blinks at me. Her face full and clear now through the red light, through the smoke. "Come on!" she calls, knotting the strips of her torn skirt, kicking off her shoes. "We can't stay here." There's a dull *whop-whop* on the hard floor as something lands near my head. "You'll need these."

Shoes.

They smell of leather, worn and tanned.

Don't stare. It's nothing. Just shoes. No big deal.

Shoes mean I can run if I want.

"Just shove them on – come on!"

Move.

Hopping into the thick leather shoes, I push forwards, everything still blurring. My hands are my eyes, searching their way down the stairs, step by step, coughing in the fug from what I guess must be smoke bombs the Hysterics threw. My spit as thick as tar, the air sharp. But...

I'm still alive!

The door swings open with a bang and I'm moving so fast my legs struggle to work, but I don't stop. The fight behind is getting quieter, the sound of Ro's breath clearer.

"We have to get Walker," I gasp.

"No time."

"What about Vik?"

"Look, you need to forget about him," says Ro. "We have to get you out."

"Forget about Vik?" I say, the anger rising in me. "He's my friend! I can't—"

The Lice cry from behind. Boots slam. The metal of their weapons rattles in their hands.

"I won't let her hurt you," says Ro. "Trust me."

"But—"

"Choose. You can stay here, you can find your friend, but only if you want to get yourself killed or worse…"

How do I show her I don't want her to rescue me, don't need her protection? But Aspiner's burn aches in my belly, reminding me that maybe I do need help right now. Maybe we both do. I can't save you if I'm dead. I've not forgotten you – I never will – but for now I have to run.

Through the front doors of High House into the cold darkness, soft sand beneath my feet, the stars blurred above.

My name is Jude Grant and I am Outside.

THE HOUSE OF SACRIFICE

~~I am my mistakes~~

~~I am pardoned by sacrifice~~

We are all your lies.

36

LESSONS IN GRACE

A few weeks before Reserves I'd turned fourteen. It was my first year eligible for the docket. I wasn't planning on putting myself up for it, but then you did.

Most of J-dorm had flunked out of Reserves. I'd fluffed my intro onstage and got no bids. The morning after, my brothers and I were in the dining room, at our regular table, hunched over trays, slurping protein shakes and doing the calculations. There was an ache in my empty stomach because you'd got a reserve. What if you were bought at auction before me?

Everyone was complaining about how much the buy-in had gone up again this year, about wasted 'promises' from their appointments – women who'd hinted they'd reserve but then never showed up on the night. Some boys, the older kids in J-dorm, had promises of buyers from their appointments today. But then there was that risk, always, that someone might outbid them, someone they didn't want. We're meant to be graceful whatever happens, to act like gentlemen.

On the next table E-dorm had started up the betting circles

for the auction itself, keeping the books on the odds between the dorms. M-dorm were monitoring the rumours and the rankings, of course, mainly the new debs (top-floor girls just turned fourteen too, the daughters of the chiefs). Top three rumoured new debs were:

1. Elean Valk – Madam Valk's daughter. House of Amalgam.
2. Reginda Neugent – top floor, House of Invention, but rumours her family out of favour with the Chancellor.
3. Romali Vor – Madam Vor's daughter. Not chosen a house yet. Rumours of vast wealth but also known for fighting and general avoidability.

Odds were low for any boys to get their bids. Debs normally waited a few years to bid on their own ward but they'd sometimes put in a reserve to practise with a boy first.

"I heard Miss Vor has actual horns," says Rod.

"And scales," Stink adds with full confidence.

"All the way down?"

"Don't be gross!"

"Does it matter? She won't bid," I say. "None of them will."

My brothers rolled their eyes. But I wasn't joking – most debs would wait until they got a good footing in their house before spending any merits on a boy they'd need to keep. We're an expense, after all.

Everyone would have preferred it if girls our own age would bid but normally it's the older middle-floor women. Not likely to end up running one of the big houses without some help, they make lower bids, live less lavishly, and a good ward can look after their apartment while they're out earning merits.

When you arrived in the dining hall, you held yourself differently. Mr Scholarship, Slick Vik. Taller. Chest puffed out. You'd been working out and there were those boys: Vinnie from your dorm and the other beefers. I didn't know their names, didn't want to know them.

"She wasn't the right one," I heard you telling your new friends as you passed. "I don't need a bid from some desperate old woman on the twentieth floor."

The relief swung through me! We'd both flunked out of Reserves.

Anyone would think you ignored me as you went by but I knew you'd waited until you were within my earshot to say you'd lost your reserve. I'm not stupid. There's no way you could have told me straight out.

Father Van had rules about his boys mixing with lower dorms, rules about V-boys showing weakness. He believed the women up top didn't want some delicate man for a ward. *They want to be a bit afraid of you*, he claimed, wanted animals to tame. *That's the trick*, he'd tell his boys: *be the beast to their beauty*. V-dorm boys weren't allowed to cry, weren't allowed to be kind, or weak, or humble. Then again, most V-dormers never made it past Reserves. Most of them were demerited for dishonourable behaviour, packed off to the mines, or worse. Not you, you said. You'd be Van's best boy.

I worried about you sometimes. But then I reminded myself you were strong in a different way. However many muscles you piled on, whoever your friends were, I knew you better. Behind their shield, you were still the boy that gave me his food that day, the boy that saved me from the dogs. You were doing what you had to, playing a part to survive. I could do that too.

37

Ro clambers to the top of a dune, her dress gathered in her arms. Wiping sweat from her forehead, she pulls off her half-mask, drops it and catches her breath.

The mask sinks into the mountain of sand beneath our feet. As I scramble to catch up, cold grains slide between my fingers like water. Fine as sugar. A film of it sticks, rough on my palm.

The moon is round, bright enough to cast shadows as we climb; cold air bites at the top. I crane my neck in every direction to see the sweeping city. The Collections say there were paths once, roads that took the Saints to the Wetlands-that-were. There were water fountains, statues – people came from all parts of the earth to wonder at how the Foundations built such a place so deep in the desert.

My calves shake with exhaustion. Walking in sand is hard – it keeps shifting and my legs are used to flat, hard floors. With every step, I can't believe I'm not sinking. "Where are you going?"

Ro points. "The old city. It's a long walk." She wants us to keep moving, get fog cover until it gets light. "We'll need to building-hop, stay inside as much as possible." She's tearing strips from her skirt with her teeth. "When the fog comes in, you feel it prickle… It floods in fast, five maybe ten minutes before you can't breathe. Cover your mouth, your nose; close your eyes if you can too. It'll buy you some time to get somewhere airtight. OK?"

The wind whips at the strips of Ro's dress held out to me. I press them to my nose to dull the stink the Outside air brings with it. We climb the sands fast, towards huge metal boxes emerging from the dunes. They're a lot higher and closer together than I imagined they'd be. Some have toppled against each other like the dominoes the cooks used to play with.

Ro's palm catches me, stopping me from falling as the sand splits underneath me. Her hot hand on my chest snaps back when she finds skin. "Sorry!" She creases her face with a flash of embarrassment. "Didn't mean to – you should…" She points at my shirt. No one's ever apologized for touching me before.

My shaking fingers fumble to fasten up the buttons. "I'm not sure we can hide from the Lice in the city for ever – they'll come looking."

"Yeah, but we're not going to stay in the city. We're going to find my mum. She's out there – at the House of Exploration outpost is my bet."

We?

"You really think she's alive?"

"Just need to find a buggy that works. There's a bunch the Hysterics have stashed, then I … we can go."

There's that 'we' again. "What about High House, the others?"

"We have to look after ourselves now," she says as she stomps

236

down the other side of the dune. The sand slides as I follow. When I get to the bottom, she's talking to herself, tearing away more layers of her dress to wrap round her own face should the fog come. "Couldn't let me have it, could she?" Who does she mean? The Chancellor? "Had to send in the troops," she mutters as I reach her side. She catches me looking at the knife I can now see strapped to her thigh. "I could've killed the Chancellor, you know?"

"Ro, about back there, with the Lice…"

She doesn't know where to look. "Olive's just trying to prove something. She's been after Vor's job since she joined as a junior a few years before me. You OK?"

Am I OK? It's bubbling, that jaw-snapping anger. Does Ro really think Aspiner was only trying to prove something to the other women, humiliating me like that, stripping me apart? "I'm fine," I lie.

"Shit!" Ro rubs at her arms. There's a bag on her shoulder, which I guess she was given by one of the Hysterics. She rummages through it and pulls out a torch, goggles. "We need to get inside. Now!"

So that's it. What her mother's Lice did to me is forgotten? One 'you OK?' and that's enough? How could I have told her I'm not OK, that I've never been OK? That I'll always have that in my head – what they did, what they touched, how they made me feel.

"Don't you feel it?" she asks. "That tingle."

Does she mean the Lice or the fog? Does it matter? Both will kill us. I take a deep breath, let the dead smell of the air in, squeeze that anger down and wrap it in the fear of the strangling fog swamping us, the Lice giving chase.

"This street. I know a place." Ro moves fast.

"Did you plan that? The raid?" I try to keep up.

"I bet the whole Tower is talking about it," Ro calls back, almost entertained by the whole thing.

"What if they hurt someone?" I say, thinking of my brothers. The smell is stronger now, curling through the shreds of Ro's dress.

"They promised not to hurt anyone – just give them a scare, cover so I could finish off the Chancellor, then get out. Well, I didn't get to kill her but –" she howls at the sky – "I can't believe I'm finally out!"

Maybe I should be happy too, right? Excited. I'm Outside!

"No more, 'It's not safe, Romali; not until you're older, Romali; we have to make it work here; it's what your mother wanted, Romali.'" She makes a noise with her tongue and gestures at the Tower behind.

And yes, despite the clawing air, it feels amazing, like the hundreds of hands squeezing my bones, my limbs, my throat, have all let go. My skin feels new, my tongue tastes dangerous air, even the dark looks different. So real when it's been a dream for so long. But then there's an ache, a naked feeling about this world without walls. An urge to head back inside the Tower and shut the door for as long as it takes for the world to feel small again.

Keep moving. One foot. Then the other.

No one's following yet. No torchlight blistering the drowning, star-freckled dark. Still, no matter how far I crane my neck, High House is still in view. If I can see it, we're not far enough away. Did you make it this far when you ran? The Lice didn't wait for the light to hunt you down.

"Jude, don't worry," Ro says. "We've got a head start! It's the fog. We have to—" She starts to cough before grabbing my hand, pulling me into a run. We wind through narrow passages, between buildings a few storeys high. The sand climbs up over old windows and I wonder how deep the floors inside go. Are there basement levels like ours that scrape the earth? We pass a stone arm reaching up, out of the sand, as if it needs saving.

In the moon shadow cast by the buildings, the air seems to prickle and hum. So that's the fog? Pulling at the hairs on my arms?

"Yes!" Ro claps as she reaches a large building, smacking a rusting metal door with a symbol painted on the wall.

"It's safe?" I ask as she tries to wrench it open.

She nods towards the symbol. "That painting, those brackets. Fog-proofed." Taking a deep breath, Ro shoves open the door. Heavy metal scratches at the floor beyond and there's the smell of animals and sour air.

"How do you know?"

"Mum used to teach me all the tricks she'd picked up from the House of Exploration. We can shelter here while the fog comes in. Look." She shines the torch closer to my arm and rolls up my jacket sleeve. "The electricity in the air makes the hairs on your arm stand up."

All I can hear is the blood pounding in my ears.

With the door sealed behind us, Ro shines her torch down the corridor. An uncomfortable quiet settles. Breathing is easier but the stink hasn't gone; it's seeped into the bricks.

"Look." Ro takes a slow breath. "I know you probably don't want to talk about it but you should know that Olive's been telling people you and her did … stuff, in your appointments."

She's bringing it up again now?

My stomach churns. "No, I, we…"

"I just wanted to say, if she comes after us, I'm going to fogging kill her," Ro says, leading me further into the building. "For targeting you." Maybe she's afraid to use the word assault. "You know you can tell me anything, Jude."

"Yeah," I lie again.

I move past her, pulling my suit jacket round me to keep warm, feeling my way along the old walls. "Be careful!" Ro says. "These places are dangerous."

"I'm not afraid of the dark," I call back.

Ro still won't let the subject drop. "I tried to tell people not to believe what she was saying. That you're not that kind of boy."

"You're right. I don't want to talk about it."

"But it happens in appointments all the time. That's what the girls say."

"Ro, you wouldn't—" I want to say 'understand' but she interrupts.

"So … she never touched you?"

"That's not what I said."

It's not the answer she wanted.

She looks away, disappointed, I guess. "Look, I get it, OK? It's none of my business. It's just…" She sighs. "Saints, I went on enough in our appointments about my problems. I could help with yours too."

How do I tell her?

I want to explain but can't find the words. Whether she believes any stories I tell her isn't the point; the truth is, if I told her, she'd never get it.

"It's OK. Forget I brought it up," says Ro with sudden bite before climbing up a stone staircase to the next floor, disappearing into the unfamiliar dark.

I follow the torch glow to find her waiting in a room with faded walls. Once I'm inside, Ro shuts another heavy metal door rigged with a light above flickering a dull green. She locks it firmly, doesn't look at me. When the light turns red, she explains, it means there's fog outside and I'm not to try to open the door.

"I'm not an idiot," I say, which she ignores. She pushes a handful of candles from the bag towards me and clears a corner of the room to sleep.

There's an upturned couch, dusty, picked half hollow. I can have it, she says, trying to be ladylike I guess, but I prefer the floor.

After spending my whole life sleeping in rooms with more boys than I can count, the idea of being too far from another person – even a girl – makes my insides curl. I lie down not too far from her. Close enough to hear her breathe. If I reached out, I could touch her hand but I won't, even if I want to.

She's really quiet when she sleeps, so different from my brothers snoring in the dark.

I bet that in the dorms no one's asleep yet. Half the boys are probably shouting at Stink for going on about the ball. I'll be one of his stories and he'll be telling the new boys that the story is true. They'll stare open-mouthed at the madness, the stupidity, the horror, until Father Jai cuts them off, because for all his blubber and bookkeeping he makes sure everyone is in bed by lights out.

In the morning, they'll go for breakfast and fight over the milk, while Father Mack from M-dorm takes the register and someone tells Stink the story of the boy that cried in the night so loudly he woke up half of T-dorm. They'll carry on like every year. Except this time I'm the one who didn't come home. And all my brothers have blind, clouded eyes. They don't see the Gardener, blood-drenched, dragging me down, down into a burning, airless hole in the stomach of the world.

When I wake up, I'm shaking. Wishing the nightmare away. It takes a second to pinch myself, test the room, remember I'm Outside.

I'm not the only one awake. Even in the dark, I can tell Ro's watching me. She's holding her breath.

"My appointments," I ask the darkness. "Why did you come?"

There's silence for a while. I roll on to my back, stare at the dark ceiling.

"Aunt Lorri," Ro says. "She was friends with Walker. Last year, after Reserves, he was upset, told her everything. And Aunt Lorri told me."

She sniffs, her breath shaking in the dark. I think she's crying.

"Next day she asked if I could check on you. Said that Walker was worried about you because you'd lost your friend."

"You came to see me because of Vik?"

"Kind of, yeah." She holds her breath for a second. "Never knew Walker was grooming you, not then."

"You kept coming, though?"

"I liked you," she sighs. No shaking in her voice, no tears now. "Like you."

There's movement in the dark. The tips of her fingers reach out; they curl against mine.

"I'm sorry," she says.

"What for?"

For Vik? Walker? The assault, the grabbing hands? For growing up without the sky, or dancing, or a family? For the auction? For Madam Vor? The infirmary, the needles, the vanished Roids? For the Chancellor?

"For everything."

In the dull glow from the light above the door, I can almost see the curve of her shoulder, the end of her nose.

"So we're still friends, right?" I ask.

Her hand pulls away. "Yeah," she says. "Friends."

38

Morning heat hits like someone's opened a huge oven door. Daylight sears through the glued-up window; it casts shadows into the dark corridor ahead. Before we move on, Ro checks to make sure there aren't any Lice.

We hardly talk as we move from building to building, always staying inside, following painted 'safe' symbols through the fiery morning heat that fills each dark and ancient corridor we find. I ask her to tell me stories from the House of Exploration to fill the silence. They were always her favourite. The art of listening, say the House Fathers, is encouraging others to talk.

With each story, it's like she's trying to convince me life is better out in the desert. The last expedition is her preferred subject, recounting the 'ten-year trek' beyond the desert edge, to what the Saints called a sea. The history books she's read say they found nothing except dust and the Saints' leftovers: fog, rot and chaos. "But, but!" Ro's eyes gleam. "Mum would swear there was more to it. When she left, she said she'd not come home until she'd proved there were survivors."

Ro's voice gets higher, faster when she talks about her mum, like she's talking over all the silence in the desert. I keep asking her to slow down.

"There are green lands out there, like the garden."

Women know best, right? She thinks it's my fault she didn't get to kill the Chancellor. I know it deep down, but I don't care. If I hadn't asked her to dance, if I'd just let her plan play out, then what? She'd be dead, that's what. And me too probably.

We move up high, passing through one of the old covered bridges leading to another building. I've never felt such heat. She points through the glass dulled by wind and dust.

"I swear! We can't be the last, the only," she laughs. All I can see on the other side of the glass is the thick fog knocking to get in. I can even smell it up here. Feel it scratching inside. Not sure we're as safe as she says we are. Does it drive you mad like the stories say it does?

"Otherwise Mum would have come home," Ro insists.

There was a hope that you survived, a hope the Chancellor gave me. It was a hope I was afraid to say out loud. We're not that different, Ro and I.

"Come on, it's too hot up here. There are old underpasses below." Ro throws me a flask of water from the bag before loosening the zip on her dress to let her skin cool. There's a waterfall of freckles all down her back, as full as the night sky.

We climb down through the next building, through rooms that hold nothing but heat and echoes. Sometimes there's an apartment that looks as if the Saints have just gone out for the day. Shadows make the ancient paint flake and curl. I bet there are ghost stories out here that would keep my brothers entertained for years.

A pinprick of pain spasms up through my heel; the soft soles of my feet aren't used to leather shoes or walking so far. I drink in lungfuls of air, right into the bottom of me. Each gulp gritty and sweet on my tongue as we get closer to the unlit corridors stretching below the desert, gaping like the throats of a waiting nest of snakes.

"Can we stop?" I ask.

"If we keep going, we can make it to the old hospital by tomorrow," Ro explains. "We can get a buggy, maybe supplies for the trek."

That was the dream once. You and me. We would scale mountains and fight monsters. The adventures we'd have. Gone now. Not dead. Gone. Is it the same dream if it's just me and Ro?

In the underpass, the Saints' lights turn on with our movement, dark ahead of us, darkness behind. I look back. The knots in my stomach reach up to my lungs, tightening each breath. The further we walk, the worse it feels to leave you behind.

We climb over rubbish abandoned in the tunnels. There are old pictures along the walls, almost completely in shreds, but in some you can see what's left of the Saints – faded *buy-this* smiles. All teeth.

My tongue squeaks over my newly bleached teeth. Maybe if I tell Ro what happened in the infirmary, about what I saw, or think I saw the doctors do to Aye-Aye, she'd want to help. Go back – get the others. Then maybe we could all go and find her mum together?

"I know about the Chancellor's vote, you know. I worked it out."

Ro stops.

"Walker was going to tell me but he didn't get the chance."

"Jude—"

"What? She's going to pinhead every single man and boy in the Tower, isn't she?"

She doesn't answer.

"I'm waiting for you to tell me I'm crazy."

"You're not. Walker should have told you. Maybe he didn't want to scare you. She's been spreading stories about some men helping the Hysterics. Then there are fears of uprisings, alliances, fights, wards attacking their guardians."

"Stories? Lies, you mean."

"It's not all lies. But ... that doesn't mean it's right, what she's doing. She has the whole Tower too afraid to think for themselves. But, if they trust her, she'll make it all better."

Stale air sucks past as Ro takes a breath. In the glow of the old humming lights above, I can't help but think she's looking at me with pity.

I need her anger. "You're making excuses for her?"

"No, but you have to understand how clever she is. She's engineering conflict to stay in power, to keep them too afraid to leave, to make them feel safe, in control, as long as no one leaves. The fog isn't as bad as it was – there are longer breaks, more regular."

There hasn't been a break in the swamp Outside since last night. How often does it 'break'? Every month? Week? Day?

"And people in the Tower can see that," Ro goes on. "The Tower's at capacity. Everyone's hungry, stressed. The building is creaking at the seams. They blame the Hysterics because that's who they're told to blame, but what they don't realize is it's mostly the Chancellor diverting funds from places they need to be." Ro shrugs, scratches at her head. "It's all about control with her. Manipulation and politics only go so far."

"So, what? We stop it."

"We can't go back," she says and moves ahead.

I chase after. "The Roids were in the infirmary because of you," I tell her. "I saw them; I saw what she did to them. That could've been me too."

"They were in the infirmary because they tried to kill you."

"And what about Vik? He tried to kill the Chancellor – do you think it's OK to leave him? And what about the others?"

And she pulls that face again, sort of angry, sort of sad, sort of like there's something she isn't telling me.

"We need to do something!"

"Saints, why are boys so stubborn?" she sighs.

"Walker thought we could stop her," I push.

Ro's green eyes burn. "You think you can stop it? On your own?"

"No, but—"

"Go back then! You think you won't end up the same as your bullies?"

Ro stomps up out of the underpass, scaling furniture, piles of dusty books, broken paintings of ancient places and people.

Maybe she's right. One boy – any boy – is not enough.

The dozen or so Hysterics who attacked the ball were hardly organized but if there were more they could get more people out. Maybe Walker, maybe my brothers – Stink and Rodders and Woody. "What about the Hysterics? Would they help?"

She stops as we get back to the surface, into another building. There's less of a stink here. I wonder how far we are from the Tower now. I swallow, my throat desert dry. Underneath the serums and injections the doctors gave me I can still feel the bruises from the Roids' noose.

"The Chancellor doesn't care what the Roids did to me," I go on. "She had the Roids pinheaded because she could, not because she needed to. Like you said, it's all about power."

Ro keeps moving, even though she's gone pale.

"I get it. You're afraid of the Chancellor." My eyebrows lift with surprise at the thought – never thought I'd see a girl afraid of anything.

"And you're not?"

Leaving you behind, leaving Walker and my brothers, that's what scares me.

"The Chancellor wanted your aunt's support on a vote. Aspiner mentioned a vote too. The Chancellor's going to get every woman in that place to vote on whether to pinhead boys like me and she'll get her way – no one with enough merits will vote against her. They'll go along with it!"

Never seen Ro so quiet.

"The Chancellor was afraid you'd stop her. Not by killing her
… it's all those merits your family has. You could have stopped
the vote! She's won. She wanted you gone and now she can do
whatever she wants."

The underpass has led us into a building with a large ground
floor, the sand-dulled glass windows glowing with light even as a
storm splits the heat Outside. No fog here. For now. Is this one
of those breaks Ro mentioned? How long does it last? Will I get
to see the sun without anything but air between us?

"Maybe the rest of the women won't vote her way." Ro doesn't
sound convinced. The rain has died down. Everything's too
quiet now.

"How long have you known?"

"It's … there's just nothing left to do. Not without risking…
Don't you get it? I can't lose anyone else. I'm not strong enough.
She'll kill you, or worse."

That's what she's afraid of?

"I'm not afraid." I am.

My name is Jude Grant and I am alive, you say, almost like a
curse.

A wall of light, as bright as the auction house spotlight, cuts
through a large, broken window. Dust flecks dance and spin.
Who knows how long the fog break will last? I have to take a
look.

Through a crack in the glass, shimmering in the distance like
it's not quite real, stretches an endless spire of rust and dust.

It seems to pierce the sun, windows glinting like the Chancellor's grey eyes.

"You really want to go back there?" Ro asks. We've come to the edge of the city, I think.

"I want to find the Hysterics, ask them to help my brothers."

"OK," she says.

"OK?"

"And then you'll come with me? We'll go and we'll find the green lands, and my mum."

Who wouldn't want to see the world?

39

By the time the storm passes and we head out, my stomach has started eating itself and my brain is thudding with thirst. But that's the least of my worries. Every second I'm checking the flesh on my arms for that telltale prickle of bumps. How long before the fog swamps us again? At the edge of the city, what Ro called the Melts, the sandy sides of the old buildings have dissolved in the heat. We're moving as fast as we can for there's less cover on the outskirts of the city. Ro has no clue where the Hysterics are. They move around a lot to avoid detection.

Hearing something, she stops, a number sixteen *wait-for-it* grin, and puts her fingers to her lips. Screeches and wails carry on the wind through the narrow streets. Taking my hand, she moves at a run towards the sound before I can argue. And I have some solid arguments.

First: not wanting to be eaten by whatever monster is making that noise.

Second: *really* not wanting to be eaten by whatever monster is making that noise.

It's coming from a few streets over, behind what's left of an old building with tall stone columns. The door is armoured and thick, its metal weathered to a soft green. On the wall there are those painted marks to say it's fog-safe. Across the door are scratches, deep, high, angry letters.

"We are all your lies," says one of the women, leaning on the door. The two guardswomen look almost the same. I've never seen twins before. She can see me staring. "That's what it says, in case you're wondering." She raises a bottle of something in salute. "Hey, Ro. Heard you've been getting into trouble."

They know her?

"Cora, Haz!" Ro greets them with an embrace. "You pulled the short straw?"

Both guards have that familiar white stripe of paint pasted across their eyes. I saw women like that at the ball. Had they infiltrated before the attack? They're clutching vicious handmade weapons. Their clothes are patched leather, patchwork armour, lashed together with belts and pins. Their muscular stomachs are hardly covered – thick red scars spread in smiles below their belly buttons. Smile forty-nine: *the-empty-ragged-kind-that-makes-you-uneasy*.

The stories say that High House banishes women to the desert for serious crimes against survival. The N-dorm collectors are obsessed with the Hysterics. They told a boy in our dorm that the House doesn't only banish the women, it takes their most precious thing.

"Whatcha staring at?" Cora snaps. She's taller than any of the boys I know, even Vinnie.

"Nothing," I say.

"So … who's your gawping friend?" says the skin-headed twin on the right. She leans forwards, her hand reaching out for my hair, but I dodge away.

"Seriously, Haz, you going to let us through, or be a letch?" Ro says.

"Last of Eli's finest honey wine, totally worth guard duty," says Haz, grabbing the bottle from her sister. Sloshing the amber liquid back before holding out the bottle to me.

"You want some, my little cutie?"

I shake my head. "No thanks."

I remind myself that the stories I've heard are lies. I still have to check: neither of the guardswomen *seem* as if they've eaten humans recently, but then again I'm not sure I could really tell. What do I expect: limbs lying at their feet, clothes made of scalps?

"She's out the back," Cora tells Ro. "Fog-watchers say we've a few clear hours but you'd still better hurry or there'll be no scoff left. We're moving on in the morning."

"Where to?" Ro asks but the women both tap their noses. "For fog's sake, fine. Let us in then."

She's out the back? They must mean the woman in charge, right? I can smell fire from somewhere, charring meat. I'm sure the screams were the sounds of dinner fighting back.

Catching up with Ro as they let us through the doors, I hear the guardswomen laugh and whisper behind me. I follow Ro through the old building, wide-eyed and pointing up at the collapsing ceilings, where painted men in robes look down.

No time to ask questions, as soon the stone steps lead out into the desert night.

"Welcome to Hysteria," Ro says.

The sky above the ancient courtyard is an endless darkness, crossed by multicoloured lanterns strung up between melted walls and bricked-up windows. The sound of jagged fiddles cuts through my ears.

"You've been before?"

"She let me come once or twice."

"Who?"

"Don't drink anything. Eli's stuff is literally lethal."

I think she's changing the subject.

Is Eli their leader? I imagine a huge woman, the size of a tree. Except I thought Eli was a boy's name. Wasn't that the name of the man Stink knew from the Agro tunnels, Eli Han, the one that he said Madam Bocharov had scarecrowed?

The lights swing in the cold night wind, making the dust dance.

"And when the fog-watchers shout you get inside fast, unless you want a gut full of poison."

Ahead, round a fire almost as high as the rooftops, a crowd of silhouettes dances in the shade of the spitting embers. "They scavenge stuff to burn from the Melts," Ro says.

It's not an animal but dancers yelling and screaming. They bang drums and tear into violins, stamping the sand, standing on tables crammed with people. Aren't they worried the Lice will find them? Even if we're far away enough to escape detection, they're mad enough to take on the full force of the Lice in their own home. Maybe they want to be found?

The air tastes of burning salt. The crowd cheers. They raise clay cups above their heads. Everything out here is strange and itchy and loud. As we get closer, music bounces from every surface – the strangled warble of flutes, the jangle of bells, the chime of cymbals. Strange and shapeless songs, all fury and chaos.

"Romali!" yells a large man. Ro groans. He looks older than me but not much. There really are *men* in Hysteria!

He has one leg and speeds towards us on his crutches so fast he almost mows us down. Half his teeth are missing and there's an ugly raised mark on his shoulder: the Mine Mistresses brand the men that work down there. The man wraps his large arm round my shoulder and ruffles my hair.

"Eli!" He burps out an introduction, filling the air with a bubbly fug of beer and laughter. Above and below the white stripe of paint, his face is scorched red with sun and drink. The dark hair on his face hasn't been barbered in an age.

"Really, Eli?" Ro shouts over the noise.

"Longest fog break ever, so the watchers say. A couple of hours. You think I'm not going to celebrate?" He hiccups and smacks his chest, introducing himself again as he drags me towards the fire. "Who's this then? That the one you—"

"This is Jude," Ro interrupts, pulling me away.

Eli scrapes his matted arm across his nose. "She's been 'specting you," he yells at Ro, waving in the direction of the fire.

'She' is probably some beast, huge and bruised and angry. The kind of woman that could snap a boy in half. I've heard stories about the woman that leads the Hysterics, stories that say she's beautiful, magical; stories that say she'll drive you mad. I doubt they're true but she must be different to all the other women somehow to survive out here, to evade the Chancellor, to build an army.

Ro keeps pulling until I yank my arm free. Eli is following behind. His hands clap my shoulders. "You need anything, you come and see me, OK?" He thumps me on the shoulder again. Looking down to catch my breath, I see he's wearing one fat boot with the laces knotted in a tight mess.

He could run too.

"There they are!" A voice comes from nearby, a silhouette against the fire. It calls Ro's name. The spindled shape shoves her way through the clutch of painted people. A cold stone of recognition drops into my gut.

"Mr Grant!" she says.

Madam Vor stretches her strong neck, flexes her shoulders the way Ro does as we get closer. The firelight burns my cheeks.

"Romali, you could have warned him." Madam Vor clocks the fear in me. She can probably smell it.

"And miss the look on his face? Not for the world," Ro drawls.

"There's no need to be snide. We taught you better than that."

"Did you?" Ro's eyes could burn through bone. "I'm getting a drink," she says, walking away.

My legs have gone numb.

"So glad you're here." Vor holds out her palm.

"You're leading the Hysterics?" I ask, before I can stop myself.

Vor's dark eyebrows lift up in amusement. A slip of her deadpan mask. "Really, I don't lead anyone, not out here. I only help keep the peace. I protect them, that's all, until they decide to leave."

My jaw tightens. All this time she's been helping the Hysterics! But she had you arrested! Couldn't she have stopped the Gardener being killed? Or helped my brothers; helped Walker? Vor nods like she understands. "My officers had orders to let Romali escape, but you? I have to say I'm surprised to see you."

"Thought I'd be in the infirmary with my brothers?"

"If you'd not decided to show off your footwork like that, I'd have found a way to get you to safety. You chose a very poor moment to buck years of conditioning, Mr Grant." I can't tell if she's impressed or thinks I'm some sort of freak.

Does she know what her Lice did to me? "So it's my fault?" My neck prickles and itches but Madam Vor's face doesn't change. All I can hear is her in the infirmary, her calm voice while they poked and prodded at me, as they stitched and bleached and dyed and waxed and cut.

She doesn't answer – her gaze is on Ro by the fire. "You're here now, that's what matters. It wasn't until we spoke that I learned of Romali's plan. Even though I planned for us to escape during the ball, I'd have rather we left without murder on her conscience. You know, I think, how stubborn she can be. She gets that from Diani, who she is also dead set on looking for without me. Wouldn't have come to me now unless forced. If you're the reason she's here, you have my thanks, Mr Grant."

This is my moment to ask for help. But would she listen? I wait for you to call me a coward. Nothing. Maybe now you think I'm stronger than I am.

"When did you last eat?" She points to a roasting animal on a spit by the fire. Its skin blisters and fizzes. I smack my lips, imagining the salty bite of a proper meal. "Eli will look after you." There's no movement in her face to tell me she can be trusted. Still as fixed as ever. "You don't have to do anything you don't want to, not here. If you're not hungry, there are places to sleep, rest. We could even find you a change of clothes." She wrinkles her nose.

It's been two nights since I put on the suit – it doesn't smell good. My hair is sweat-clogged and sandy, but I kind of like it. It's been a long time since it's felt OK to look real, no make-up, all my scars, all my bruises and ugly edges.

Vor walks away.

Ro returns with a drink, two glasses of murky-looking water for us both.

"Maybe something stronger?" I ask Eli, at her side. A proper drink, that'll give me the courage to ask.

"I've just the thing." Eli slaps his chest.

Ro sighs. "Don't say I didn't warn you."

"Beer! Now that's my house." Eli, the man who doesn't seem to take orders, leads me away. He sits me down near the fire before pushing into the crowd, shouting, "Let's put some fur on 'is lungs!"

40

More jokes. More stories. More toasts to the Gardener, honouring her sacrifice. As the fire crackles and the music swells, the painted Hysterics stamp and drink and smoke and laugh. Men and women come and go, talking at me fast, asking questions. The blisters on my feet don't hurt, I tell someone. I think I've eaten half the pig, I tell another. How long have you been a Hysteric? Do you really eat people? I was in the kitchens, you too? Someone tries to get me to dance and I don't fight them away.

"If you're sure," says Eli, after I rush from the crowd and ask for another drink. He tops up my cup again. "How many is that?" he asks.

I shrug, burp. Lost count.

"Think this should be your last." He winks from where he's sitting.

When I look up, the coloured lanterns swing and sway. I squeeze my eyes shut to stop the stars from moving.

"Heard you were a sharp-stepper!" He laughs as I stand. "Let's see those moves."

Eli claps a beat and I think of Walker. "Come on!"

"No. No. No!" Waving my hands, I land heavier than I intended on the bench beside Eli and have to hold on to him so I don't slide off.

My brain hates me.

He pushes me up and plants me on my feet again. "Go on," he says and then points to his leg. The one Madam Bocharov let him keep. "You show me your moves, I'll show you mine."

I shuffle around a bit. Trying to remember the steps Walker taught me.

Eli laughs. "Tha's not dancing. That's just moving to music."

I thought they were the same thing?

"Haz was telling me 'bout you and Ro at the ball. Now that sounds like real dancing." He smacks my chest with his palm so hard I almost fall off the bench. "Gotta use this." He hits my chest again. "Not this." He flicks my forehead.

"That's going to bruise," I slur.

Eli pulls himself up on to his crutches fast. He starts to clap a beat, yelling at me to stamp my feet. Faster, he says. With passion, with drama. It's fun. I can feel each stamp vibrate in my chest thanks to my new thick soles.

"Romali!" he calls into the crowd as Ro appears. She's angry, storming towards the fire away from Vor. Maybe she asked her for help? Maybe Vor said no. "Dance with this guy, will you?"

"You OK?" she asks me, folding her arms. She's the only person who ever asks that. My tongue's fat, my eyelids heavy. I hang my head between my legs and realize I'm babbling again, trying to explain about the boys in the dorm, their nicknames.

Stink and Rodders and the others. Maybe the Hysterics can help them too, I say.

Eli pulls me up, rolling with laughter. I'm not sure I was trying to be funny. "Sure, nothing like a suicide mission t'round off the evening."

"Eli, don't," Ro says, pinching the bridge of her nose.

"Yeah, humour him, tha's great! He wants to go and get 'is head spiked? Be my guest. You think Cora and Haz wouldn't've got every last kid outta that place the other night if they could? It's not possible. Your mum got it right – get out, stay out."

A rush comes up from my gut and I feel like I'm going to be sick.

"Eli! Vor told you to look after him!" Ro swears and starts shouting, but I can't focus.

"Kid needed to loosen up." Eli winks. "Give the guy a dance, will you?" He shimmies his vast shoulders.

Ro sighs. "I'm not in the mood. Besides, he's off his fogging gourd."

"I thought…" I remember dancing – there was dancing. "You were good."

Did she smile? What number is that? I can't tell any more. There was a list. Walker gave me a list. "Where's Walker?" I say to Ro, to anyone. Swaying slightly where I'm sitting. No one answers. "I lost him," I say. "He needs to know where I am."

I lost Walker. I lost you too. You'd know what to do.

"He'll be really mad."

You always knew what to do.

Where are you? I can't hear you.

Squinting, I see Aye-Aye in the dance, between the blurred Hysterics. Vinnie and Toll too – except where their eyes should be there are great gaping holes. They're not dancing, just standing there, expressionless. Bodies push me this way, that way. There's a lot of stamping feet.

Eli grabs my shoulder, hands me another glass. I tip my head, peer at the lanterns swirling above. Someone pushes past. Was that Stink? He's here too? Did the Hysterics break out all the boys from the ball? Am I the last one to be free? The ache shakes out of my toes, my fingers as the music gets faster. Louder. I could burst, I'm so happy.

Then there you are! Your skin laced with grey dust as you fling your arms into the night and howl at the moon and cry freedom and dance, dance, dance. Is that you? Are you real? I push through the crowd but the ghosts disappear, leaving only Ro behind. Motionless. The crowd dances round her. I'll show her that out here I'm not a boy. I'm a free man and I can dance, and we can escape into the fog and we can slay monsters and climb mountains and fly.

"Are you angry with me?" I ask. She's been weird ever since that first night. "I thought you said we were friends."

"I'm not angry about…" She pulls at the knots in her hair. "Look, Vik's not here. You keep asking people for him. Stop it!" She's about to say something but instead starts worrying at the remnants of her dress. She won't look at me. There's something she's not telling me. There are bubbles in my stomach. It might be the alcohol, but it's not. I felt this ache before I went to the Chancellor's rooms.

A chant begins from the blurry mass. "We are all their lies!" Over and over. "We. Are. All. Their. Eyes." The sky shakes with it.

"You said you'd never lie to me. In our… When you came to see me in the appointments. You promised you'd never lie. What aren't you telling me? We're friends." I hiccup. "You said!"

She tries to leave. I hold her arm, hold her still. She could pull away easily.

"Jude, don't."

"No, you're my friend, you are. I don't care what you say. Whatever it is. Tell me – you promised you wouldn't lie. Vor said no, didn't she? You don't need to protect—"

"Secrets aren't the same as lies, Jude."

"Ro, please."

"You've got secrets too. You think you're perfect? Maybe you don't want to know. Maybe it's better you don't."

She's right. So I tell her. Right there, with the Hysterics swirling round us, I tell her everything. I tell her about the appointments, about Aspiner and her grabby hands. And I'm not ashamed, I shout, because I didn't do anything wrong. And I tell her about the fight with the Roids and Swims and even about my deal with the Chancellor.

When I'm done, there's a lightness, the pounding in my head gone for a moment. "So?" I say.

She looks like she wants to hold me, but she doesn't.

"I can't, Jude…"

"You think Vik's dead, right, that the Chancellor lied to me. That I'm stupid for falling for it." The swirling world has started to get clearer, my heart beating fast.

Cheers shake the clouds in the sky. I look up at the endless dark. It's the most beautiful thing I've seen. I could touch it.

"You're not stupid. Saints, of course I don't think that. I think you're so kind and smart," she says. "Maybe it'd be better if you weren't, maybe you'd be happy, but you know life in there isn't right. We go back, we lose and she takes your mind, or worse she actually kills you and it's all wasted. And why? For a boy who could be long dead. Jude, you don't owe him anything!"

"Course I do!" I try to explain about the kitchens and the dogs and how you got hurt, but my brain is all hooch and heat and I can't put it into the right words. "She promised she'd let him go."

"My entire life I've never known the Chancellor to make good on a deal unless it suited her. Look, I feel bad about what happened, I do, but … he could be out here now, with us—"

"You tried to get him out?"

"The night of Reserves, Vor had learned about Walker's plan. The Chancellor likes… She played this game with men who tried to get her attention. She'd invite them up to her floor, let them flirt, then get them to run. Then she'd send the police after them. Most of them ended up decorating the atrium the next day. Vor sent Cora and Haz to help last year, but … your friend, Vik … he wanted to stay."

It takes all my brain to follow. "Why?"

Ro rolls her eyes and throws up her arms. "Beats me! Boys make NO sense."

"You're lying!" I shake my head. It feels weird, like my skull isn't attached to my face. I'm going to be sick.

"I promised I wouldn't!"

"Maybe he knew about her plan, didn't want to run away like a coward."

Her eyes shine in the firelight, her lips pressed tighter. "I … I thought this is what you wanted?"

"Hiding in old buildings? Running away?"

"I'm not running away! I'm running *to* something, to see the world. To Mum—"

"So where is she?"

"She's alive. The stories are all lies, I told you—"

"If she cares so much, why did she leave?"

Ro stiffens, her neck straight, her mouth twisted tight. Her whole body shaking with anger. I need to take it back, the second I say it, but I can't.

Say sorry, tell her you're sorry, you didn't mean it. My mouth opens to speak.

"Don't," she says.

"But—"

"Don't, Jude. Please."

People are still dancing round us, smiling, trying to get us to join in.

"You said we're friends," Ro says. "Maybe we shouldn't be." She turns into the crowd and I don't follow.

41

The morning after and the world smells like the bottom of a pickle barrel. I'm not sure where I am; another building full of ghosts.

Lifting my hand to my head, to prise it from between the slabs of stone it seems wedged between, I find the stones aren't stone but piles of old clothes. I scratch at clumps of my hair, which also somehow hurt. My eyes are thumping! Thumping, thumping. There's a full-sized person inside, beating on my eyelids, trying to get out.

Even the idea of moving my head makes me ill. My mouth aches with thirst as if I spent the night sucking on old gym slippers. I crawl through the ache of my brain, past the throbbing and the thudding, to try and find some place to sleep.

It's an hour, maybe two, before the patter of water above is too much for my head. Another roll shakes the sky.

Ro coughs, shuffles her feet. Her hair's wet, the red of it as dark as mahogany. She's carrying a cup of brown-looking water. There's a dance in my chest when she hands it to me like maybe we're OK.

"Heard you moving from downstairs," she says. "Fog's clearing.

We're moving out." They need to keep changing location, Ro said before, to avoid Lice raids. Why do I feel like the Lice are Outside right now, waiting?

"Thanks." I try to smile like *this-is-totally-normal-and-not-awkward-and-weird-is-it?* What number am I up to now on the new list? All that training from Walker – those instructions he gave me, to smile, to put on a show, anything to make a lady feel better – it doesn't seem to be working.

She shrugs.

"I'm coming," I say.

I expect her to be angry, or upset, something, anything. But I can't read her at all. She's switched off. Outside, the sky rumbles again.

During the storm the Hysterics move out in groups of six, taking different routes through the Melts to reach the hospital. Ro's in one of the first waves to leave. I'm to go with the last group, with Eli and some of the more vicious-looking Hysterics.

Eli asks me about the Tower. He says he tried to get into the House of Boys when he was younger than me, but didn't have my looks. He remembers Stink, he says; glad he got in, despite the teeth.

"They're not that bad actually," I say.

As we clamber through the dusty old buildings, he tells me stories about the mines, shows me the scars on his body from all the work, the tattooed lumps he marked on his body for every man they lost. He tried to get more men out but they weren't strong enough to make it. Boys too, he says, but I don't want to hear about that.

"Mr Grant?" Madam Vor is waiting in the next room we reach. "Might I have a word?" She waves Eli and the Hysterics past but I don't want them to leave. Why didn't Eli warn me? I'm not ready to be alone with a woman like Vor.

"Romali told me last night that you wanted some of the ladies out here to try to help your friends?"

I was right, she did ask! "I ... well, I thought—"

"Friends like those boys who, from what I heard, tried to snap your neck?"

"It was a trick, to scare me. They wouldn't have—"

"Mr Grant, they've put dozens of boys in the infirmary."

"So that made it OK to pinhead them?" The words fall out before I can catch them.

"I didn't see them pinheaded and no law stands to do such a thing to boys. Do you have proof?" Her long fingers dust a ledge to perch on. "Romali tells me you think the Chancellor plans a vote? Convince me."

Is she playing with me? She must know! It's a test – it has to be.

I've heard of the Mind Absolution Act, the one Madam Hyde put in place, but that was for women. It doesn't cover the boys yet. Is that what the vote is about?

Or maybe I'm wrong...

What did I see? Needles. Doctors. Blood. But did I really see any of them pinheaded? Am I even sure I saw what happened to Aye-Aye?

My memories scrape through the night with the Gardener,

269

the 'one vote' the Chancellor wanted from her. Walker's lecture to the boys at Swims. *What if this was the last-ever auction –* wasn't that what he said? Then Aspiner, how she said boys like me wouldn't fight after 'the vote'. I try to explain it all to Madam Vor.

She nods, sighs. "Holding the threat of pinheading her rival's wards, or the boys they favour, would make sense. I heard her talk of applying the treatment to the House of Boys... We've been able to get more men out, to the House of Exploration outpost – an old airport where Diani ... where she was last seen alive. Repopulation, Mr Grant, outside the walls of that Tower requires a few more of your kind. My wife hoped one day to prove that every man and woman could leave High House."

"Are you sure the Chancellor wouldn't rather pinhead every man in High House than let them leave?" I ask.

Madam Vor stands and watches out of the window a while. There's a prickle at my neck – fog's coming in. The daylight has started to darken.

"I'll lead a few women back to extract those they can. Men, women, your brothers, Walker." She leads the way to the door into what I guess is our destination.

"There's a boy, at the infirmary," I say.

"Pinheads can't survive in the desert."

"Viktor Perrault, he's called. Vik. He's there because of me."

Madam Vor's eyes narrow as she remembers. "The boy Walker sent after the Chancellor last year?"

"Can you get him out?"

270

"If he's there. If he's able, willing," she says. "But as soon as it's safe tonight you're to leave with Romali. She refuses to go to the outpost without you and it's not safe for her to stay here. The Chancellor will send my officers after us. If they follow their training, they'll wait until the best moment. I won't let Romali venture to the House of Exploration alone and, of all the places in the city, the Chancellor knows the hospital is the best staging post to make it into the desert."

Ro wanted to come to the hospital. Is that where we are? The shadows seem to make the ancient green-blue paint flake and curl. There are wide stairs beyond the door and ancient paintings rotted in their frames. Above, the crooked remains of a chandelier. It must have been a grand entrance to the building once, like the Saints' palaces from old fairy tales.

"I can ensure the Hysterics provide cover for her, you too and as many as can make it. You understand me, I hope."

"They're coming. Here?"

She nods. "My bet is they're waiting until there's good reason to attack. They won't want to return without a significant number of bodies. We embarrassed the Chancellor. She'll retaliate tenfold."

"You're willing to risk—"

"If it gets my daughter to safety."

I nod. "You'll follow, right? With Vik, the others? What if the Chancellor tries to stop you? Will *you* kill her?"

"Killing her would only empower those who agree with her. She needs to be discredited. Once we get those we can out, I'll stay."

"But she must know you've betrayed her by now."

Vor's expression returns to its usual unreadable mask. "I'll claim I was kidnapped as planned. With my sister-in-law's and my wife's merits to my name, if there is a vote, perhaps I can stop it. Perhaps I can even arrest her, build a case, put her on trial. I'll assist your friend, the others, while you accompany my stubborn daughter so she gets to some form of safety?" She holds out her hand. "In the old days, the Saints would shake on it."

I take her palm. It's firm. And I believe she'll do it, I really do.

42

The storm's still raging outside the hospital walls. Knock, knock, knocking to come in. It could be my eyes but I'm sure it's darker inside. Old lights struggling above. The walls feel strange, like being inside the Tower. Most of the windows here have been bricked up with clay; the doors are thick and locked firmly when the fog comes in. And out there, somewhere, the Lice will be planning their attack.

Eli, the other men and I wait in a hall that has thick windows a few storeys high. I don't take my eyes off the rainwater as it washes down the glass. We're at the edge of the city, no more buildings, just desert and the world beyond that waterfall blur.

Below, through the pipes, come the distant voices of the women. Vor has them working in the basement, getting the buggies started, Ro says as she sits beside me. Her face is caked in grease. She wipes her hands on her knees. The dress she wore at the ball has long been shredded into rags and now she's wearing trousers, armour, like the rest.

Between the sounds of the women below there's a grinding noise, the smell of fuel. Vor said the Hysterics and the old Explorers dragged the Saints' vehicles into the basement after digging them out from under the sand.

"Brought you something to eat." Ro throws me a cooling potato, sweet-smelling, its skin baked crispy black.

"I could've helped, fixing the buggies," I say. "Used to help with the generators when I was a kid."

Ro shrugs, still acting cold.

There's music in this place. The dripping of rain through pipes. Ro sighs. The scuttle of mice. The nervous tap of my foot. "Look," I start, needing to apologize for our fight.

"It doesn't matter." She gets up to leave. I don't stop her.

The ache from the alcohol has passed but that familiar anger is banging at my head. Being shut up like precious cargo while the Hysterics work below. It's no better than being at the House of Boys.

I tug at the waistcoat I kept from my outfit at the ball. The men washed my shirt while I slept last night; it doesn't stink so badly now. I donated the suit jacket and tie to ghosts behind us.

"You could help clean up after dinner," Ro says, pointing to a handful of men in the corner who have been cooking for the last hour.

"I did my stint in the kitchens, thanks." I lay on the sarcasm, because is that all she thinks I can do? We watch Vor return with a dozen Hysterics who clap each other on the back and cluster round the men to order food. They must have left the basement but I can still hear knocking. Maybe it's from the storm.

"How long?" I ask.

"Soon." Ro shrugs. "It's been a few months since the buggies have been started. There are always a few people here to guard them, keep them running. If the Chancellor knew about what was under here, she'd have burned the place to the ground. Vor kept her away."

"No." I fold my arms. "I mean how long have you known about Vor?"

"Really? You want to do this now?" She rolls her eyes. "You think I'd blab that to anyone, to a boy? I know you guys gossip about us."

The knocking wind seems to have got louder, and it sounds less and less like the wind. It's not the storm. There's no rain on the windows, only the water-distorted distant view of the desert.

Vor, at the end of the table opposite, has got to her feet.

"What is it?" Ro asks, her forehead creasing as she stands. "Vor … Vor? Mum!"

I've never heard her call Madam Vor Mum before. Vor turns – she seems surprised too.

The knocking sounds slower this time. Vor holds up a hand. "Stay there," she says. "Stay back."

The knocking comes again. The voices of the crowd settle into silence. The knock is clearer. Deep, clunking, repetitive.

One.

Two.

Three.

Someone's at the door.

What if it's me?

That voice of yours is quieter these days, the more time I

spend with Ro. It's the Lice – it has to be.

She's let me go.

At a twist of Vor's wrist, a dozen Hysterics are on their feet. Weapons clink and clatter, pulled from hidden places, from skirts, shirts, boots, shoulder straps.

They're going to kill me, you say. *An army wouldn't knock. Let me in.*

The Hysterics are armed with knives, bats with nails in, long-barrelled guns handmade from pipe and hunks of metal. Vor, her breath held, waves her hand again and the mass of limbs clambers noiselessly over tables towards the main door.

I'm on my feet, convinced I'm right. "Wait," Ro says, and follows fast.

"An army wouldn't knock," I tell her.

Another movement of Vor's hand brings a second wave of Hysterics to their feet around us. Behind, a third crowd of women hurry the men out of the kitchen, including Eli.

There are nearly twenty heavily armed Hysterics by the front door. I have to fight my way to join them, not get scurried away like the rest.

They wait. Vor rests her hand against the old metal. Everyone watches the red light above the great door. Fog's still out. The light wavers.

The knocking comes again.

One.

Two.

"Open it," I say.

Three.

Vor shakes her head. The knocking comes again. And again.

You're out there and you're choking. I can feel the rope of dust and fog eating into your lungs and squeezing.

There's no more knocking.

Vor takes a deep breath, searching in one of her pockets for a key. Her face sours as she slips it into the lock to override the safety. The whole building creaks as the door opens. Vor wraps a cloth round her mouth and steps out into the thick cloud. "Stay here!"

Cora and Haz push the door almost shut behind her but I can still smell the egg-sour stench of the fog as it begins to seep in.

The horde of armed women fight to keep everyone back but Ro pushes forwards, shouting at the guardswomen to let her pass as she shoves through to the open door and dives into the fog.

What if you're out there? What if they waited too long? What if they let you die?

In a heartbeat, Vor and Ro crash back inside, dragging something between them. The world is slow, grey, when the door slams. As the Hysterics part, knives and guns clatter on the stone. I push to see through the sinking haze.

They're carrying a body. A man. He's wearing a fog mask like the Lice wear.

My gut aches the moment I recognize his suit, the sweep of silver in his hair. Walker.

The white tips of his shined shoes have been dragged through puddles, the legs of his trousers splashed with veins of muck and dust. There's thick gauze wrapped round his eyes. Vor orders her army to make space, make room, give him air as she lays him down on the dirty stone floor. They unclip and remove the fog mask, messing up his always-perfect hair .

"Move!" I tell her, not caring about the rules, what's right, what's proper. "Move!"

Vor works fast, snapping free the gauze with her knife, unwrapping it. There's a pain in my head again. It pushes right through my eye like a needle.

"He's alive, right?" I ask.

My hands shake as I drop beside him. He's half covered in dust and so wet his skin is almost see-through. He's warm. Still warm. On the right side of his perfect face there's a deep bruise, his eye swollen purple and black with it. Through his ballooned eyelids he stares straight ahead.

"Get up!" I shake him, my voice cracking. "She pinheaded him!" I tell Vor.

His perfect mouth sits in smile zero, *at rest*.

A thick tear of blood leaves the corner of Walker's eye, crawls over the bridge of his nose and drips on to the old stone.

"Jude, please." Ro tries to pull me away.

There are worse things than death, Walker told me.

"We should've gone back!"

The rage pulls up from the floor but there's nowhere to put it, so it spins inside me. No more dancing. No more laughing, or winking to the crowd. No more *it'll be OK, kid*. No more *I can fix this*.

I can hear the Chancellor's beetroot-pink tongue click. *We simply take their minds*, she said.

He's not dead. I wish he was.

*

Seconds. They pull me away.

Minutes. They carry Walker up to the top floor as I follow. Everyone's talking. I want to know if they can they fix him and what does it mean, and how did he get here and why?

Hours. He hasn't moved and neither have I. I'm waiting for a twitch, a blink, a shuffle.

There's no smile. No wink. No *only kidding, son*, which will make me hate him for a second and then never, ever, ever again.

He's only here because of you, you say.

No. I refuse to believe this is my fault. This is her. This is the Chancellor.

In the corner of the room on the top floor of the hospital is a folded suit on a lonely chair. The sand-splattered toes of his shoes peep out from underneath. I tried to hang his suit up. There was nowhere to put it. His jacket still smells like him.

They don't think he'll survive. Vor said the procedure the doctors performed on him wasn't successful. She didn't say it out loud but it's obvious that they botched it on purpose.

The Hysterics have already started leaving, dozens of them, out into the desert. I won't go, not until Walker is stable, not until they can take him too. And I know what's at stake. I know the Lice could come any second, and I know Ro won't leave without me, but I can't leave him.

My heart's hot and then I'm tearing at his suit fabric, the perfect stitching, the neat seams. There has to be something! Something to tell me everything will be all right, that I can do this. That I'm not alone.

Walker designed his suits himself, had Madam Cramp put secret pockets in the lining. I shake the contents inside on to the floor: a merit book, the slips torn away; an old folded map of High House; a tin of black boot-polish; a tube of hair oil. That's everything that's left of him. As I flip through his merit book, a small piece of paper flutters from its pages.

Everything slows down as it lands. It's folded into a shape. A perfect paper dog.

My hands shake as I bend to pick it up, see the little pin marks in the paper. I run my thumb over them.

⠏⠕⠺⠙⠗

Coward.

As Ro sweeps into the room, the lantern in her hand swinging, I push the note behind my back. She's flustered, angry.

"Are you coming?" she asks. "Everyone left is going back with Vor."

I'm holding my breath. My whole body has gone cold. Is the message from you to Walker? Or is it to me? It's like the note before Swims, the one the infirmary prentice delivered.

Clang go the doors. Click go the lights – little red boxes above the doors to warn of the fog.

"We've missed the storm window. Fog's in. But … we can make it, Jude."

"We can't," I say. Vor said pinheads won't survive the desert.

"There are plenty of fog masks."

Vor made me promise to go with Ro. But now…

The note crinkles in my fist.

"Jude, are you listening? We have to go. He didn't walk to the hospital. The police are distracting us. Waiting. We have to go!"

"Not without Walker," I repeat.

✳

Hurrying with torches in our hands, we follow Cora and Haz who carry Walker between them on a makeshift stretcher.

There's energy below. Hysterics laughing, clapping, ripples of excitement up and down. Ro's nervous, I can tell, keeps looking back, stopping at strange sounds. At one point she even reaches out to take my hand, but I jump. Your note's still held tight.

"What *is* that?" she asks.

I close my hand tighter and try to keep moving but she fights for it. Convinced she won't be able to read it, I finally let go.

"Where … where did you get this?" Ro snaps, unfurling the scrunched-up paper.

"It's nothing."

I've got to know her face well since Reserves: the scar on her chin; the nick in her ear (a birth defect, she said); the way she rolls her green eyes when Vor talks, or lifts an eyebrow when I make a joke that's not funny. But I've never seen this face: she's worried. She runs her finger over the bumps. She can read dark-text?

"Jude?" she says. Her hands are shaking. "Please, she's playing you. Using him. It's what she does for entertainment, for power. When she wants something, she takes it, or she takes what you love and she twists it!"

We're alone, the twins and Walker lost in the distance. Why is everything suddenly so quiet?

Ro takes a breath, about to speak, when a boom rolls under us and the whole hospital shakes.

Through the Hysterics' screams comes another whoosh; an explosion shreds the floor below our feet.

Barricades from the ancient windows shatter around us. Rubble and dust and wood and smoke.

And then we're falling.

43

LESSONS IN PATIENCE

Three days until last year's Reserves.

It was the final chance to put our names forward to our House Fathers. If I hadn't done it that year, then I'd have only had one more year left. At seventeen, without a guardian, Father Jai would sell me to the mines. After that, we get too strong, he says, less trainable, so no woman would buy us. The nightmares had already started, of ceilings so low I could never stand, of darkness and dust and a dry mouth, of scraping at the rock with torn nails.

Last year's auction was a fail for both of us but at fifteen this would be our best shot. Still, I wasn't going to put my name in without knowing you'd done it too.

That year Rodders could afford to buy his way in but he decided to wait a year. In his appointments, one of the top-floor madams promised him she'd consider a bid if he took more care of himself.

He smacked his gut. "No more extra shakes for me, boys. I'm hitting the gym. This time next year I'll be twenty pounds lighter and so hot the ladies will have to cough up much meritage. To the treadmill!" he proclaimed, standing up at the table. "Oi, Judy, you coming?"

"Really... Judy? We're going with that now?" I'd sighed.

"Meet you there." It was Saturday – no appointments. First to the gym could get in an hour's work before your beefcake friends tossed them out.

You were over at your regular table with the gym boys. I knew you'd been working with Walker. It was no secret. Mr Walker's favourite. He'd paid for your entry price. He'd arranged a special audition for you. And so on.

I kept wondering what would happen if you found out it was all because of me.

Two older prentice from the House of Entertainment had come into the dorms one day looking for the boy that wore the silver ring on his thumb. We all wondered if you were in trouble for bragging – good boys don't brag.

Not long after that the rumour started: Walker was grooming a successor. Was I wrong? Had you impressed him more than me at your first audition, after all? Either way, you were back, and I had nothing to do with it so it was safe to tell you about the audition now, right? We'd laugh about it, and you'd be grateful and we wouldn't tell anyone, it'd be our secret. But Vinnie and the others kept guard over you. Shut me out of the gym when I tried to talk to you. And if you weren't in the gym, or lessons, you were in endless appointments.

So I made a plan. A note on a scrap of paper I'd saved ... spent ages learning to fold it into a little man, like you could.

I was going to bribe some V-dorm boy to slip the note on to your lunch tray. I knew if I got caught I'd risk a beating from your mates, didn't want that before auction. Bruises don't get bids. But I had to get your attention…

⠠⠺⠑ ⠝⠑⠑⠙ ⠞⠕ ⠞⠁⠇⠅⠲

We need to talk.
JG

44

Every breath of air coughs out of my body. There's a jamming ache in my ribs that stabs as I try to stand. The smoke spikes at my eyeballs when I blink through it. Dragging myself forwards, searching for shapes in the swimming black. This isn't a normal darkness. I'm climbing through a black soup that burns in my chest. When I call out for help, I can't hear my words for the ringing. Everything is dark and I don't have my ears.

Can't stop. Must keep moving or I'll choke.

"Ro?" I shout, searching through the debris. I don't know this place. In the appointment rooms, I'd rely on my other senses but here there's too much noise.

I find fabric, an arm, and move my shaking hands with care to reach the familiar twists of Ro's hair. She doesn't stir. There's blood in her hair, sticky and warm. Calling her name again is useless, so I pick her up with one huge shout, to stifle the pain in my side. It takes both arms to carry Ro, her body clutched against mine. I fight through the thick smoke, coughing against the brick dust clagging my throat.

Not just smoke, there's that acrid stink too as the fog seeps in through the shattered walls.

The click and whine in my head starts to pop and I hear shouts up ahead. Or it could just be the sound of my aching head collapsing in on itself.

Bootsteps pass. I stumble forwards until a wall stops me. Us. Her heart's still beating. I can feel it against me. Maybe we're dancing, that's all, dancing like before. The Lice aren't coming. We have time. For a beat, it feels true.

A hand grabs at me, trying to take Ro away. I shout out and the noise is from somewhere animal inside. Kicking against flesh, swinging at shadows, over and over and over.

"Fine, then keep moving!" shouts a voice. Vor's, I think. "Basement, now!"

A handful of Hysterics push ahead of us and I follow. My arms are shaking under Ro's weight as the floor slopes, spiked with broken rubble.

As we move, a single slender needle of green light slices through the black beside me. At first I think it's my eyes, damaged by the blast.

Then there's another. Another. Coming from behind us, and Vor's voice shouting louder.

I keep moving, biting down hard to stop myself from crying out from the pain in my side. Above my head bullets squeal through the air.

There's a thud beside me.

And another. Another. Everywhere a green light touches, a Hysteric falls.

Thud. Thud. The corridors fill with flashes, the tang of hot copper and smoke and panic, as one by one, around us, the Lice fire into the dark.

I duck, move to the side.

Did some of them get out? Vor promised the Hysterics would go back for my brothers, for you! They can't help if they're all dead!

"Jude?" says a voice in the chaos. Ro's hands hold tight round my shoulders as she opens her eyes.

"Jude, I'm OK." She pushes against me until I put her down. She's limping, coughing too, but she can walk. So we keep going together, as fast as we can, dodging the lights, scrambling over rubble, bodies, through smoke mixed with curling dark fog, holding each other up until I can't move any more. There's a strong smell of oil and engines. We have to be close to the basement now.

"Keep going," I say. "I'll catch up." Dizzy, sniffing away the sting in my nose, coughing and spitting on the floor until my lungs have emptied of smoke, I take a breath, catch my side as it sears with a pain I've never felt before.

Ro tries to help as I cry out but another group of Hysterics floods past, torches burning in the dark. This time I've not got the strength to stop them as they sweep Ro up. I can hear her trying to get back to me, calling my name. In their disappearing light, when I look down, there's a glint. Something sticking out of my side. When I put my hand on it, I find a hunk of glass, as sharp as a knife, buried deep in my flesh.

As I lay my hand on it, everything in me seizes up from

the waist down. But it's not from the glass; it's from the voice getting closer, bellowing orders at her officers.

Aspiner's sharp shouts scratch at my ribs.

45

My nails drive so deep into my palms I'm certain they meet bone. But all my energy's gone. I can't walk. Can't run.

"We'll have to do two trips," Aspiner tells her officers with that biting voice of hers. As the smoke settles, I can make out the open door that leads down to the basement, its struggling red light like a dying heart.

If I can keep the Lice away – stall them – it'll all be OK. Vor can get to safety. She'll send people to help you, Ro will go out into the desert and find her mum and—

"Hello," Aspiner says from behind me, through the suck and hiss of her fog mask. "The Chancellor said we'd find you here."

She flips a switch on something in her hand and I turn, bracing myself for the electricity of her baton to flash and burn my stomach. Instead, it's torchlight she brandishes in my swollen eyes.

After a lot of blinking, I make out the other officers halfway down the corridor, searching through the bodies at their feet.

"Get the rest. Dead go on the truck, men to the mines," Aspiner shouts. "You heard me!"

"No sign of Romali, Spinny," squeaks one of the officers.

"That's Madam Aspiner, Officer Holt," Aspiner corrects her. Madam? Does she have enough merits now to lead the House of Peace? What if Vor's been replaced already? Can she still help? "Check down the hall. No one'd be stupid enough to try to leave the building. Not with the fog out there."

Aspiner turns to me. "What's down there?" she asks, casting her torch beam towards the door.

"Pardon?" I say, remembering how she pretended not to hear me when she assaulted me at the ball. Show her I haven't forgotten, that she doesn't scare me, even if she does.

"Maybe you should show me?"

"Sorry?" I say with Walker's *butter-wouldn't-melt* special. "I didn't catch that."

She looks me up and down, repeating louder, "I said, maybe you should show—"

"Sorry? The explosion." I point to my ears. "Maybe if you said please."

She finally gets it, I think.

Aspiner pulls off her fog mask to look right at me, moving so close I can hear her swallow. "Funny boy. Half dead and still teasing, like you've something to prove." She laughs, pushing against me.

Her torch picks out my wound, blood dropping red rain into the dust between us. "Tempted to go out into the fog?" she says. Catching me staring at her fog mask, she drops it at my feet. "Let's see how far being pretty gets you."

Then the worst happens. Ro calls my name from below.

Aspiner snaps into action, backing away, reaching for her gun.

"Wait, take me instead. You can let Ro leave," I say.

Ro calls up again.

There's no time left. I jam my fingers into the wound in my side and fumble for the glass. I try to imagine I'm digging out a bone from one of the slaughtered animals they brought to the kitchens. Not me. Only meat.

Aspiner won't hesitate to lead her Lice below, to shoot Ro.

The peppery dew on my fingers from the smoke sears through every nerve as I drive deeper, pinch the hunk of glass and pull.

Launching myself forwards with a roar of pain, I crash into Aspiner. As she hits the floor, I raise the shard of glass and drive it down.

46

Aspiner rolls on the ground, howling and pawing at her burst eye.

Dropping the shard of glass and grasping my wounded side, I plough through the broken building towards the basement.

I just needed to get away. Didn't mean to—

Don't think! Run! Don't look back! Out of the torchlight there's just dark but my senses are sharp now, even in the dust. Hurried breaths bounce off walls, rubble. The firm fall of my feet, moving until I find the doorway, shut it, smack, lock it. Stairs, my feet tripping over each other as I claw my way down into the guts of the earth.

Always fun when they run, the Chancellor said.

Is it the fog or my wound making me dizzy? I feel my blood, warm, oozing through my skin, over my fingers. But I don't stop.

Aspiner shouts from above as I hunt along the wall, searching for the end of the staircase with my fingers. I hear the Lice firing at the door, trying to get through.

Darkness breaks into light but I can't stop looking at my shaking hands. Everything beyond them is a blur. There's a mix of dust, blood. Mine? Aspiner's? They don't seem like my hands.

The fingers seem longer, stronger, curling in and out slowly as if their grit-lined nails could scrape chunks from the world. These are the hands that put glass in Aspiner's eye. Not me, not my hands.

"Jude?" Ro puts her rough hand to my neck, and I jump. "You're shaking."

She's fussing at my side while I tell her it's fine, fine. Maybe she's pretending not to hear me.

There's a bang above and the shaking in me stops. For a second, clarity. "Aspiner," I say. "They're coming."

We're trapped down here. In the dust and dry, everything as solid as the dorms except, even though I'm surrounded by people, I feel alone. So very far away. Things start to come into focus. Someone is shouting orders I can't quite make out – Vor. Eli is searching for something to bind my side with. It's bleeding too much, Ro says, stop shaking. Anyone any glue? Where's the kit? Cora!

Why am I so cold? Is it cold down here? The air tastes of oil and copper. Pressing my hands in my armpits will warm them, hide them, stop them shaking. Everything reeks down here, like the kitchen generators but worse. It sticks in the nose. Ro presses a cloth to the gash and it brings out a growling swear word from my throat. Good boys don't swear.

"Don't think about it," she says. "Whatever you did, you had to do."

"She's not dead," I say. "I couldn't." Maybe I should have. Maybe that's why I'm shaking, because I know she won't stop, not now.

"Listen," Ro whispers.

It's quiet. Too quiet.

"We've got time," she says, climbing kind fingers up my arm. Her hands. Her steadying hands. "They don't know what we've got down here. They won't waste bullets. They'll wait it out."

Long lights clunk on above, on and on and on, into the distance.

M-dorm were always droning on about the Saints' engines. They'd talk of things with wheels that could devour distances in the dunes, about the House of Exploration dragging some into the Tower to study, dismantle or even bring back to life.

And here they are! Those mythical machines. Cars. Trucks. Tanks. Buggies. Buses and bikes. Long rows of vehicles stretching into the dark. Desert-ready. One M-dorm kid drew diagrams and tried to explain them to me once but there are things here I can't name. Things with huge scoopers on the front, ploughs for moving sand.

The hairs on the back of my neck are itching.

"The police don't know there's a way out. Vor kept that a secret," Ro says. "We're leaving. All of us."

The Hysterics fan out, starting as many of the vehicles as they can. They jump on bikes, pile into cars.

It's happening. It's really happening.

Ro helps me into a sturdy-looking truck with thick metal doors, grilles at the windows. "Best of the beasts," she says, shutting the door on me. "Vor's orders."

Inside everything is bare metal. Fabric and leather stripped away from seats, only shreds left like skin clinging to the bolts with defiance.

"Got to go now, while the fog's in. It'll pass soon." Ro gets in the other side, behind the wheel.

I'm only half listening. As I wipe my palms on my body, the blood smears but doesn't go.

Don't think of the scrape of glass on bone, the crunch as her body hit the ground, the ache in my arm as I snatched it back. The clitter-clatter of the glass as it dropped to the ground. The animal noises she made. Maybe she won't follow. Maybe she'll bleed to death? There's a splinter in the meat below my thumb that I can't dig out.

Does this make me what they say we are? Violent animals that need to be protected from themselves.

Ro is about to shut the door but hesitates as Vor pulls in close to the buggy, her needle-thin shoulders straightening as she looks through the window and straight at me.

Vor blinks and reaches out to Ro. Her long arms hug her daughter close – she holds her tight. Like she'll never let go. That's when I see Madam Vor smile. Walker called it the *heart's-desire* smile. Mouth stretched and thin, eyes bright. Grateful, free. She whispers something into Ro's ear, takes a deep breath and with a sigh turns away.

Around us there's the slam of truck doors, car doors, a roaring howl of tyres and engines, hollering Hysterics.

Determined, angry, Ro pushes herself into the driving seat.

"Is Vor coming?" I check.

"She's going back to High House, to stop the vote," Ro says. It's OK. It's going to be OK. "Hold on!" she shouts, and slams her foot to the floor.

"To what?" But my words are lost in the deafening noise as our truck, with its time-cracked seats, stripped floors and rattling doors, crunches into life. Leading the pack with a growl that shakes through my boots, we surge forwards, my breath left behind as my body flies ahead.

Front lights, shining from the pack of vehicles, pick out the concrete and columns flying by in the dark. The world moves too fast under me. My sticky hands grab at dials, clutch on to latches on the panel in front, hold on for dear life as bikes speed past, *wvroom-wvroom*, towards a dot of light that – with a clunk – starts to spread into a smile. A gaping bright mouth of heat as the bikes catapult up and out into the dense fog.

We plough into hot winds of dust, and sparks spray in through the open windows from the wheels. Angry sand spatters my face as I battle to close the window, as Ro reaches for the compartment in front of me and clicks it open. She grabs a pair of goggles for herself, yelling for me to put a pair on. Snapped over my eyes, the desert plunges into deep orange.

Wrestling off my shirt, trying not to cry out at the stab in my gut, I swoop the fabric round my head, my nose. One-handed, holding on to whatever I can reach. We rumble along – road beneath us – until the sound softens as dunes swallow it up.

Ro revs fast to climb mountains of sand dunes that lunge

towards us in waves until we tip over their peaks, the nose of the truck falling – for a second, I don't weigh a thing – then crashing down. The other buggies pull alongside as the road catches us again.

Inside the fog, a storm rages, howling at the grilles of the truck, clawing at the doors, the windows. Lightning crackles in clouds above.

And it's beautiful. And I wish I could slow it down, hold my breath, tell my brothers that the world is alive.

A growling black monster, twice the size of our truck and made of huge lights, swipes us, almost tipping us over. One of the other Hysterics, lost in the fog? We land again, the driver's-side wheels jolting, to see the monster ramming into us again.

Ro swears under the scarf she's wrapped round her mouth.

Aspiner. Driving so close alongside I can see the burst veins at the edges of her remaining brown eye. Of course she'd follow! Of course they have their own vehicles! How stupid to hope she'd let us go.

Catching sight of the shotgun, I duck, pulling Ro down with me as Aspiner fires, the shots smacking into the metal of the cabin around me. Ro veers the truck to the right. Another shot. This time it pierces the back of the vehicle. Another as Ro swerves again, the shrapnel ripping into the side. Ro cries out. I think the shot hit her but there isn't time to check as she turns the wheel sharply.

The sand beneath falls away and we fall with it. Rolling. Over. Over. Crunching. My brain twisting in its casing. Those hands, my hands, pressed against any surface – ceiling, window, then floor. Ro's steadying palm again, pushing against my chest so hard she could break through my ribs and crush my heart.

We stop. It's quiet. Sand against the window, deep, dark, drowning.

Moving fast then, we kick at the windows, the grille, door handle, anything to get out before we begin to sink. We work at the same door, scrambling to the back of the truck. Kick. Shout. Punch.

The door opens. The shotgun pointed at us like a cannon. Aspiner looks down as the fog begins to clear around us. She's strapped dark gauze round her head. It's darker where her eye should be, gummy with blood that crawls down her cheek, as thick as syrup.

"Out!" she growls, pulling us both up.

She drags us, fighting against the sliding sand, so we can look back to see the Hysterics driving into the distance, leaving us behind.

Aspiner wants us to see we're alone.

Did Vor get out? Send anyone back to the Tower? As our truck sinks into the sand, there's that vengeful look in Aspiner's remaining eye.

"Romali Vor's head and the safe return of her potential ward – minus an eye, terrible shame but accidents happen. *And* I get to tell the Chancellor that Madam Vor is in league with the Hysterics... My bloodline will run the House of Peace for a century!"

There's nothing left for me to fight her with. Even Ro looks beaten, shaken.

"No," Ro mutters under her breath, shaking her head.

At first I think she's going to try to fight but she's up on her feet, moving faster than I could believe in the opposite direction, back towards the hospital.

She's running? Leaving me. Maybe she's going for help.

Aspiner laughs. "Don't worry, she won't get far," she says, turning. Then she swears, reaches for her gun. Because Ro isn't running away. She's waving her arms, yelling as a bike screams out of the fog.

"Stay here." Aspiner runs to her truck, dragging me alongside. As we reach it, I scoop up a hot handful of sand and throw it in her good eye.

Crying out, she drops me, rubbing at her streaming eye as she rushes to get inside the truck. There are threats: she'll come back for me; an eye for an eye, or maybe two. I don't need to see to be loyal.

The door slams and the monster grinds towards Vor's bike, speeding through the dust.

Ro's ahead of me as I try to run through the sand towards her, my feet slipping, every fall another stab to my side. There are bruises and wounds from the crash, but I keep going. Aspiner's truck speeds through clouds of sand. It'll crush Vor and her bike like paper. Vor must know that. But, as the bike gets closer to Aspiner, she swerves, turning side-on. Then the whole of it is swallowed under the wheels.

The sound of crunching metal makes Ro stop dead.

I catch up with her just as Aspiner's truck crunches to a halt, the spines of Vor's torn-up bike grinding underneath.

Vor jumped clear, right? That black body in the sand between us and the truck. Vor's just winded, and now she's going to fight Aspiner and everything will be fine because ... because it has to be. Vor must've known that angling the bike like that would disable the truck. She must've seen Aspiner follow after us. She knew her. Knew she'd never give up. Vor would risk everything to stop Aspiner from snatching her daughter's dreams away.

But Vor isn't getting up. Ro pulls away from me, runs towards her mother. Aspiner has less distance to travel, hobbling forwards with her gun raised. Spitting out sand, wiping grit from her remaining eye, she reaches Vor's bruised body first.

Maybe Vor jumped too late. She isn't going to fight. Not today. Not ever.

We get close enough to see the gloating Aspiner kick Vor's bruised body. Close enough to make out Aspiner's face as she sees Vor's still alive, as she takes a breath to gloat. Close enough for Vor to recognize her daughter ploughing through the sand towards her. Close enough for Vor to raise her palm.

Stop, it says. Stay there. Stay back.

Ro shakes her head, shouting, drawing Aspiner's smirking glance a second before the grenade in Vor's hand takes them both.

47

The sky boils dark with storm clouds as a handful of Hysterics relight their torches. The ones that stayed back with Vor. There are only a dozen, Cora and Haz among them.

By the time they returned, the blaze was almost out.

Ro is on her knees, still lost in tears. I don't know what to do, where to look, how to make it better. So I sit beside her, my shoulder warm against hers, until she folds into me.

"You shouldn't look," I say but Ro won't move.

Last time I heard her cry was in that appointment. I took her hand. Our bloody palms press together now. Ro squeezes tight, roaring into the dust until there's nothing but a crackle to her voice and her grief becomes the fierce grip on my fist.

It pricks at a part of me that sound, the strength of it. The dorm Fathers taught us about families, their structure, their purpose, but not about how it feels to have a mother – what Vor meant to Ro. I can see how it hurts.

Flanking us, a handful of Hysterics stand silent, disciplined. They raise their hands in salute as Cora and Haz run over to us. We hold our breath as they get closer.

"Let the desert have her," says Haz. She rests her hand on Ro's head. "We should move out, stay ahead of the weather."

Ro's as stiff as stone. "I'm not leaving my mother to the desert."

It takes a while for the rain to come, thick, driving. The sand gives up a strange earthy scent as the clouds douse the flames. Ro still hasn't moved. The Hysterics find a way to cover us from the rain – sails of fabric are draped between the cars. The ceilings patter and applaud.

"At the party … you asked why she left?" Ro sniffs, wiping the rain from her face. "My mum, Diani."

"Ro, you don't have to…"

So she's quiet. Behind us, the air twists and dances where the horizon meets the sky.

The twins collect what's left of Madam Vor, wrapped in a rough cloth.

I go to check on Walker, stashed in the truck. No more forever smile on his face. He seems at rest, for the first time, curled up against the window. I wonder if he dreams now.

Around us there are more tents being assembled to protect us from the rain. The twins dig out our shot-riddled truck from the dune, check on the engines. There is singing, sad, mournful. Light passes, carrying grief in it like stone. No one speaks as they work. Eli guards Ro, his scorched cheeks stern, thick arms folded.

We stay until the fog-watchers deliver their warnings. Vor's remains are lifted like they're a glorious thing. Laid on a truck flecked with spots of rust and green glittering paint, metal leaves gripping its metallic bark. Through the rain, I can smell the charred cloth and try not to imagine what's inside. Picture her sleeping, like Walker.

"Mum wanted to explore – it's all she ever wanted," Ro says. It must've really hurt, what I said when we fought, to keep bringing it up. "There were lots of people who wanted her to run for Chancellor. Then suddenly this opportunity comes up, the big trek. I tried to make her stay. Vor did too. But 'what if?' she'd say. 'What if there is life Outside?' She left because the Chancellor told her there was evidence, proof."

The words fall out between long pauses, heavy breath. There are too many things inside and she can't keep them in. "She lied. The Chancellor. I know it, even if I pretend not to. I just… I didn't want to… Why can't it be true?"

"There's no one out there?"

Romali shakes her head. "I don't know what's true any more. Vor was willing to let me go and find out. Even if she never saw me again!"

She needs to talk so I don't interrupt. Let it come.

"Mum, she cared, but she never wanted a kid, not really. It was Vor who wanted a kid but she couldn't so Mum… I didn't know, not before… Aunt Lorri told me when I moved in. I was old enough to understand, she said. And I … I was mad. Didn't believe her. I needed to cry, to let it out, so I came to see you. There was nowhere else I could go. No one else I could talk to. You held my hand. You were different."

The Hysterics are taking down the tents. The rain's all gone now, along with the blood from the cracks in my knuckles.

Ro wipes her nose on her arm. "Vor, my mother, she stayed behind. Everything she did, every disgusting thing, she did to keep me safe. Making sure the Chancellor thought her loyal, even when she hated it…"

I can still see the hospital in the distance, then the Tower, High House, veiled behind dark curtains of water like something out of a legend. It doesn't seem so scary, though, from here. "You told me stories your mum read you. The ones with fairy godfathers, evil kings, wizards and stuff?" I say.

"You laughed at them."

"Remember the one where the princess saves the handsome prince from the mean dragon and they ride off into the sunset happily ever after? I laughed because there were songs. You sang them. Repeatedly."

"Oh Saints, I did, didn't I?" Ro grins, all sideways. Catching herself, she buries it fast. It was good to see her smile. "Don't read too much into those things – they're kids' stories."

We're standing still but my heart's thumping like we're dancing again. "What I'm trying to say is you need some new stories. Not princesses and magic but adventurers, noble leaders, discoveries. Whatever's out there…"

Pay attention. Look at her. Really look. Take in that face they didn't want me to see. The smear of her lips as she twists them, not knowing what to say. Count her freckles, find where they hide – by her ears, in the line of baby hairs framing her face, the creases of her nose. After this, her face will change. Her skin is mottled with dust. There's sand in her red hair. Any softness will harden.

I've seen it in boys I knew. There were things that made them men. Ro won't ever be that girl again.

It takes a second, a blink. Ro pulls away as Cora calls her to get the wound in her shoulder looked at. Haz checks on my dressing too. I don't like the face she pulls, the complaints about me not taking care, as the Hysterics climb into the fleet of vehicles, juddering and sparking them back to life. They raise their burning torches and bow, rev their engines and chant Vor's name. They shout the oaths of Hysteria.

When Ro returns, she's clutching something in her other hand: Vor's blast-dented badge of office. A single metal V for the House of Peace. Only the Chiefs of House get badges like that. Ro holds it to her chest.

I look back towards the Tower appearing through the haze of passing rain.

"Jude?" Ro asks.

"What?"

"No lies, no secrets," she says. "This isn't a fairy tale. You can't save Vik. You know that?"

"I know. He's dead. The Chancellor lied so I wouldn't shoot her." It makes sense. Saying it out loud makes it real. And I can feel it, like aching heat being lifted away by a cold wind. My eyes tingle. I look up to the clouds to stop tears coming. But then I let them fall because out here I can.

I've been wishing you alive. Keeping you in my head. But you're not gone – you're dead. There's just your ghost left. Little paper notes, the hope, it was all a game. She likes to watch us run, she said.

Maybe we shouldn't run.

"No, it's— You don't owe him, or anyone, anything. Not me. Not Walker. Definitely not Vik." Ro stares back, towards her mother's remains, and I think she might break down again, but she doesn't. In the light from the torches, her features seem even more fixed. "Before we left, Vor said if I l-liked you I should let you go."

"I'm not some prisoner."

"I don't think she meant it like that." Her smile seems forced. A number twenty-eight: *if-I-don't-smile-I-might-cry-or-scream* kind maybe?

"We're not that far from the hospital. You could make it back to the Tower, you know," she says. "There are meds in the hospital and if you reach the Tower there are doctors."

Of course I remember the doctors. Everything hurts and everything's heavy. Ro's eyes lock on to mine. I can see the grey in them, twists of blue, of brown.

"You were right before. It's suicide." She blinks when I say the word like she's surprised I'd use it. "I don't want to die. But ... you heard her. Aspiner wanted to take me back *alive*. The Chancellor doesn't want me dead. After all, she got what she wanted, didn't she? She wanted you exposed, out of the way."

"Maybe, but you still can't help everyone on your own," she says. "You were right too. We need to help. Nothing will change if we don't work together."

"But your mum?"

"If she's alive, I'll find her one day. We'll all go. You, me, your friends and a thousand more, as many as we can get out. So many inside just need an excuse, one act of defiance."

I don't want to deflate her but, "Ro, I can count, you know." I look at the small remaining gang. "Even if all of us go back…"

"We'll get the others from the outpost," Cora interrupts. "If anyone can persuade them, it's our Ro."

"And there's plenty of people in the mines too, hundreds," Haz jumps in.

"But they're men. Don't you want to protect—"

"Of course," Ro says. "But we've also seen Eli fight."

"No matter how many people we have … we can't just go in without a plan. We need a distraction," I say.

"A distraction?"

"Like … like the Lice did with Walker. Like when we danced. She needs to be unprepared, looking the other way." An idea's forming in my gut, Ro can tell.

"You? You want to go back?" she says. "Now?"

"Aspiner said the vote would be after the auction. Another day or two and it'll be too late." I try to count the nights since the ball on my fingers. "The Chancellor. She still wants me, right? Why else would she send those notes? She wants to win me back."

"What if you're wrong?"

"Trust me, please. I can do this." I need to do something on my own. I need her to believe in me.

"Just … survive," she insists.

308

"It's what I'm good at." However strong I try to appear, I know the chances are slim. This is what I'm really worth – a day, two, as much time as I can stall the Chancellor. It's more than enough. It has to be...

"At the auction I get the mic, like at Reserves. Except this time I'll tell a story. About you and Vik and the Gardener and Walker, the Roids, Vor. I'll tell them all her lies."

She wraps her arms round me, holds me tight. I've never felt that wave inside before, heat, like everything will be OK.

As they pack up to leave, we plan how I'll get to the Tower: the best route, how to get back in, ways for me to get a place in the auction.

The sky clears as I head towards the hospital – there's time before the fog returns, as if the world wants to help. Even the wound in my side, the pain in my legs, seem to pass. There's a feeling like I'm flying: those hands that once suffocated me have started pushing me forwards, holding me up.

THE HOUSE OF PEACE

Justice above all else.

Justice at all costs.

Justice for all.

48

LESSONS IN HONOUR

The night of last year's Reserves.

That night.

Reserves had finished two hours ago.

"Seriously, kid, you can do better than the Chief of Agriculture. Bocharov's a rude old clot. You need to learn some showmanship," Walker said, leading me down the cramped, damp concrete stairwell. The rough blocks of stone were as familiar as the dorm. We descended fast.

Madam Bocharov had reserved me for five merits. Despite waiting for her in her rooms for hours, when she arrived, she passed out drunk but not before calling to cancel the reservation. The man that came to collect me wasn't Father Jai. A cold sweat broke on my neck as I recognized the face at the door. Mr Walker. His hair was black then, his nose fixed, the thin moustache on his lip like a drawn line. On trend. Straight teeth and smile.

You were the boy he'd favoured. He should have gone to fetch *you*! I was just an amusement to him years ago. You're the one he'd been working with all that year.

Go back, you interrupt. *What happened before Bocharov?*

His slicked hair was mussed up so he ran his fingers through it before tidying it with a comb. "Put on a show. Where's that movement I saw, all that pizzazz?"

I swear he's speaking another language. "I don't ... I don't do that any more," I said. "Where's Father Jai?"

"I offered to let him rest – busy night. I gave you a chance, kid. What would you say to some private lessons?"

What about you? He was helping you?

"No need to look so nervous, kid. I hate to see promise wasted. And you owe me, or did you think I forgot? Well, that's the price – teaching you how to use what you've got."

Alarms squealed up and down, up and down the endless staircase in a wail. Walker shook his head, sighed and swore. He led the way down a few more stairs. "Keep up, no dawdling!" he shouted until I caught up with him on the ground floor, the one with a big 0 painted on the wall. Walker flashed a plastic card against the security pad of the nearest door. "Stay here," he said. "I have a horrible feeling she made him run."

"Who?" I asked, but Walker had already made his way through the door into the atrium.

It was the first time I'd seen front of house. The only way out. *I* could run. I looked down at my slippered feet. We were meant to run together. Or did I dream that? Was it just me wanting it to be true?

The front-of-house doors to Outside flew open, hard. I froze, held my breath. The fog would come in and drive me mad, or rot off my skin.

A steaming swarm of Lice piled in and I choked. I couldn't hold it long enough. For a breath, I could taste the dry Outside air, sandy and cold.

The Lice lunged on something. No. Some*one*. One of the madwomen maybe? They were shouting and kicking and swearing.

Not a Hysteric.

"Vik?" I called out, but didn't feel my lips move. Everything was disconnected.

You saw me. You stopped kicking.

"Jude?" Was it surprise in your voice? Worry? Anger?

Whatever it was, that's the moment the Lice struck, pushing their batons into you, firing electricity into your veins.

I hadn't had a single misdemeanour since the dogs. I'd been a good boy. Not any more. My numb legs carried me forwards fast, but Walker was faster. As your body juddered and gave up on the marble, Walker caught me by the collar and dragged me into the stairwell. The black cloud of officers swarmed round your body.

"There's nothing to be done. He's gone," Walker said as he shut the stairwell door with a clang.

Gone.

Not dead.

Go back.

"They can't do that!" I'd break my way through the door. "Let me go!"

Every single bone inside me was shaking with that familiar anger as I beat on the door, punched and kicked the glass until my knuckles crunched. He pulled me away. My fists hit him then and kept on hitting. I didn't care what punishment I'd get, but the way he looked down at me, that was new. None of the House Fathers ever looked at me that way, none of the boys in the dorm, or the cooks back in the kitchens. Weirdly, I thought maybe he was proud.

Eventually, there wasn't any fight left in me. "It'll get you in trouble that temper." Walker smiled.

Smile twenty-one, his *I-can-work-with-this* smile.

"You can help him, right?" I said. "You have to."

Walker tidied his moustache. "No, but I expect you can help me."

You skipped over it, you interrupt again.

No.

You skipped it! Go back.

49

The rain falls warm on my skin, washing me clean. Each drop drawing away the prickling dust, the smattering of other people's blood; the heat from the wound in my side; the sweat and the muck and the dance and the doctors' stitches, tweaks and drugs; the Roids' bruises... Until there I am in the garden, afraid to my toes, remembering the Chancellor saying, *Don't worry, I've got you. I won't let you go.* She needs a new ward. She wanted a challenge. I'm ready, even if she plans to pinhead me.

I couldn't save you but I can save my brothers.

Soaked through, splashing through puddles on the stone steps up to the hospital doors, I clutch my side and stumble in the rubble the Lice left behind.

The skin on my arms prickles. It's getting dark and another wave of fog is coming in – too fast for me to make it to High House. The air tastes like the kitchens, boiled-up eggs. Holding my breath, I search for Aspiner's fog mask in the hall. Finding it, I loop it round my neck then climb the central stairs, hunting for the box of medicine Ro said was in the room where they took Walker. Dizziness is setting in but finally I make it upstairs, past the hole in the floor, sliding along the wall to keep me up.

My bloody hand paws through the box as the other tries to hold tight to the wound in my side. The blood's dry now, the cotton of my shirt stuck to it. Pain rips through me as I tug the fabric free from the bloody gash; gummed closed with sand and blood before, it bleeds fresh and hot. If I die of an infection before the night is out, then all the plans in the world will be for nothing. Chewing down a big pink pill that I hope will stop an infection, I tear a hole in the lining of my waistcoat and throw in a handful of pills and a few of Walker's things. Then I search for something to bite down on as I pour alcohol on the gash, before squeezing a tube of wound-glue into the hole. It stings so much I discover I have a gift for swearing that'd make Father Jai blush.

Using the torn fabric of my shirt, I tie the shredded fabric round my waist until it bites and grab Walker's boot polish, needing the stench of the tangy fumes to wake me up, bring my brain bright. The perfume reminds me of the hours he spent working his shoes into a shine while I tried to remember his steps.

Closing my eyes, swaying in the fumes, I see Walker leap out of the bunk like nothing happened, tap his heels on the floor and then stroll off to get his hair fixed. *Come on, son*, he says, *work to be done.*

You're seeing things, you say.

I knew you couldn't be far

"I'm coming," I tell you. "For all of you."

You don't answer.

By the time I'm downstairs, I can't see the door. The fog

thickens with every breath. My fingers shake as I stretch the cracking leather of the fog mask and pull it on. Finally I can breathe.

Should I wait?

Bandages, glue and painkillers aren't enough. I need a doctor. With a pile of pills rattling in the lining of my waistcoat, a torch in my hand and a long beam from the fallen ceiling to help me walk, I head out of the front door into the cold desert night.

Let's see how far being pretty gets you, Aspiner said.

The boy that took her eye, was that me?

That boy … the things that boy could do.

50

Dawn light diffuses through the thick fog. In the distance, there's a faint, tall shadow getting closer with every slow step.

High House.

Ro explained the quickest way back is to avoid safe houses and head straight down the 'main road', a wide stretch between the buildings. It's been hours in the fog, bumping into walls and moving aside. Feeling my way. My breath echoes inside the mask, warm round my cheeks. In. Out. The filter clicks. Swimming my arms in the fog as the walls guide me.

Once the fog has gone, the sun is right above me. The baking heat begins to bite, cooking me from the inside out.

I pull off the mask and drop it to the ground to bask in real air, sand battering my face as I arch my cheeks towards the sun to remember every second of it.

Are those birds? High above. Black dots moving. Circling.

Could I just stop, sleep?

My bones tingle as I take one wavering breath, then another and another, blinded by the sting of the day.

No, keep moving. Not far now. I wonder how long before the fog returns as I follow the walls stretching ahead, leading the way. My fingers brush shadows of old red, blue, yellow paint; they dance over tiles dotted like dark-text. Here, the air twists and changes with every street. The light moves with the sun until a huge shadow is cast by High House, swallowing me up. There's the arm of that statue, drowned by the desert. Nearly there.

Then the hairs on my arms stand up again and I turn to see the green haze flooding the street behind in a great sparking wave of sand and cloud. How long ago did I drop the fog mask?

Run, a voice shouts in my ears but it doesn't sound like you any more.

I can't run. There's nothing left in me.

Go back, you say. But I'm done being buried by the past. Done blaming myself. I don't want to die today, not any day.

Forwards, I have to keep moving forwards, but it's too hot to move fast. The tiredness in my blood weighs like cement. The buildings around me get higher. Huge posters and paintings look down from every wall. Faded messages from the world that died while the Foundations held tight to hope below.

Run! Is it the Gardener's voice in my ears? Scratchy and dying.

The vast burning glow of the sun is starting to green. I yank the cotton from around my waist, crying out as the wound in my side tears, and wrap it round my face. Try not to swallow the air.

Run! Maybe it's Ro's voice.

Move! Maybe it's Walker's?

Can't see the Tower now – my eyes are watering.

Go back, you say.

No. Even High House seems to hold its breath as the poisonous air reaches into me and takes hold of my lungs. Squeezing. Thanks to the Roids, I can hold my breath for a long time.

Taking a deep gulp of air … one.

Kicking off my shoes, I need bare feet to feel the world in the dark. For the first time in days, my feet feel like my own. Steps, I can feel steps.

Two…

Curl my toes in the burning sand.

Three…

Rushing, I can feel the soles of my feet blister in the hot sand then I crash into the marble steps. Even if I can't see it, I can feel the Tower looming Saint-like over me. I stub my toes, cry with pain, knock to be let in, let me in, let me in.

Coward.

What?

Ten… I don't want to be out here, let me in. My trapped breath squeezes behind my ears.

It's like the day I killed the dogs. You don't want to think about it. You skip over it. You don't tell the story. You lie.

Thirty… I pound at the great heavy doors, the ones the Lice dragged you through, after you ran.

Fifty. Fifty-one and a half…

Coward. You blamed Vor. You blamed the Chancellor. You blamed Romali. Walker. It isn't their *fault I'm dead.*

NO!

The glass opens ahead of me and I'm stumbling forwards,

pushing past shapes trying to hold me, gasping for air until it floods inside, and I blink through watering eyes at the bright atrium, the familiar murals staring down and every single woman staring back.

The doors slam closed behind me, echoing through the vast space. Two Lice stand guard, but they don't grab me. They hang back as I push my way in, eyes streaming from the fog. It's almost like they're expecting me.

In the centre, the fountain of water trickles over black rocks stacked high. There are women moving round me, shapes through the sting of my eyes as I blink to see straight. I tear the bloody fabric from my mouth, my nose.

"Please. I need…" I begin, coughing up handfuls of sand. The hall echoes as the women around me draw breath.

This is where I last saw you alive. It's where I danced with Ro.

"The Chancellor. Please…"

They pretend not to hear me but I know they do.

My feet slip, squeaking through their space, then I stumble, grabbing the women's robes. They push me away, unsure of what to do, a boy, his hands, the dust. I catch hold of someone to stop myself from falling and this time I won't let go. The woman yelps and struggles to break free.

"It's important," I say. "I need her."

I can smell the green water around the twinkling fountain. It's a wide pool, leaves the size of plates floating on the surface. Orange and white shapes swim in the dark. My eyes are actually burning now so I let myself fall, crashing into the cold water.

Swallow mouthfuls that taste of weeds, the copper cloud of blood from my side. The women peer into the pool. Their faces swirl into ribbons.

And I smile.

Smile number screw-the-list: *kiss-my-ass*.

51

After they haul me from the fountain, the doctors are sent for as a handful of Lice hurry me to one of the appointment rooms. Out of sight. I am grateful. I am dignity. I am pure fogging obedience. You'd be so proud of my performance and Ro would laugh. Walker would raise both eyebrows and roll his eyes and ask me if I'd hit my head. The good boy I was once, asking for the Chancellor.

The doctors arrive. White-coated, white-masked. Eyes and needles, that's what they are.

"Delirious," they say as I ask to see the Chancellor again.

I screw up my eyes, expecting their long needles, but I don't struggle as they help me to a stretcher.

When the elevator doors ping open, they rush me into the infirmary. High-merit women walk around in dressing gowns. Slippers shuffle like the ones they make us wear in the dorms.

Ro said they'll have to fix the wound in my side before they can do anything else. No point pinheading a dead man. While they get to work, gluing, stitching, sticking my arm with needles, giving me blood, fluids, I wait. Count the bolts in the ceiling when it hurts. There's one missing.

It's a small room. The soft furnishings torn away, leaving the cold walls bare. It's cramped, stacked with folders and medical machines that gave up working a long time ago. Now they're used for hanging gowns, stacking glasses, dirty plates.

One of the doctors remembers me and tuts to see what the desert has done, all her hard work ruined. They cut away my clothes but before they can take them away to burn I salvage the contents from inside the lining of the waistcoat – specifically Walker's merit book. They *aww* and *aah* like I'm a wounded animal who needs looking after, sweet that he covets such little things. They ruffle my hair and mew over the trauma I must have had, stroke my cheek, all the time asking when I've got the emergency doctors' all clear so they can take me upstairs for the full 'procedure'.

There's a reason I need Walker's book. It's where he kept his security card, pushed into a pocket in the cover. If it could get him into front of house, it can get me out of the infirmary.

The Chancellor wants me to fight for the right to be her ward. She wants me to win her, not the other way round.

I'll show her fight.

There's still heat in my side, a biting, sick, churning ache. But I don't need to stay to see what they'll do when they're happy it's fixed up.

No. I need to get to the dorms.

What about me?

There's that idiot hope again, that you're alive.

*

When I get up, the ache from the stitched-up gash hasn't gone, but feels deeper, curling up my spine, down into my heels. The doctor watching over me warns me not to try to walk, her voice soft behind her cotton mask. I need the bathroom, I tell her, except I call it the 'little boys' room'. Her laugh is muffled. She thinks I'm sweet, helpless, stupid and I'm letting her believe that but with all the meds in my system it's not hard to sound pathetic. She'll show me the way, she insists, being ladylike. I'll get there on my own, I insist. Give me this, a little bit of freedom. My hand grips Walker's merit book so tightly my knuckles are white.

The doctor, Mareesh she says her name is, looks around before pulling her mask away so I can see her face, a small act of defiance on her part too. Ro said there were women who would just need an excuse. I didn't believe her. Maybe there are more than I thought? The woman crying for her ward in my appointments was just the start.

You go, run, the young doctor's face says, that expression of pity and hope in her eyes as she hands me a gown.

As I slip it on, I'm counting the days since the ball. If I'm right, the auction hasn't happened yet.

I limp down the corridor, holding my gown closed as women stare and whisper. Most of them don't look at me, refuse to move out of my way as I stumble ahead, so I have to weave round them. They sigh, shaking their heads. "Boys these days."

I keep scanning the walls for the emergency exit. Do I care if they see me use the card to slip into the stairwell? How soon will the alarm sound when I don't return?

Gritting my teeth, I fumble for the card in Walker's merit book, pinching inside the cover until I find it. I think of how he could have used it to get free too, to escape the Lice, the doctors. How after all his years at the Chancellor's side she threw him into the desert like a broken doll. No. I don't care who sees me. With a swipe at the wall panel, the door clicks open and I dip inside.

A hundred floors down are my brothers, my dorm. I can warn them at least.

My bare feet still sting from the sand but I start moving, as fast as I can, one foot after the other, imagining their faces. The tales I'll tell of Outside – of Eli and the Hysterics, the buggies and dunes.

Before last year's Reserves.

Are you going to tell them the story, or shall I?

As the stairs extend above, below me, I can almost hear Walker laugh. *You need to learn some showmanship*, he said. I can hear his feet tap.

There's no one following. No Lice stomping down the stairs from the infirmary. No doctors. When I reach floor zero, I keep going. You're trying to tell me it's my fault but I ignore you like you ignored me from the moment we joined the House of Boys.

Not going to answer? Suddenly so quiet?

At floor minus two the air gets thicker. There's no air conditioning in the stairwell and the stifling heat chokes. My hand hesitates at the door to the dorms. I rest my head on the metal. There's no way the card will open the front door; the Chancellor would never give Walker that kind of freedom.

Inside the dorm corridors there's no one. My brothers must all be at their appointments, right? I'm not too late, am I?

Stumbling into J-dorm, I make my way to my bunk, the bedsheets untouched since I left them. Need somewhere safe to stash Walker's card for now, so I reach underneath for my bag of stuff. Everything's there: sweets, pens and the note I never gave you.

We need to talk, it said.

It's all there except … the paper man you made. I pull off the bedsheets, tearing up my bunk to find little pieces of paper. It's been ripped to shreds.

Did I just do that? Maybe it fell apart when I pulled at the sheets?

My brothers clatter into the dorm, alive, laughing. Stink's face explodes into a grin when he sees me. He bounds across the room and flings himself against me with a hug. Rodders joins him and tries to stick a wet finger in my ear, saying that he's a lot of pranks to make up. I shout as they hold tight, too much of me broken, but I don't shake them off, even when others join in the pile-on. When I finally push them off, they start applauding.

I've heard a lot of applause since I joined the House of Boys. Most of it empty. Most of it unwanted. Not this. My stomach swells with it. My side is a patchwork of stitches and glue. Head swirling. The paper pieces fall from my hand as they congratulate me for coming home.

52

When everyone heads to lunch, Stink lingers like a bad smell. "Before you ask –" he grins, showing off a long line of gleaming white teeth – "Quinn likes good pegs. Stings like pepper paste but worth it, right?"

His face looks wrong with such new teeth. "They look great," I say.

"So you want to hear a story?" he asks.

"No," I joke. I've missed this.

"Go on, it's a short one."

"Fine," I sigh.

Stink takes a deep breath. "Here it is. I should've helped, when Vinnie and the others came after you. I was afraid. I'm sorry."

"I'm alive, aren't I?" I shift from foot to foot, remembering Aye-Aye fighting in the infirmary. Could I have tried harder to help him?

"We thought you'd been sent to the mines by the Lice. I kept thinking about it. That was the most insane thing ever, dancing with Madam Vor's daughter. Mad."

"Yeah." I try not to smile. "I mean, there were the Hysterics too. They did attack…"

"Which was scary, sure … but, Jude, you asked a girl to dance!" Stink laughs. "Look, I'll make sure the others don't bother you. My way of making it up to you for being a useless bunk-brother?"

"Sure," I say.

He's about to leave.

"Justin?" I call and he turns. "Thanks."

"That's what brothers do. See you up there, Superstar!" he beams.

"Up there?"

"She sent you here to get ready for auction, right?" he says. He thinks I've been with the Chancellor all this time.

"Yeah," I say. I figured I'd be a day early for auction. That I'd have a day to get them out maybe? "Tomorrow, right?"

"No, it's tonight, that's why we're off appointments early."

It can't be tonight. I thought we had more time. Stink bursts out a laugh. "Wait, that reminds me. There's something you have to see!"

*

Bzzzz

The speaker rattles in the dining room. By the clock, there are four hours until curtain-up. I thought there'd be more time, time for Ro to get back with the others. Did I count the days wrong?

Stink persuades me to come to the dining hall, even though I'm not hungry. "That's the place to get the best look at them," he says.

"At what?"

"You'll see."

Most boys try not to look at me, or at least not get caught. "The numbers of boys have gone down," I say.

Rodders nods. "A lot have gone. Since the ball, even the most trivial misdemeanour and the House Fathers pack them off. What was it that kid in L-dorm did?" he asks Stink.

"Full-blast spat at Father Lim! It was glorious, splendid, *a-may-zing*, my friend." Stink kisses his fingers. "But instead of going to the mines they said they packed him off to the infirmary! What a treat."

"He went to the infirmary?" I say, a cold, creeping feeling inside.

"A-MAY-ZING," Stink reminds me, up close. Displaying his shining new teeth. Clearly *amazing* is word of the month.

"That's where you got your teeth done? And they let you leave?" I ask.

"Er. Yeah, why wouldn't they? I mean, I've got to go back for more work, though, they said. Everyone's been offered treatments, even the troublemakers, and for free! Since you came back hot as hell after Swims –" Stink won't stop grinning – "everyone's been jumping for it. Amazing, right?"

"The infirmary isn't somewhere you want to go."

Rodders shrugs. "Hey, just cos they made you up and you don't want the competition—"

"It's not that, it's…" I'm trying to find the words to warn my dorm mates about what happened to Vinnie and his gang, when Rodders' name is called. Excited, he runs off and returns a few minutes later with a suit box in his arms. "Pressed and perfect and pure, gentlemen, I give you…"

He drops the box on the table. Stink stares in awe, not noticing his water has tipped over and is drowning his protein porridge. "Wow," he says as Rod pulls out the white suit and dances up and down the aisle, wiggling his ass. The dining hall whistles and whoops and cheers.

Every boy at the auction gets a pure white suit.

"Sorry, brother, there wasn't one at Jai's for you," Rod tells me. "Hope you're not going up onstage in your pants like in Swims? None of us'll get a look-in!"

"Walker insisted his tailor make mine," I say, while the boys around us laugh.

"*Oooooo*," they sing in unison.

"Nice," drawls Stink. "So it's true then? You were working with him?"

I forgot it was a secret. "Sorry, I should've said." It feels good to talk about him.

"Mate, he was hardly subtle with his crushes, you know that. At least you didn't go on about it like… Anyway, you seen him since Swims? The rumours are mad. He was meant to show up for auction prep the other day but we got that lackey Fry instead. The guy could hardly keep everyone under control, kept crying every few minutes."

I shake my head. Another lie and by the way they all look at each other I bet they can tell. Stink shrugs like he doesn't actually care.

"Well, here's to Mr Walker." Stink raises his glass. "And to whoever gets to fill his slippers."

They all look at me as we crash our glasses of water together.

"Here they come," Stink splutters, smacking me on the shoulder. He points at the entrance as everything goes quiet.

Three boys. No, not boys. They're too big.

Vinnie. Toll. Aye-Aye.

Should I look? I can't help staring as they walk together in a line. They don't look at any other boys. The expressions on their faces don't change.

I remember the laughter, how they posed and preened in the dining hall. Their bodies seem larger than they were before. Veins thick in their arms. And here's the creepiest thing – they seem even more handsome, at least by the Chancellor's standards. Set zero smiles as empty as the masks the women wear at Reserves. It's a perfectly choreographed performance. Perfect poise. Perfect smiles. Perfect men.

If you were still alive, she'd have pinheaded you too, right? You'd be back too.

"Pinheads," Stink whispers. "Serves them right, eh? No one's going to pick a fight now!"

As I stand, the sound of our bench shifting back makes the Roids' heads turn slowly. Their once-bright eyes seem clouded, cataract white. There's nothing behind their eyes when they look at me. They collect their suit boxes, turn and leave silently. Good boys. Quiet boys. Graceful boys who know their place.

After they've gone, not one boy in the dining room says a word. I search their faces but they look away, at their food, at the walls, the floor, anything but me.

They're not in awe of me: they're afraid.

∗

Bzzzz

Three hours till curtain-up.

Father Jai sent a note. My suit's waiting in appointment room forty-two. Music pipes into the room, skipping like before. There's the same path I'd worn in the floor. Jai brought up a mirror. My suit, ordered by Walker, is the best I've ever seen. Soft cotton, sharp creases, buttons made of bone. The silk lining is black. The tie too. But the material isn't white like my brothers' suits. It's blood red.

There was another smaller box that Jai gave me. When I tear at the paper, it comes away easily. Lifting the lid, I pull out the bag, untie the string and look inside.

Shining shoes, black leather, firm heels. When I put them on, I have to stamp on the floor. I can feel Eli's hand pounding my chest. Shoes for dancing. Shoes for running. Shoes for standing tall. Are they from Walker too?

"You'd be amazed how thick the armour of a good suit can be," I say, slipping into the suit, mimicking the pauses and tones of Walker's voice and winking at myself in the mirror because that's what he'd do.

In my new face, there's Walker's catalogue of smiles. His wink.

The skin of the boy who never saw the sun has been scorched. Everything is squarer than I remember. Solid as stone. Stubble on his cheek. This face belongs to someone who isn't afraid to take what they want.

*

Thirty minutes to go and Jai comes to get me. I didn't hear the buzzer. Too busy pacing, worrying. Jai's huge frame walks me along the line of my brothers in the dorm corridors. Stink pats me on the arm and whistles at the suit. Rodders winks. Jai leads me to the head of the line.

"You will make your dorm proud," says Father Jai, striding past the other House Fathers who have boys in the auction. There's pride in his walk; the other Fathers show respect too. Another result of having the Chancellor's favour, I bet. Don't mess with his superstar or your boys will end up like the Roids.

"Yes, Father," my brothers repeat.

"You will make your brothers proud!" shouts Father Jai as he disappears down the line.

"Yes, Father!"

I'm not joining in with the chant. Father Jai nudges me. "Stand up straight now, son, please. You will make your house proud."

My new shoes are snug, made for less well-travelled feet.

"Yes, Father."

"Thank you, Jude," he bobs, softening his voice. Jai sweats through his make-up as he tidies his flattened-down hair. It's the only time he's ever called me by my name. He's afraid too as he hands me the basket of white velvet ribbon.

"You know the drill," he orders.

I pull out a ribbon and he passes the basket to my brothers. "We blind ourselves to beauty," they chant as they wrap the ribbon round their eyes. "Our speech is sacred. To love is illusion."

Today. Tonight. Now. It's really happening.

Why can't I shake the feeling that we're all still playing the Chancellor's game?

"Don't ruin this, son," says Jai. "She pays what she promised for you and every boy in your dorm after you benefits." I forgot J-dorm gets a cut of my bid. He pulls the ribbon from my fist, reaches round my head and ties it so tight that I swear. As I try to adjust it, he pokes me in the side. Right where my stitches are. "You'll be grateful? To the dorm that groomed you?" he checks. "You are honour and charity and grace. You are silent and respectful. Understand?"

Stand up. Stand tall.

"I don't have to do anything I don't want to," I say. I'm here because I chose to be. I chose to do this. Whatever happens, this is my choice. My life. No one else's.

53

"Five minutes to curtain. Stay still, please," says Madam Glassey over the microphone. "Set the stage."

My heart is drumming in my ears. I want to take off the blindfold but, for now, I have to play along.

Even though I know my brothers must be on the stage with me, I feel alone, picturing the vast space of the theatre as a gaping mouth, the rotten red chairs its teeth, the chandelier its tonsils rattling as it prepares to swallow.

Beyond the blindfold, the spotlights give everything an orange glow. Then there's breath, chatter, the sounds of squeaking shoes, the shuffle and coughing of the crowd. I imagine Stink grinding his new teeth as he prepares to remember every second for the stories he'll tell.

My whole body is shaking. It's not nerves. Something's wrong. The pressure of the high waist on my trousers helps with the pain of the wound in my side but when I press my hand against it the wound burns hotter than ever.

Perfumed women gather round me, laughing, adjusting my suit as the burbling sound of the audience grows beyond the curtain. I grit my teeth as they spray my hair, rearranging it on my head until it's right. I cough in the haze, my side stabbing with pain each time. But I am obedient. I am loyal.

"Smile, sweetheart," says one. "He's too grey – can we get some foundation over here?" There's the smell of oil paint as they slap cover-up on my cheeks. "This is your big day."

"Thanks," I say through gritted teeth. *Not* smiling.

One last small victory.

Music starts: booming, floor-shaking drums rumble with triumph through the theatre. A microphone whistles as I picture the masked audience. Their eyes wide, they lean forwards, hungry for the echoing voice of Madam Glassey. She says each word slowly, swallowing the ends of her sentences. "Ladies, welcome to … to the Great Theatre for the last event of this season's auction," she stutters. "Lots of memorable nights but, erm, none more so than tonight."

Beyond the curtain, only the fabric of their dresses rustles.

"I've a sad announcement." Madam Glassey swallows. "In the last few days, you'll have noticed the absence of our good friend the … the…" She chokes on her words. I don't think it's an act. "Mr Russal Walker sadly passed this week."

The rage bubbles up through me. I clench my stomach where the grief sits.

From behind the curtain come cries of shock from the audience. My eyes ache underneath the blindfold, pricking with tears as I bite my tongue to stop myself from screaming out, *He's not dead, she pinheaded him!* Soon I'll tell them. I'll tell them everything.

"In honour of Walker and his tireless commitment to our beloved Chancellor, we must acknowledge him," Madam Glassey adds with a sniff.

The audience applauds in a disorganized trickle.

"Raise your glasses to Russal Walker, last of his name."

A wall of voices shakes the curtains. "Russal Walker, last of his name."

Every bone of me wants to break their rules, shout his name. I wait for my brothers beside me to react. There's nothing. Silence.

Wrong, says a voice. *Something's wrong.*

Vik?

You there?

Vik?

The anger in my gut turns to terror as I reach out, waving my arms blindly around me. In front – nothing. Behind – nothing. Beside me – nothing!

Tearing at the blindfold, I scan the stage to find I'm alone. My whole body goes cold inside the armour of my suit. Where are my brothers?

On the other side of the curtains the sweeping shadow of the Chancellor parades in front of her audience. Her shadow looms large against the fabric. Powerful applause erupts round the Auction Hall.

"Ladies, ladies," says the Chancellor's swimming shadow. "You're too kind. Beautiful, wonderful. Each of you here today is part of something amazing. As you know, today is meant to be our annual auction," she says, soft and sweet. "And, as was agreed with our Council, it is to be our last one."

Last? Did the vote already happen?

My back teeth clamp as the women chatter, as some applaud. What did she do with my brothers?

"We have a break with tradition this year. What can a girl do? I fell in love."

There's a sick feeling inside as the audience hums with glee and soft laughter. Is she talking about me? She's lying. She has to be.

"I know we normally wait until the auction to finish the affairs, settle our bills with the tenacious Sophia here."

"Please, Madam Chancellor," says Madam Glassey. "It was nothing."

"No, no, we all know you never let a merit slide, Chief Bookkeeper. But, well, I couldn't wait for the event tonight so a few days ago we managed the paperwork to complete our oaths and I invite you all to celebrate here, now."

She wants to make me her ward before the auction starts? Should I play along? We need a distraction – what better than an oathing? Maybe she really wants me. That has to be why my brothers aren't here. They'll be held in the stairwell until all this is over, right? Why won't you answer?

Think fast. No auction means no speech. Any moment now the curtains will open and I'll smile your number thirty *I-did-it* smile, all *ear-to-ear-love-me-I'm-yours-and-I-can't-believe-I-won*. Flapping at my cheeks as they warm, wiping my tears of humility away. Thanking my House Father. Blessing my brothers ... and when we're alone – if Ro hasn't arrived by then – I'll have to finish what Walker started.

Careful not to move too much and aggravate the burning stitches in my side, I tidy my suit, my hair. Wipe the sweat from my neck, my forehead. Do I put the blindfold back on? My fingers and thumbs fumble with the ribbon in my hand. The curtains shiver. I take a deep breath. But a new shadow appears on the other side at the Chancellor's hip.

Slim, muscular and as tall as me, smart-cut suit. I swear I can even smell his boot polish. My head screams Walker but I know it can't be.

"Ladies, debutantes," the Chancellor coos. "May I introduce my new ward. Our new Head of the House of Boys, Viktor Perrault!"

54

Someone took all the air out of the world. Someone took the floor away.

"Madam Chancellor," says your voice. You but not-you. You but deeper. You but hers. "You're too kind. After everything you've done, I can't accept your affections without offering my services." The long shadow of not-you bows, almost right to the floor.

She asked me to kill the Gardener or run. Run. You ran. What choice did she give you? What did she offer you?

"Pshh!" the Chancellor says, following with her musical laugh. "Let me tell them. Ladies, debutantes, this brave, incredible young man is the reason we have successfully obliterated the pernicious Hysterical element beyond our walls."

Waves of cheers and screams of adulation. I'm dizzy and I want to go home. Curl up in my bunk and hold on to my knees and let the earth swallow me up.

"A year ago," the Chancellor continues – even with my hands over my ears, I can still hear her – "I encouraged this brave boy, the first I hope of many in our midst, to rise above his nature. The Hysterics, led by the murderous Romali Vor, corrupted his innocence, sent him to kill me."

Gasps from the audience as the Chancellor puts her shadow-arm round your shadow-shoulder.

I'm falling like when the Lice blew up the hospital. The stage veers underneath me, so I bend and touch the rubber tiles, gripping the curling tape markers with my fingers to hold on, until my nails ache.

The Chancellor's voice is soft and light. "But he resisted, instead offering his support for our cause. This, ladies, debutantes, is a good boy. Worth all his brothers combined. Truly, the best I have met."

Applause.

Think! It has to be a trick, has to be.

Maybe it's not really you?

"Madam Chancellor," you say.

Maybe you're going to kill her; maybe you've been changed like the Roids.

Or maybe not. Was this what you wanted all along? Top floor, that's what you said. Top floor. The best.

55

LESSONS IN LOYALTY

There's a story I never wanted to tell – before Bocharov, before you ran, before I agreed to help Walker – the one I wanted to bury in the sand, that was easier to pretend away. It happened just before last year's Reserves. I was searching for you backstage at the Great Theatre, pushing my way through the queue to find you, past other smart-suited boys. For a moment, I thought maybe you weren't even going to go up for Reserves. I took a risk paying my way in, to talk to you.

When I found you at the end of the line, it was the look of disappointment that hit first. You were the last one up for the bid, too much make-up on your face to hide the red stripes in your cheek, your lip.

"Vik, please," I said, pulling you aside. "Can we talk?"

Your beefcake friends hadn't put themselves up. I hadn't seen them in the queue. Maybe you told them to hold back. Maybe you didn't want the competition?

"What do you want?"

I had all these things I wanted to say. Nothing.

"So? Say something."

The buzzer hummed; only a few minutes until curtain-up. Theatre prentice pushed past us, boys practised their speeches, tidied their hair, pouted into small hand mirrors.

"You've got a buyer already?" I asked.

You smiled. A full *wouldn't-you-like-to-know?* grin.

"Top floor." You said that last year too. "The best, you'll see."

"And then we'll go?"

"Go?" You screwed up your face in confusion.

"Outside," I said. You had the same dreams as me I thought. You wanted to get Outside, have real freedom.

You buckled over, laughing. "Oh Saints, you mean it. You're an idiot."

It hurt. It really hurt.

You didn't stop. "I'm not going anywhere. You'll see. I'll be running this place in a month. And there isn't anywhere Outside to go to, my friend, only up," you said, pointing to the ceiling.

I didn't move. Were you lying, pretending, or did I get it wrong?

"But we planned it, in the kitchens—"

"Oh … you're the kid from the kitchens!" you said. "The one that couldn't get it up to pop a couple of puppies." You made it seem like it was nothing, like you didn't remember me, but I knew how you cried, knew how you shook on the floor at night and couldn't sleep. I saw the bites they took out of you. I knew where all your scars were.

Still I took the bait. "Jude," I reminded you. "My name's Jude Grant."

You nodded like you'd just remembered. "Oh … yeah." You spun the ring on your thumb. Walker's ring.

"You're joking, right? You're messing with me. Playing a joke, pretending you've forgotten my name."

"It doesn't matter." You shrugged. "Your name."

The anger came up from my soles. The anger that would later pick a fight with the Roids; that would take out Aspiner's eye; that could kill the Chancellor…

All you cared about these days was who'd buy you, I shouted, but there was a whole world Outside. Didn't you want to see it, taste it? We had dreams once.

I told you I hoped some bottom-floor woman bought you. Pulled out every cooks' insult. You were pathetic, a sewer rat, it'd serve you right. They say jump, you say how high; you'd jump off the Tower if they asked. The fact they want to pay for you doesn't make you worth something! You think you'll get a good buyer? You're too short. Too fat. Too old. Too ugly.

"Keep going," you dared, turning, your fists clenched. "If you think you can hurt me, you'll have to try harder."

And I knew, I knew how much I'd hurt you, but you'd hurt me too. You'd been my friend in the kitchens, the only one I'd had. How long had you hated me? Since the dorms, since the audition, the dogs? Maybe you'd never been my friend. I didn't stop. The words kept falling out.

"You'd be better off finding a guardian from the Hysterics in the desert," I said. "Then no one would have to look at you."

I wanted to make you feel like I felt.

"Go on," I said as you stepped towards me, your nose to my nose, hot breath, bared teeth, burning eyes. "Hit me. Go on."

"You're not worth it, my friend. The Chancellor's going to buy me and I'll be Head Ward and—"

"You wouldn't be here if it wasn't for me," I blurted out.

"What?"

The boys around us bristled. Eager for a fight.

"You're only here because of me!" I said. You were used to insults about your face but all this time I'd let you believe you'd got in on your own. All you'd ever wanted was to prove yourself and I took that away from you. "Walker picked me, not you."

"Go back," you said. "Say that again." It was a threat but your voice shook.

I couldn't lie now. "Walker. He picked me. Not you. It was meant to be only one of us. He gave you that ring because I asked him to. You think you're so special? I bought your way in."

The boys around us tried not to laugh. Someone goes to fetch their House Father but the others are chanting for a fight.

That inside voice getting louder, wanting you to hit me. I needed it. It hated me for what I'd just done to you. It wanted you to hate me. After what I did to your face, I deserved it. I waited. But the House Fathers arrived.

They tell us our speech is sacred. It's not. It can kill. But you were a good boy now; you wouldn't start a fight, not with everyone watching. Not just before Reserves. There were tears in your eyes as you turned to get back to your spot in the queue.

"Coward," I said as the House Fathers pulled me away.

56

It bursts out of the darkness, that anger Walker was so interested in, that made me so cruel – surging through me again, sending me lunging towards the curtains. I need to see your eyes, to know it's really you and not some pinhead version of you.

"I'd have made twice the sacrifice for half your affection," you tell the Chancellor.

Did Ro know? She said you didn't want to leave.

Did Madam Vor know, or Walker?

Gone. Not dead.

As I search for the break in the fabric, her shadow turns. And I swear and I curse. I bring up every bubble of bile in my stomach and I spit it out. The audience takes a breath but I don't stop. Can't stop. Won't.

I didn't realize – why didn't I? – the bone sculpture in the Pent House that looked like you. And you were running *back* to the Tower, not away from it.

"I was broken, lost." You raise your voice above my shouts. "You offered me hope, protection, the chance to make a difference."

That dream, to leave, to adventure. You were joking. I wanted it to be true.

It'll get you in trouble, that temper, Walker told me. I know that but I didn't fight my way back for nothing! I have to know – are you *you*?

"To work with my brothers and ensure they don't fall prey to the same corruptions."

No. She gave you a speech. You're playing along. You're being a good boy, right? Where's that boy that got thrown out of his prenticeships? Were you being so good that night last year? You betrayed Walker, told her he sent you to kill her, expected her favour…

You weren't running away, you were running *back*. To her.

A tearing sound fills the auditorium. I look up. Above, the curtain rips and ring after ring pings, stretches and slips free. Everything slows as I back away, cover my head, duck. The poles clang like bells and a wall of fabric crashes down heavily on top of me.

Over the muffled screeches from the audience, I'm crying out from the pain in my side. My stitches have burst but I don't stop fighting my way free, crawling, dizzy, into the limelight.

The Chancellor steps between us, a protective wall. Her dress white, as bright as your hair. Your eyes are clear. She didn't pin you but the boy you were has gone, like Walker said. Not dead. Gone. He's been eaten by the unscarred, perfect skin of this man. How long were you in the infirmary? How many procedures did she pay for? This man, this man she made you into, is an old copy of Walker from my audition, even down to the fur of hair on his top lip, his pinned-back ears, perfectly parted blond hair.

My heart drums in my ears. My fingers twitch. The audience hums with shock.

"Vik?" I pant.

Of course, this is what you always wanted. The truth curdles through me. Viktor Perrault was never really my friend.

You were never him. You were a voice in my head, the friend I wanted him to be.

"Stay back," the Chancellor seems to plead. Can't everyone tell it's an act? Her grey eyes still bright, in control, even as she holds up her hands as if afraid, performing for her audience.

I should look at her but I can't. I keep remembering my nightmares from the infirmary. Your hands round my aching throat. I thought it was the drugs, the nightmare of that place. But you were there. You've been helping her all this time. Her good boy. Her best boy. Walker was wrong – she didn't want a challenge. She told me what she wanted, back in the garden. She wanted loyalty.

Blood oozes out, spreads through the red of my suit, turning it black. My heart's beating too fast.

"Mr Grant, Jude?" I know that smile. That shark smile. "No need to get emotional…"

I wanted to tell them all the Chancellor killed the Gardener, that she had Walker's brain scrambled, that there are boys that lost their minds. But the words aren't there. Neither is the anger, that forever ache in my head. It's gone.

What's the point in telling them? I'm not born to be believed. I can't convince them, not on my own.

"Ladies, sad to say but this boy is what will become of our men if we do not vote to address their worse natures."

"What? No!" I take a deep breath, in through my nose, out through my mouth, to focus as the Chancellor keeps talking about how she knows I organized the attack at the ball with Romali, how she failed me, failed to see I was being used, how she tried to forgive me for the Gardener's murder, for Madam Vor's abduction.

"No!"

How she tried to help me, fix me – I push forwards, bloody hands spread. That's not what happened, shut up, shut up, liar, LIAR.

"So, regrettably, now the time has come to officially table a vote to give us the power to protect them from damaging themselves and others. To end this corruption in our gentlemen once and for all. To extend the Mind Absolution Act immediately to all the men in our care."

"No, you can't, not now."

"Let's do them this kindness. Free them from the tyranny of their sins, those toxic instincts; give them peace."

She doesn't need them to vote but she wants them to, not just so they agree but to make them own it.

"How say you, ladies?"

The house lights rise.

Well, aren't you just gorgeous? Walker said, the last time I saw all those faces.

There's a world where I become everything they reduce us to.

Where I kill her. Seconds, and the Chancellor will turn back to you. Arms steady, I'll reach out and snap the white ribbon round her neck, pulling so tight it creaks. The Chancellor's silvery eyes will roll back in her head as she chokes.

The audience will run screaming for the doors, climbing over the ancient chairs, tripping on skirts. Some will shout at me to stop, masks flying from their faces, as others tell me to keep going. In this world, the Chancellor kicks and chokes; her heels will scrape the floor behind me; her fists will pull at my hair, scratching at my face with her armoured nails. I won't kill her, because she knows I don't have it in me. But I'll give her all the votes she needs to pinhead every last one of my brothers. That's her game. Lose/lose. I can picture that world so clearly I can taste it.

She needs a killer. Proof for all her lies. Proof that we're all the same, us boys. Proof she can do what she wants. Proof her people should give her unquestioning loyalty, rather than see her as human like them, like us, like me.

No, it says.

It's not your voice, not any more. Maybe it never was. It's my voice. And it's shouting.

I'm not a killer. Not today… Not ever. I'm more than they say I am.

She's still waiting. Holding her breath. Thinking she's found the right button to push, to tip me over into playing her game.

There was a time, on this stage, when all I wanted to do was run. Instead, my breath sticks me here. It makes me wait.

It pulls my spine straight.

One.

Ro isn't here.

Two.

It's up to me.

Three.

Four.

There's one last battle in me.

My heart pounds a beat. A distant *dum-da-da*. I step back, stamp my foot to the thump in my chest. With a creak, the spotlight, juddering, leaves the Chancellor and her new ward and turns on me.

57

My body moves and I follow. The energy comes up from the earth. Every last bit of being alive that the Chancellor mocked me for being proud of; it's made of soil and sweat, blood and tears, face paint and dust. All the wounds in the world wouldn't stop me.

Did you hear the story of the boy who danced? He never knew the moves but he refused to stay still.

The Chancellor is calling for the Lice to take me away, I guess, but they haven't come. No one in the audience has gone to fetch them. She's almost screaming, that calm, soft voice cracking in her throat.

And then, instead of voting, a pair of hands in the audience claps together and another woman joins in, another.

"You'd rather he fall then? Like the rest?" she challenges her women, calling for her Lice again. Still no one comes. Where are they?

My jacket is too heavy so I take it off. Find the music in the breath of the audience, the creaks of the lights, the stamp of my feet on the floor.

"A hundred merits!" a woman shouts from the dark.

She should be voting but instead she's bidding. It's not enough to buy my brothers. She's bidding for me, I think. But she's giving away her merits, any power, even if it wouldn't work, to vote against the Chancellor, for what? I'll be dead when I'm done. Can feel it with every step, the wound inside me stretching, tearing.

The Chancellor barks at them to wait: I'm not for sale – I'm broken. But I don't stop. I'm not dancing for them or their bids. I'm dancing because I still can. There are moments when I hear Walker counting out time, moments when it's as if there are a thousand bodies onstage lifting me, twisting me, throwing me. Picking me up again. But with every move I keep my eyes on you.

"Two hundred!" adds another voice.

"He's meant to go to the infirmary – he planned to kill me," the Chancellor croaks at Madam Glassey, who moves out of the way as I spin round the stage.

You point to your waist and then mine, with a twitch of your head, telling me to look down. I put my hand to my soaked side and feel my shirt heavy with sweat and blood, but I died long ago.

I take off my shirt, discarding Walker's armour on the stage because I don't need it any more. I keep moving, now with the space to stretch my shoulders, as the women point and whisper.

"Really?" the Chancellor shouts. "This is ridiculous." But she knows I'm not going to play the game by her rules. If she wants to pinhead my brothers, me, it won't be because I gave her an excuse.

"Five hundred!" bids a woman from the circle.

Six … seven … nine… The numbers climbing, over and on top of each other, each voice rising, more women jumping to their feet now. They may not live our lives but they're hungry too, I guess, trapped, controlled, angry. Even if it's only a small change, standing up to her, it's enough.

Another spotlight joins me from the rafters. Music too – the band in the pit striking up strings and drums and swells of sound.

One thousand! Not enough to beat my reserve. Maybe the Lice will take those women away too. Maybe we'll all be dragged off together. But still the Chancellor screams, still they don't come. I kick off my new shoes: it's better barefoot. My feet squeak as I twist. My eyes on you, your eyes on me. Daring you. You thought I was the good boy but I wasn't. You're the one who's trapped by the rules. You forgot – there's always another way to be free.

As I trip on the curtains, my body lands on the stage with a clap. You laugh. But this is how I won you your life when Walker saw me dance. He's here now, watching in the dark, applauding.

I drag myself up. I'll move until my body gives in and maybe the audience will tell the boys that follow – that's what keeps pulling me to my feet.

"Five thousand?" Glassey shouts at the audience, joining in with defiant glee. She even winks at me from behind her mask. "We can do better than that!"

My body is heavy. It stumbles and drags, this way and that,

from the edge of the stage, catching the light, letting it chase me. The string inside whips and tugs and jumps until parts of me begin to go numb but I won't let that stop me. I'd move my little toe if was all that was left. I'd dance with my body glued to the floor. Even if my brothers don't survive, the stories the audience tell will. *Put on a show*, Walker said. Tell them a story. It's what I leave behind that makes my life worth living.

Madam Glassey can't keep up with the bids now.

Despite the blinding lights, I can see the faces of the women in the dark. No more masks. They're out of their seats, massed up against the stage. Over the music and cheers and bids and applause, I can hardly hear the Chancellor shouting. She's the one on her own. And in those grey eyes, for the first time, there's something like fear.

The gash in my side is on fire as if someone is reaching inside, up through my ribs and squeezing my heart. I grunt through the pain, pushing out the last of my energy, and I jump, I spin and land on my back, smack.

I hear shouts, tens then hundreds of thousands.

Just one push, Walker said. He meant the Chancellor but maybe that's all the women needed too. Every bid against her, defying her. They climb so high I can't follow. I'll let the stage swallow me whole.

High above, the lights burn like the desert sun. With my eyes closed, I can go back to that. I can lie here and slip into dreams of it, of the rain hitting my face in the dark. The Lice probably went to stop Ro and the Hysterics but in my head they're safe, and free, and I'm Outside, running, fighting monsters, with Ro, with my friends, with the friend I thought you were.

"Six hundred thousand? Your very own rebel to tame!" Glassey laughs. The bidders have beaten the Chancellor's reserve. I'm not hers. Never will be.

"Any more? Going, go—" Glassey begins to close the bid as the Chancellor snatches the gavel. The music stutters to a halt.

"He's not for sale," she spits.

Pain sears through me in a scream as a foot presses down on my side, over my knuckles where my hand holds tight to sticky split stitches. The pain is like cold water crashing through me. Your shoes are polished white, perfect, except where they smear through my blood.

"Are you done?" you say to me.

"No!" The Chancellor tries to stop the bidding but the women keep shouting. "I have the reserve and he's broken; he's going to the infirmary," she insists. "Mad. Mad from the desert. You saw, in the atrium, you all saw," she says, quiet now. Not shouting for her Lice. Not pretending. Her plan hasn't worked, no one voted, but she isn't done.

"Fine. Let's do this another way. How much for the all the rest?" the Chancellor says. The sheen of her falls away, exposing the real her, underneath. Calm. Powerful.

The audience stops. Silent.

"The rest?" Glassey asks quietly. "But you can't … there are rules…"

"I wrote the rules. I own the House of Boys – I just need to cover their reserves," the Chancellor snaps back at Glassey as if she's an idiot. "The other boys' reserves – all of them. How much?"

Get them out, Aye-Aye said. All of them. In the dorms, are my brothers being rounded up, are they being taken away, are they fighting back? She'd planned this all along. They're probably already in the infirmary.

The Chancellor turns to the wings. Her doctors are waiting there.

"Jude, I said are you done?" Vik asks again. It's the first time you've said my name in years. It doesn't sound right. The Chancellor's silvery gun is in your hand, the one that shot the Gardener. Meant to stop me if I attacked the Chancellor, I guess. I was meant to attack, you were meant to save her and her vote would pass without debate.

The women operating the spotlights don't know where to point their beams. The Chancellor clicks her fingers but their beams land on me, not her.

"Don't you care about the others?" I ask.

"They can be better," you say.

And then I'm laughing and can't stop. Because in the dark the audience are shouting, protesting. She'll have to pinhead every woman in High House.

"Stop it," you say. Your fist comes out of the dark with a solid thud. You've been waiting a year to hit me that hard.

"You're meant to fight!" you shout.

The Chancellor goes quiet as he follows with another hit.

He's strong, like the Roids, but I won't hit back. "I'm sorry," I manage to say and I mean it. I wanted a friend and when you weren't that I hurt you.

"Hit back!"

I take each punch, each blow trying to drive me through the floor, through the concrete dorms, the dusty tunnels we grew up in, and into the mines.

"I'm sorry," I say again and again until you stop. And there you are, the boy you were, before I let you down.

I'm dead already. You know it too. We both knew it the second the stitches in my side burst.

The Chancellor hands the gavel back to Glassey. "Call it," she says. "Now."

Silence drips through the stalls. Even the ancient chandeliers are still.

"Call it!" the Chancellor orders.

There's a cough. "Excuse me?" a voice shouts and the room catches its breath.

Finally. I've been waiting for that voice.

The house lights go up, flooding the Great Theatre, showing every flaw in burning white light. The auction guests are surrounded by hundreds of dust-covered Hysterics, men and women, their weapons ready to fire as Ro steps up on to the stage.

58

Ro addresses the crowd. "No need to panic... Ladies. Ladies, settle down!" she shouts until Glassey hands her the mic. "If we can all contain ourselves – sit, sit – you'll soon be happy and at home. Let's keep this peaceful, please." Ro sounds like Vor. Her face fixed, no smiles.

Despite the loud complaints of the crowd, Ro's army of Hysterics surrounds the Chancellor. She doesn't run as they troop up the aisles, come in from the wings. What does she know that they don't?

Where are you? You've gone.

"We'll find him," Ro says, catching my eye. "Cora?"

Cora waves at me before she disappears with a few of her friends into the wings to arrest you.

"My brothers?" I ask as Ro reaches me.

"Safe," she says. "Otherwise we'd have got here sooner. We went straight to the dorms, the infirmary. There were Lice guarding them – it took some time."

"Ms Vor." The Chancellor smiles and then sees the Chief's badge of office on Ro's collar. "Or should I call you Madam Vor now?"

"Call me what you like but it'll be a waste of your last words," Ro says as she points her gun at the Chancellor. "This is justice. For Walker, for my aunt, Vor, my mum ... for everyone you've blackmailed, starved and killed, and lied to, for years of blaming. Call it a mercy."

Vor didn't want anyone else to die. I try to stand but my head is so light it's like I've drunk a gallon of Eli's hooch. "She wanted a trial," I fight out. "Vor." Every breath is a struggle now.

"Vor's gone, Jude," Ro reminds me, straightening as she says it.

They say we're killers. They say we started the Last War. They say we need protecting from ourselves. They say we're dangerous. But we're not that different.

The Chancellor shakes her head, amused, as if I'm some animal that's learned to speak. She pinches the bridge of her nose. "This is ridiculous, Romali. Shoot me and it's you who is committing the crime. In front of all these people too. Not clever." The Chancellor appeals to the audience. "A million merits and the position of Chief of Peace to the first to end this childish display."

Ro checks her weapon.

"Ro," I beg. "Don't."

What the Chancellor is offering her women – merits, freedom, power – it's more than any boy could dream of, even you. It's enough to cover my debt ... enough to cover yours. It's a deal anyone might take a life for, I think, as you aim the Chancellor's gun at Ro. I watch it flash as you fire.

I'm already dead when I push Ro out of the way.

Air catches in my throat, sour with smoke. I hear the bullet before I feel it. Can smell it too, that gunpowder, the cooking coppery blood. After the shot, the silence is a wound.

Somewhere Ro's army is wrestling you from the creaking wing staircase to the ground. You keep firing but in vain. The Chancellor only gave you one bullet. I wonder if she planned to have you pinheaded too.

Somewhere the Chancellor is buckling with anger as my insides burst. Somewhere Ro is catching me. She won't let me fall.

"Don't you dare…" she says. "Don't." But it's not up to her what I do. I took the bullet because I wanted to. Because I could. I'm glad that the last thing I get to see is my friend. She knows I'm more than the skin I'm in, more than the blood in my veins. I'm the things I do. Did.

"Who bid on Jude?" Ro asks Glassey. "The auction, who bid? How much?"

"We didn't close," Glassey says.

"Take everything, every merit. My bid, it's enough for him, right?" Ro asks Madam Glassey.

I try to argue. I don't want anyone to buy me. I don't need her to save me. But I can't talk.

Ro stiffens her jaw. "All of it. Check the books, my mum, Aunt Lorri … Vor too." Those merits were meant to stop the vote, I try to say, but there's not been a vote. "Everything!" she insists.

"But that would mean—" Glassey protests.

"I know," Ro says. "Do it."

"No, I don't want—" I try to say.

"Shut up, Jude. Trust me, I know what I'm doing."

"Sold!" Madam Glassey sings.

As the gavel hits, Romali Vor, my friend, my guardian, lifts her gun and puts a bullet in the Chancellor.

One shot. Done. She doesn't even look back.

59

The House of Life doctors operated for days. Good doctors, Jai says when he comes to visit. The infirmary doctors are under arrest. I'm now missing something called a spleen. Nerve damage too. They tell me I'll limp for the rest of my days and dancing won't be so easy. "We can fix it for you," they say, behind their surgical masks. I tell them no so fast they jump.

The House of Life isn't like the infirmary; no one cares about luxury here. These doctors are scientists, they say, interested in how my insides fit together not the shape of my nose. Everything seems to beep. Seventeen years ago, I was an egg in a dish up here. Feels right to be back as today's my birthday. I'm a man now but I don't feel like one.

"It's a shame," Father Jai says, trying to be nice. "You weren't that bad a dancer."

Father Jai snuck in a dictionary and a book that translates our dark-text into their letters. He says I've earned it. He'd been given it years ago by a woman who had favoured him. The first thing I look up is *spleen*. My reading is improving every day.

"You don't need a spleen, you've got plenty to go around," Jai jokes.

Spleen: *an abdominal organ for the production and removal of blood cells. Part of the immune system.*

Or

Bad temper.

Father Jai is sort of funny, I guess. Nice to see a familiar face, even though he's been behaving strangely since the auction. Not afraid, not mean, friendly even. They say he was the only one of the House Fathers that fought to keep the doctors from coming into the dorms. It's probably thanks to him that my brothers didn't get their heads spiked before Ro's army intervened. The Chancellor started the process before she'd even got on to the stage, while I was getting pampered, preened, prepped to play my part. They lost a good dozen boys, Jai says.

The second thing I look up is every swear word I've learned. That passes the time. Not enough time.

I need to know what happened to you, to Ro, but no one will tell me. Beyond the windows of the House of Life, the sun rises and sets. I won't ever tire of it.

*

Without a mask, Madam Glassey's face isn't what I expected. It's as round and bright as the moon. She flips through a big book with my name written on the spine. Licking her fingertips to turn each page, she shows me the last entry. My eyes bulge at the size of the number at the bottom. The book is my namesakes' merit ledger.

Glassey is almost excited. "Quite frankly, Mr Grant, you're more merited than half the women in High House. If you were a girl, you'd be eligible for my job. Maybe even that will change now," she says hopefully.

I run my fingers over the bumps of the tattoo on my ankle and wonder how much debt is left against my name. "But what about my debt?"

Glassey sighs. "Oh, my dear boy, you don't understand. You have no debt. Quite the opposite. Romali Vor paid the Dunn family's *entire* fortune for you. I have all the paperwork if you need to see it."

"But what does that mean?" I say, scratching at the stitches in my back. "Where is she? Aren't I her ward now?"

Madam Glassey rubs her warm cheeks. "It means … a big change. We've never had a free man in the Tower."

"I don't have to go to the mines?"

"Do you want to?"

"No!"

"Would Mr Walker's rooms do for you, when you're ready? The rent is surprisingly affordable for a top-floor apartment. Unless there's somewhere you'd prefer?"

There isn't.

"You'd be a good candidate for Head of the House of Boys too," Glassey adds.

I try sitting up straighter. "What about Vik?"

"The mines… Since you survived, the Council agreed that the crime should be downgraded." Madam Glassey leans in.

"If you'd like, the House of Peace can overturn the decision?"

"No," I say. I don't want you dead. "He only did it because of the Chancellor."

I'm not sure Glassey agrees. "Madam Lay offered him a defence – she heads up the House of Law. Argued insanity."

Even though you shot me, tried to kill Ro, it wasn't insanity; you weren't some broken toy. But I guess they need stories too.

"Now, of course, normally we'd keep you here for observation but in light of your windfall – and the disappearance of your guardian…" Madam Glassey reaches out and puts her hand on my arm. Is this care? The woman who has sold thousands of my brothers, and me, cares?

I pull my arm away and wince as the sudden movement makes my back spasm. "She didn't disappear, she escaped custody, right?"

"Jude, please. The point is … you're a free man." Madam Glassey blinks. "The first in our history."

It takes a while to sink in. I'm not sure it ever will. A free man.

"And if Ro comes back?"

Madam Glassey closes the book in her lap. "Well, I mean the auction, it was truly a disaster as far as the Council is concerned," she explains. "Given that your benefactor shot the Chancellor, we should arrest her and seize her assets."

"Does that include me?"

"Unclear. The laws don't really cover that eventuality."

"Ro was trying to help but you'd still arrest her?"

"Yes, yes. Our dear Chancellor, a great woman, truly a great woman." I don't think she really believes that herself; she's just trying to clean up the mess. "But we have a few candidates. Lots of changes we hope. My merits are on Madam Cramp. Talk of expanding living accommodation to the Outside, reinstating the House of Exploration, adjusting the population, maybe even allowing natural births. We haven't had an election for so long! It'll be a great show."

"A what?"

"Oh, don't worry your pretty head. Luckily you won't have to concern yourself with the stress of voting and you can keep those merits safe. Spend them on nice things, a few suits, a haircut. Maybe you could decorate your rooms – wouldn't that be fun?"

I guess if merits give voting rights that only applies to women. Maybe I can persuade them otherwise?

Free: *to be able to act or be done as one intends; not under the control of another.*

I looked that up too.

Release from confinement or slavery. Without cost or payment.

I'm not sure what definition Madam Glassey is using. I feel like I paid a high price. I feel like freedom is just the start.

As Glassey leaves, she says the stories are true. I can pick any name I want now I can afford to pay for the paperwork. She says it like it's a small thing. It's the hugest. If I'm not what they made me, the name they gave me, the debt I carried, then who am I?

I roll over. Walker lies in the other infirmary bed. I watch him until I fall asleep. Ro brought him back.

*

I finished reading the dictionary yesterday. I give it to Stink before he leaves this morning. I invited him and Rodders up last night, paid double for their time and asked them to bring me my stash of stuff. I spent the evening telling my brothers everything that happened. I'm going to fill them up with stories.

"You coming to visit?" Stink asks as he slips the heavy book into his bag.

"You can book an appointment," Rodders says, and I can't tell if he's serious.

I laugh. "I'm not sure that's how it works."

He grins and punches me in the elbow. "You'll figure it out."

As Stink gets up, he wonders out loud, "So what are you going to do with all those merits?"

"What do you mean?"

"They say, you know, rumours, they say you're richer than half the women." Rod raises an eyebrow.

"Yeah," Stink agrees. "They say you could pay off the debt of most the boys in the dorms. Just an idea."

"It's not a bad idea," I tell them. If the merits I have don't give me the power to vote, then what's the point? Maybe more of us need to be free.

Stink shrugs. "You know the Roids were sent to the Surrogacy to help, and the others that the Chancellor had pinned. No one wanted to book them for any appointments so they weren't making their House Fathers any merits."

"That's good, right? They won't try it again?"

"What name you going to pick?" Rodders keeps asking as I show them to the door. I can't shut him up about it. He has a lot of terrible suggestions. Mostly rude ones.

"I don't know," I say. But I do.

"I'll send up a list of suggestions from the boys." Stink helps me usher Rodders out, laughing. "See you next week, Superstar! Get me a good story, won't you?"

✳

The doctors have been ordered by Madam Glassey to discharge me from the House of Life today. I'll keep paying for Walker's treatment. Maybe they can help. I tell Walker the name I chose as I get dressed to leave and dig his pass card out of my stash. I know what I'm going to do but there's somewhere I need to go first.

60

It looks so different in the sunlight. I squint and shade my eyes with one hand. Calls from the birds above, squawking, chittering. They don't care about me. The leaves on the trees glisten with water. The damp heat clings to my cheeks. Life. It's a deep breath. The greatest theatre of all. Even the silence up here sounds like hope. If the garden can survive, maybe we can too.

Although the Chancellor had a private elevator, she wasn't the only one with access to the garden.

When the door to the maintenance elevator opens, my whole body collapses into the grass and I lie there a while, bathing in the light.

And I know I should be afraid, sad maybe. The memories of the last time I was here aren't gone, they're woven into my skin, but I was a different person then.

I follow the sounds of water. Where the Gardener died the grass is lush and thick. Someone, I'm guessing Vor, has planted something there, a tree sapling. The only thing that makes me nervous as I walk is the thought that the Chancellor's dog will jump out at me but I can't see her anywhere.

The garden doesn't care that the Chancellor is dead. It was

planted before her, it'll survive her, and when we leave it will probably take over.

Just one push, Walker said.

I open up the balcony doors. Throw them wide.

The air out here is cooler than at ground level and the wind pushes me back, whistling in my ears. I'm so far above the fog here. It's as if I can see to the edge of the world.

A small bird hops over my feet, out from the stuffy heat of the dome, and takes off. Maybe he'll come back. Maybe not.

As I make my way to the pool at the far end, shielded from the whipping wind by high glass panels, I slip off my shoes, let my bare feet press into the cold stone. My shirt. The stick I use to help me walk. The rest of the journey is a limp but that's OK.

I can't swim yet, but I can learn.

I lower my bare legs into the water. It's warm, smells clean. There's a strange scent on the wind, peppery and sweet. Something from far away. Stink won't believe me when I tell him the pool exists, or where it is.

The water comes from a waterfall inside the garden and the pool passes under a gap in the glass dome. Half the pool is inside, the other half Outside. After years dreaming of some magical way to fly through the High House walls, the price of a deep breath under the water seems too small. Not that I could go far from here. It's a long way down.

The pool goes right up to the balcony edge, the high glass side reaching below the surface, almost invisible, sending streams down the building as if the Tower could weep and wash away the dunes below. When I close my eyes, I hear the babbling water, the hum of the vents, the peace of being alone. Free. I don't think I'll ever get used to the word.

There's another sound too. Footsteps. The pad-pad-pad of soft paws, long nails on stone. The smell of the garden in fur. When I turn, fast, I slip and land with a splash in the cold water.

My arms are flapping as I try not to swallow the whole pool, coughing it up and trying to find my feet until an arm reaches in and pulls me up.

"This isn't me saving you," Ro says. "Please don't drown, OK?"

I spurt out the sharp water from my nose. "Then don't sneak up on me!"

She looks at the water and jumps in. The Chancellor's white dog barks and dives in after her, trying to save us both. When Ro bobs up, soaked, still dressed in the same ragged clothes she was wearing days ago, she laughs. "Needed a wash," she says and tries to stop the dog from making too much noise. "Dee, shh, shh. We'd better get out or he'll never shut up."

Funny, I'd assumed the dog was a girl. "You're up here for the dog, right?" I ask.

"Lorri said the Chancellor kept him in the garden – couldn't let him starve. Needed to make sure he was OK."

"You've got to get out of here – they'll arrest you." I move my arms like her; it helps me float. We're so high up I can almost imagine we're flying. Another few birds take flight through the door I left open to the garden, disappearing into the distance.

"You too," she says. "If they catch me, that is. Or are they still debating whether you're my property or not?"

"You were listening to Glassey?"

"I just know how this place works," she jokes. "Worked."

We pull ourselves to the pool edge, wipe the water from our faces, watch the dog battle his way up to the steps. He shakes dry his fur.

"You can make a difference, you know. Now," Ro says, perching on the edge.

We both look out into the blue sky. She's going back out there. "Still looking for your mum?"

She nods. "You don't need me."

I want to go with her. Not today but maybe one day.

"There'll be another Chancellor, you know," she adds. "Maybe not so bad. But this place won't get better unless there's people here to change it, to set an example, to keep fighting. I'll find somewhere safe. I'll come back."

"I know."

"You're going to live, OK? Not just survive. You're going to live. Promise?"

"Promise." She's right – there are still monsters to fight inside the walls. Maybe, when she comes back, we'll fight side by side. As friends. As equals.

"You know, I didn't come up here just for the dog." She laughs. "I needed a way to see you." She takes my hand.

There was that time she took my hand in our appointments. Remember what he wanted to do, that boy, back then.

"Can I – just once?"

Any other girl wouldn't wait to be asked. She nods, smiles. It doesn't have a number but she blushes and looks awkward and shrugs *sure-I'd-like-that*.

I thought it'd be difficult but kissing Romali Vor is easy. It's dancing with my eyes closed.

There's a ladder that reaches over the balcony, which she heads for. "Look after Dee. He needs feeding, walking, a friend." The dog stares at me, wide-eyed, and scratches behind his ears.

I don't know where the ladder over the edge of the roof leads but I know she'll get out. It's impossible for her to stay, even if I want her to.

When she's gone, I sink back under the water, holding my breath in the perfect silence.

Maybe I'll take a new name, maybe I won't. Truth is, Jude Grant could be any one of a hundred boys. A name is a story that gets passed down and twisted by time. This has to be the start of more than one story, so it needs more than one name.

I'll be a boy. Just that.

A boy that started something. A boy that went to Madam Glassey and insisted he pay off the debt of as many in the dorms that he could.

They can ignore one boy.

Not a hundred, more maybe.

Freedom for as many of us as possible. There's more power in that than anything.

I'm not just going to live, I'm going to fight. We all are.

Dear Reader,

I'm so excited for you to hold *The Boy I Am* in your hands.

I came to this story wondering what kind of feminist I wanted to be. Writing this book helped me process my own experiences from years working in a male-dominated industry. There have been so many great times, but they're pierced by moments when some men I worked for reduced me to something to flirt with, dismiss, or sideline when unwanted advances were met with polite declines.

Each moment sticks with me. I over analyze whether I dealt with them the right way, then wonder if there is a right way, then doubt my memory, then beat myself up for taking the burden of anxiety on myself, and so on… Sound familiar? You don't need to be a woman to know these feelings, far from it, they come wherever there is disparity in power. And there's a lot of that today.

The proverb 'absolute power corrupts absolutely' kept circling my mind as I found Jude's story. If we are all equal, are we all equally capable of abusing the power we have? If so, how do we choose to be better?

See, I told you I over analyze.

From where it began, soon my research took me to some places full of sadness:

To forums teaching men how to manipulate women, where young men believe their worth is only in relation to their ability to be with a woman, or where they are radicalized and pressed into dark causes to compensate.

To charities raising awareness of the hidden problem of child marriage for both girls and boys in a world where thirty seven countries have no real minimum age of marriage, including the USA, and where the rules can be exploited, not only for straight and cis people, but often to force young LGBTQI people into marriage.

I saw the worst extremes of both gender rights movements and questioned my own identity and beliefs.

But…

And it's a really important but…

I came out the other side with hope because of people I met along the way, working together despite their differences: activists for gender diversity and equality, for disability and anti-racism. I also came out with the comfort that things are, slowly, getting better. But it will take all of us working together to stop them from getting worse.

The realization I came to is that I am an unfinished feminist. And that's how I want to be, always learning about the power I have, the systems I am a part of, and how I can work with those around me to strive for a better, more compassionate world.

I hope your journey of discovery is as powerful as mine.

K.

IF YOU ENJOYED *THE BOY I AM* ...

Here are different perspectives on some of the themes in *The Boy I Am*:

The Burning by Laura Bates
A Change is Gonna Come, collection by various authors
The Belles by Dhonielle Clayton
Blood Moon by Lucy Cuthew
Wonderland, Clean and *Meat Market* – London
Trilogy by Juno Dawson
Proud, collection by various authors
I Will Not Be Erased by gal-dem
And the Stars Were Burning Brightly by Danielle
Jawando
Orphan Monster Spy by Matt Killeen
A Very Large Expanse of Sea by Tahereh Mafi
Only Ever Yours by Louise O'Neill
All The Lonely People by David Owen
Gloves Off by Louisa Reid
Gender Explorers by Juno Roche
Surrender Your Sons by Adam Sass
The Boxer by Nikesh Shukla
The Hate You Give by Angie Thomas

ACKNOWLEDGEMENTS

Long before I was offered any chance to publish I used to lie awake thinking of all the people who had supported me and helped me learn and hone my writing. You are holding up every word on these pages, I'm so sorry I can't acknowledge every one of you.

To Alice Sutherland-Hawes, for your courage in me and this strange story. Rachel Boden, Katie Jennings, Mattie Whitehead, Charlie Morris and Lauren Ace, Tom Truong, Kimberley Chen and Marg Hope, you are the champions and passionate partners I could only dream of working with.

To Vanessa Harbour, you were the first person in the professional publishing world to take a risk on me, and you remain my guiding light. To Imogen Cooper for the Golden Egg Academy, and all it does. And to Lucy Coats and your incredible support.

To Sara Grant, and the Undiscovered Voices team. Since my knees gave in on the day you called to tell me I had been shortlisted, they have not grown back. Your commitment to new writing is phenomenal.

To all of my friends who invested time and patience into early drafts of this and other stories: Amy Carpenter, Will and Charlotte Cohu, Kasha Shana-Turner, Emma and Sophie Cox, John Smith, Kate Brewer, Athena Stevens and the KEHS green sofa crew. To my writing family from WordTheatre,

GEA, and SCBWI (particularly my zoomies). A special love to my Boot & Floggers – Mandy Rabin, Charlotte Teeple-Salas, Jenny Rees, Helen Simmons, and Olivia Wakeford – this book simply would not exist without you. And to Miss Warne, Mrs Moule and librarian Mrs. Maloney who nurtured my love of the literary.

To my parents, who have endured me being hunched over a laptop or notebook on too many family occasions; my brother who encouraged me not to 'give [my] writing away'; my best sister Sian; and to my fabulous husband, who read an early draft of this book before our third date, and didn't dump me.

And to my Apple and my Rain. You are every reason why.

ABOUT THE AUTHOR

Made in Birmingham, K. L. Kettle lives, works and writes in London. *The Boy I Am* was shortlisted for the SCBWI 2018 Undiscovered Voices competition. She has won competitions and been highly commended for her flash fiction, including being longlisted as part of the 2017 Bath Flash Fiction Award.

When not writing Kathryn can be found traveling and working around the world working to solve big technology problems. Kathryn has a husband and twin children.

@klkettle